THERE ARE NO SAINTS

STEPHEN KANICKI

Black Rose Writing | Texas

ISBN: 978-1-68433-643-2 (Paperback); 978-1-944715-93-9 (Hardcover)
PUBLISHED BY BLACK ROSE WRITING
www.blackrosewriting.com

Printed in the United States of America
Suggested Retail Price (SRP) $18.95 (Paperback); $23.95 (Hardcover)

There are No Saints is printed in Baskerville

*As a planet-friendly publisher, Black Rose Writing does its best to eliminate
unnecessary waste to reduce paper usage and energy costs, while never
compromising the reading experience. As a result, the final word count vs. page count
may not meet common expectations.

In loving memory of my mom and dad:
Gregory and Ravanina Kanicki

THERE ARE NO SAINTS

CHAPTER 1

I had enough sense to break the fall with my suitcase, which I clung to for dear life. Unfortunately, my mouth slammed against the hard edge, and it split my lip like a grape. Blood splattered everywhere, over my white shirt and onto the ground. My demon-fighting bag struck the side of my head just moments later (the conductor had both a strong arm and good aim). Next came my soapbox. It flew like a cannonball and nearly decapitated me before slamming against a rock where it broke into several useless pieces. I heard the conductor yell something about not having a ticket, but I told the tawdry little man I couldn't find it; it wasn't exactly a lie. I really could not find it.

I stood up and shook my fist at the conductor. "Hey you. Peckerwood!" I shouted. "What about my bottle?"

The conductor held up a finger as if to indicate I should hang on a second, and so I did. He disappeared and returned a moment later clutching my whiskey bottle, which he then chucked at me. It would have struck me in the head, if it weren't for my quick reflexes. I walked over and picked up the bottle and, to my dismay, found it empty. It may have been empty from before. I don't remember. It was a damn long trip from Ohio.

The engine rolled as its boilers fired and protested against the heavy weight it dragged behind. I should've been grateful he stopped the train before throwing me off—I haven't always been so lucky—still, I was angry, and I shouted at the trained monkey conductor as he pulled away. "Hey, you, peckerwood!"

With the train out of sight, I shook the dirt from my clothes and assessed my bearings. Using my hands to shield my eyes from the sun, I scanned the horizon and saw I was in luck. In the valley below, the town was in sight. It didn't look too far off, and the weather was fine for walking, so I picked up my bags and made the final trek of my journey on foot.

They call it Drake's Well, so named because some fella named Colonel Drake drilled a well there and struck oil. Apparently, God saw fit to place a river of crude underground near this town called Titusville, Pennsylvania. It's a tiny town, no bigger than a postage stamp, but this oil thing is kind of a big deal. Men found it, refined it and turned it into useful things like Kerosene. It's worth a lot of money and its discovery turned Titusville into the gold rush town on the east coast. The way people are acting—losing their minds and their dignity at once—you would think it were real gold spurting from the ground. I read all the headlines before jumping the train:

"BIRTHPLACE OF THE OIL INDUSTRY!"
"DRAKE'S WELL STRIKES OIL!"
"THOUSANDS FLOCK TO TITUSVILLE!"
"TROUBLE FOR TITUSVILLE!"

Oil is everywhere, they say. It permeates the soil, seeping through every nook and cranny and saturating every pore like honey on a cracker. Even the water is so infected. I know this because I stopped to rest at a river and to wash away the grime and blood from my face. There was a rickety sign near the bank that read: *Oil Creek.*

Yes, it was aptly named. The water was reddish and tasted like rotting cabbage. I managed only a few sips before spitting it out for the poison it was. However, I splashed some on the back of my sweaty neck and was grateful for its soothing effect. It's the craziest water I've ever seen or tasted, but I must admit, it left my skin feeling soft and silky smooth.

Off in the distance, I saw the tall derricks sprouting from the land like overgrown corn stalks. They towered over the hillsides like macabre and grand cathedrals. I guess it's to be expected. Oil, after all, is the new religion in Titusville.

I walked alone, but the sights and sounds distracted me from my loneliness. Birds whistled from the treetops; the wind rustled the leaves and moved the golden wheat stalks in a choreographed sway. Soon, the countryside faded away and a peculiar aroma filled my nostrils, causing them to flare. I couldn't say for sure it was oil I smelled; it could've been cow shit for all I knew. I suppose It wasn't so bad; I've smelled worse in the bowels of Hell's Kitchen where piss and human excrement mixed with rotting pig flesh to create a fine, but twisted bouquet. It's an acquired taste, I admit.

Closer to town, I hobbled past a row of newly built mansions with their fresh coats of yellow and pink paint. Yellow I can stomach, but pink? Wealth does not guarantee good taste. It only proliferates poor judgment.

Yes, this poor farming community was blessed, but there was a cost too. The money brought greed and gluttony and sordid characters from all walks of life. It was in all the papers, sensational stories of instant wealth; once-poor farmers turned millionaires, losing their minds and souls in the process, leaving their families behind to rot as they pursued misguided exploits with women of ill-repute. I read about the drunkards, the gamblers, shady businessmen and the general godlessness that has run amok in this town.

I see it in their faces too as I walked down the main road, past the church and saloons. Humans turned to moving stone statues, many ignorant of their plight or too jaded to care. As I made my way to the center of town, I watched them, studied them actually, because that's what I do. There was something in their eyes—dark and hollow; they stared into nothingness. No one smiled at me. Not one made eye contact. Instead, people turned their heads away as I walked past, pretending not to see, nor hear me as I greeted them in a friendly manner. They were all ghosts to me. Good people, gone bad; their bodies and minds inhabited by evil spirits.

Yes. The Devil came to Titusville, and that is why I came. I am Dexter James, demonologist extraordinaire. Some people call me an exorcist, but I prefer the term demonologist because it sounds more academic, and less religious. I cast off demons, devils, spooks, spirits and evil minions from the unfortunate souls who have crossed paths with such malevolent creatures.

I am not a saint; I am a hired gun. I charge five dollars for my services, an outrageous price by some standards, but well worth it in my opinion. I offer a money back guarantee. If I fail to cast out the demon, I'll refund your money minus a four dollar and ninety-five cent sitting fee. In the unlikely event of re-possession—a term used to describe the re-infection by a demonic agent—I offer a special price: one dollar for an additional cleansing. Most of the time, a single cleansing is enough, but some demons are pesky devils and require due diligence to send them back to the unholy lairs from whence they came.

The life of a traveling demonologist is not an easy one. I am prone to agonizing introspection and self-doubt, long bouts of loneliness followed by debilitating depression. Maybe I should have been a gambler or a prize-fighter. Surely there are easier ways to earn a living than following the trail of sinners, cleaning up after their messes and restoring them to the pure vessels they were meant to be.

Who does this line of work? Few have the inclination, and I can't say I blame them. I keep telling myself it's God's work. It's a calling. These people need me, and I need them. Demonology is my calling and so I must heed this call wherever it takes me. Today, it is Titusville, Pennsylvania. Tomorrow? Who knows?

I arrived at the town's center just before dusk. I walked the rickety boardwalk, and It clacked and creaked beneath my feet as I found myself next to a building with a freshly painted sign hanging over its door: CLEM'S BOARDING HOUSE.

It looked nice enough, and I was too achy to look elsewhere, so I walked in and strode up to the front counter. An old woman with pale, wrinkled skin greeted me. Her grey hair was pulled back in a bun, and she looked like she sucked a lemon just moments before I arrived. I didn't mind the sour expression so much. I was just happy to have a place to set my bags.

"Good evening," I said, removing my hat and placing it over my heart. "I've just arrived in town and I would like a room. I'm not sure how long my stay will be but judging by this crowd, my work will be rather arduous and lengthy."

The old woman looked me up and down suspiciously. Then, she zeroed in on my face. I could tell by her expression an explanation was in order.

"Oh this?" I said brushing my fingers over my wounds. "You see, I was involved in a rather nasty spill this—"

"Are you an oil man?" she interrupted.

"My dear lady, do I look like an oil man?"

She scowled and said, "No. You look like one of 'em fancy college professors who's just been wrestling with a mountain lion. Are you one of 'em fancy college professors?"

"No ma'am. I'm a demonologist."

The old lady's eyes lit up. "A demon you say?" She turned over her shoulder and yelled to an unseen body in the back room. "Hey, Clem. We got out ourselves a demon over here at the front desk."

"Oh that's great," a man's gruff voice returned. "We need us some demons here like we need another hole in our goddamned heads."

"No ma'am," I said, trying to stifle a laugh. "You misunderstood. I'm a demonologist. I study demons and exorcise them from people who are possessed. I don't claim to be a demon myself."

The woman peered over her glasses and stared at me for what seemed an inordinate length of time. I tried to return her gaze, but I was no match in my exhausted state.

"Look," I said. "I've just had a twelve-hour train ride that ended with a rather nasty spill. I'm weary and would like a room."

"Five dollars a night," she said.

Either I suffered brain damage from the fall, or the old woman said, *five dollars.* "What?" I said. "No, no. I asked for a room, a single room with a single bed and amenities for just one person."

"Oh," she said, laughing and shaking her head. Her cackle was infectious and so I joined in. "Well, in that case," she continued. "That will be five dollars."

I immediately stopped laughing and wiped the sweat from my brow. "How can you charge so much for a single room?"

"Haven't you heard? They struck oil here. That's the going rate. In fact, you're lucky to even find a room. We've been booked solid for weeks. So have the other boarding houses and hotels. Some poor fella drank himself to death just this morning. That's how this room opened up."

"Oh, dear God. Did he die inside his room?"

"Okay," she said nodding her head. "Let's say he didn't."

I looked into her eyes, but they gave nothing away. "Does that include board?" I said.

"Dollar extra."

I shook my head in disbelief. "Madam," I said. "Surely, you can do better than that."

She looked at me with her beady eyes. "You an oilman?"

"I told you I'm not in the oil business. I'm a—"

"Oh, that's right. You said you chase off demons or something?"

"That's correct."

"That line of work pay well, do it?"

"Provided you have enough people who are in need of such a service. Speaking of which, do you reckon this town has a need for a demonologist?"

The old women's eyes lit up. "Well, I should say," she replied. "Seems like the entire town is demon possessed ever since they discovered oil here."

"Yes. That's what I thought."

"Yup. It was a quiet town ya know? Everyone knew everyone. Some people struggled from time-to-time—bad harvest or illness and such—but ain't no one ever let ya go hungry."

"And now?"

"Well, you've seen it. You walked down Main Street, didn't ya? Seems like the place is swollen with folks, and not the good kind neither, if you know what I mean."

"I do."

"Yes, I think this place needs someone to chase away these demons mister—mister? What you say your name was?"

"I am Dexter James," I said. "But you may call me Dex."

"Well, I'm pleased to meet you Dex. I'm Lucy Ford. My husband Clem is in the back. Hey Clem, say hi to Dex."

"Uh huh," the tired voice called from the back room.

"Well, it's nice to meet you, Lucy."

For the first time, Lucy's face softened, and she smiled warmly. "Well," she said. "I reckon I can do a special rate if you plan on staying a spell. How does a dollar a day strike you?"

"Expensive," I answered quickly. "But throw in three meals and we have a deal."

I held out my hand. "One meal," she said, shaking my hand.

I'm a sharp negotiator, but the old woman could more than hold her own. Besides, I was too tired to argue, so I surrendered.

"I'll get Clem to carry your bags up," Lucy said.

"No need. I just have my suitcase and my little black bag."

"Oh, and what do you have in that black bag of yours if you don't mind me asking?"

"This here is the culmination of over fifteen years of demon fighting," I said clutching the black bag to my chest. "Inside are artifacts and tools for plying my trade, demon-fighting arsenal as it were, some very rare."

"What sorts of arsenal?"

"Well, let's see. I have my Bible. No demonologist would be caught dead without his Bible."

"Oh, yes, the Good Book. I have one that's been passed down from—"

"This isn't just any ordinary Bible. This one comes from ancient Jerusalem and was salvaged from the burning temple of Niamm on the Aegean Sea."

Lucy looked duly impressed.

"Yes," I continued. "The entire temple burned to ashes, nothing but black soot and molten rubble left in its wake. But you know what they found amidst the smoldering ruins, still intact and as pristine as the day it was inked?"

"The Bible?"

"That's right! The very one contained in my bag."

"Oh my," she gasped. "How did you come by it?"

"I won it."

"You won it?"

"Yes. Five-card stud. The gentleman was short on funds; I took the Bible instead."

"Oh dear. What else you got in there?"

"Oh, the standard assortment of demon-fighting tools. I have a book of spells to ward off evil spirits."

"I bet you got a cross in there too."

"That I do, but not just any cross; it's a special one made of genuine iron. It's shiny and was blessed by the Pope himself."

"For real? The actual Pope from Italy?"

"From Vatican City. That would be the one."

"You went all the way to Italy to fetch it did ya?"

"Well, no, not exactly," I said, chuckling. Miss Lucy stared and waited for me to expound. "I—well, I won it too."

"What? You won the Bible and the cross in the same card game? The Dickens you say!"

"Well, it wasn't exactly the same game. They were two separate occasions."

"My, you must be one lucky fella."

"Ma'am, I assure you luck had nothing to do with it."

"You're good at cards, are ya?"

I winked at Lucy and said, "Well, my nickname is Dex; short for Dexter, but it also stands for decks as in a deck of playing cards."

"Well then, you shouldn't have much trouble finding yourself a game here in Titusville."

"No, no. I gave up gambling for a higher calling."

"Oh, it's just as well. Ain't nothing but trouble anyways. Say, you been traveling all day. You must be hungry. Head up to your room, and I'll bring you a hot meal."

"Thank you, but I'm fine. If you'll be kind enough to point the direction, I'll just head up and retire for the evening."

✝

The door swung open with an unearthly groan reminiscent of a haunted castle. The first thing I noticed was a quarter-full whiskey bottle lying sideways on a dresser. I remembered what Miss Lucy had told me about the previous occupant, and I cringed at the image now stuck in my brain. Other than that, the room looked pleasant enough, sparse but nice. Against the wall stood a bed flanked by a nightstand. Off to the side, was a round table that I could use as a desk. A view of Main street was provided by the glass-fitted, double doors leading to a balcony.

The décor was uninspired; ugly-green paint splattered the wall and could perhaps explain why the poor-chap before me had drunk himself to death. It didn't matter. This was to be home for the next several weeks. Besides, I've spent enough time in rat infested holes. This place was a step up, a regular palace by my standards.

I didn't bother unpacking, nor undressing. I sprawled out on the bed and read my Bible until my eyes grew heavy and I could no longer keep them open. I fell into a deep sleep more akin to a coma than a restful state. The bed was comfortable enough, but I spent a rather fitful night, tossing and turning. I dreamt a lot. Most of the dreams were the normal, standard fare. I dreamt of being thrown from the train, while the conductor and other passengers laughed. I dreamt of Holy Cross church in Hell's Kitchen. I recall seeing fragments of stained glass, the altar, and the face of the monsignor looking every bit his age. He smiled at me and I kept asking him what he was doing here, but he never answered.

They were weird and wonderful dreams, but nothing unusual. Then, I had another dream, every bit as riveting but hardly as peaceful. It was the last dream before I woke up. I was playing poker—five-card stud—with the Devil, a priest, and a small child (a girl with pretty, long blond hair). It was the perfect setup for a bad joke, but this was no joke. It was a nightmare in which I could not distinguish the dream state from the waking.

I had a winning hand—no surprise. The Devil kept changing, however. Sometimes he was himself, sometimes he was the priest, and sometimes he was the little girl. It was when he took the form of the little girl that frightened me the most, for the two of them congealed into a single entity that was one part pure, innocent and sweet, and another part, evil. It was as though the girl was imprisoned, trapped inside a hideous shell made of grey, rotting flesh. I recalled winning the hand: ace-high straight flush. I was happy; I slammed the cards down and collected my winnings, only to find the pot had turned to a pool of blood. I looked up from my red-soaked hands and saw the Devil smiling at me, nodding his head. It was all very strange and yet, real as if it were something more than a night terror—something I could not explain.

CHAPTER 2

It sounded like someone trying to break the gates of hell. I tried ignoring it, but the person on the other side of the door was a persistent soul and would not stop.

"It's me," a squeaky voice called from behind the door. "Lucy."

"Oh, Miss Lucy," I shouted back with mock enthusiasm. "Yeah, if you could go away, that would be great."

I dove back under the covers hoping my gentle rebuke was enough to shoo her away, but of course, my luck was never so good.

"Naw, I'm not going nowhere," she said. "I thought you might like some hot coffee seeing how you didn't eat last night."

I had to admit, coffee sounded good, so I invited her in. She walked through the unlocked door, wearing a big smile and holding a pot in one hand and a mug in the other. She strode up to my bed, placed the mug on the nightstand and poured the steaming coffee.

"You take cream or sugar?" she said.

I sat upright in bed and took the mug from her.

"Black is fine," I said.

"Sleep well, did ya?"

"Well, actually, I was visited in the night by some rather troubling spirits."

"Oh?"

"Yes. They seemed hell-bent on making my sleep a rather fitful one."

"I'm sorry."

"Eh, it's not your fault," I said, raising the mug to my lips.

"How is it?"

I saw the near-empty bottle sitting on the nightstand and poured a squirt into my mug.

"Be careful with that," Lucy said. "The last feller had his fill of the stuff. More than his fill, actually."

I looked into Lucy's grey, sullen eyes and plopped another splash into the mug before taking a swig straight from the bottle.

"Ah," I said. "That hits the spot."

"How 'bout some breakfast?"

"Oh, that sounds wonderful. I'll have steak and eggs, sausage, toast and some freshly squeezed orange juice."

"Toast and grits coming right up. Oh, and by the way, you'll be getting your first customer soon."

"My first customer?"

"Yeah, my cousin Ethel. She'll be up here anytime now."

"What's wrong with Ethel?"

"She's demon possessed. I don't know why I didn't think of it earlier, but she's been bewitched going on a year now. Poor gal."

"Is that so?"

"Yeah, I reckon so. Well, you just sit tight. I'll go fix you up some grub. Want me to bring it up when it's done?"

"No, I'll be down straight away after I freshen up a bit."

"Now don't forget about Ethel. She should be here any minute."

"Yes, I'll be waiting with bells on I'm sure."

Lucy pointed a twisted finger at me, smiled and then left. After she closed the door behind her, I slowly rose from my bed, picked up my mug and dragged myself out to the balcony where I had a birds-eye view of the street below. I guessed by the angle of the sun it was roughly eight. Titusville didn't seem fully awake yet. Hell, I wasn't fully awake yet. My brain felt groggy, and I still ached from the unfortunate spill yesterday. I hadn't looked in the mirror, but from feel alone, I knew my face was bruised and swollen. The Irish coffee helped.

I watched the pedestrians pass below my perch and took long, deep pulls from my mug; I felt melancholy. I was pleased to be here, but I was alone, and loneliness is troubling in my advanced years. I miss the gentle touch and sweet scent of a woman. Not just any woman—I've had plenty of those—but someone special. A sweetheart to share my thoughts with, my dreams, my aspirations and my life—a partner in crime if you will, a woman I can talk to, laugh with and if need be, cry on her shoulder. I've never had such a woman and at fifty-three, I reckon I never will. I may have ten good years left in me; maybe not that long. I could be dead tomorrow. I should have been dead thirty years ago. I simply beat those odds.

I looked down at the nameless faces passing by and then I saw her. She looked different from the others. Her hips were round and full, and her chest practically spilled from her dress like rising dough from a pan. Yes, I had a very fortunate view from my vantage point high above, and I am slightly embarrassed to say I took every advantage. However, as endowed as this lovely vision was, it was her hair that captivated me the most. It was—for lack of a better term—big, and it bounced too in the most provocative way. Long, blond curls reflected the sunlight and radiated the most astonishing golden hue into my eyes. I watched intently as she strolled down the street; her hips swayed as she moved with a confidence you don't see in most women. The rest of the crowd seemed inert, white statues standing motionless as she sauntered past. My heart stirred just a bit.

"Now, there's a woman," I spoke out loud. "Now there's a woman I could fall in love with."

A sharp knock on the door woke me from my dreamy state, and I walked back into the room.

"Come in," I said.

The door slowly swung open with a dreadful creak, and a lithe, old woman walked in. Her hair was long and scraggly, and her wrinkled face bore a slight smile that looked vaguely familiar.

"Hello, hello," she said.

"You must be Ethel," I said.

"And you must be Dex." Ethel waddled up to me and extended a limp hand beneath my nose. I didn't know if I was meant to shake it or to kiss it. I chose the latter. Ethel blushed and giggled. "Oh my, Mr. Dex. You are refined," she said.

"Well, I've been called many things in my life dear, Ethel; refined has never been one of them."

"Are you from the city, Mr. Dex?"

"Originally."

"Pittsburgh?"

"Oh, I've spent some time in Pittsburgh. There and Philadelphia, Chicago, Denver, Utah, Boston. I've traveled overseas, spent some time in Europe. I'm originally from New York City, Brooklyn."

"Oh, New York City. I have some kin up there. Do you know a Miss Emmy-Lou Blythe?"

"Uh, no, I don't believe I've had the pleasure. You know, New York City is a pretty big— "

"Oh wait, Miss Emmy-Lou ain't from New York City. She is from New York, the state that is, but she's from a town just outside of Buffalo called Jamestown. Have you ever been to Jamestown?"

"I don't have a recollection."

"Oh, you should go sometime. Pretty little place, lots of shops. It's not too far if you got a good horse and buggy. Do you have a good horse and buggy, Mr. Dex?"

"No. I'm afraid not. I travel by train and I hoof it the rest of the way, pun not intended."

Ethel laughed and waved her hand in front of her face as if she were shooing a fly. She looked positively smitten and this worried me.

"Oh, Mr. Dex," she said. "You are too funny."

"Yes," I said. "So, you think you're possessed?"

"I am possessed," she stated emphatically. "No doubt about it."

"And how did you so become inflicted?"

"I had relations with a chicken."

I studied Ethel's face looking for a sign, some clue, anything that would reveal a hint of tomfoolery in her message. However, her pale, stone-cold expression gave nothing away. I looked at the bottle on the nightstand and was pleased to see it contained another sip or two. I needed a good swig—straight up; no coffee.

"Uh," I said. "Excuse me, Miss Ethel. Come again. I've had some Irish coffee this morning, and I'm afraid I may have tipped the bottle a wee bit too high. I thought you said you had relations with a chicken?"

"Yes, sir. That's right."

"So, I heard you correctly? You had relations with a chicken?"

Ethel paused and blinked her eyes several times. "I'm not proud," she finally announced.

I pulled a handkerchief from my shirt pocket and wiped the sweat from my brow. "I see."

"You believe me, don't ya?"

"Oh, indeed. I'm quite familiar with the Incubus, and his tricks."

"Who?"

"The Incubus; a male demon who has relations with a female. Though I must say this is the first time I've seen it take the form of a chicken. What on earth possessed you to have relations with a chicken anyway?"

Ethel leaned in and turned her head left and then right to make sure no one was eavesdropping. "That cock was a sweet talker," she said in a low, breathy voice.

I made the mistake of sipping my coffee as she spoke and only the last-second turn of my head spared Ethel the alcohol-infused shower that ensued.

"Are you okay, Dex?"

"Uh, yes," I said between hacking coughs. "I'll be dead by noon, I'm sure, but I'm okay now."

"Oh, my."

"Yes, well," I said after regaining my composure. "You should beware those sweet-talking cocks."

"Now you tell me. So, do you think you can help?"

"Indeed. First, let's discuss your symptoms."

"My symptoms?"

"Yes, what is happening that makes you convinced you are possessed?"

"Oh, lots of things. For instance, I get these hot flashes."

"Hot flashes?"

"Yes, these burning sensations that light my loins like the very flames of Hell. And I get night sweats. I'll wake up in the middle of the night and my sheets will be wet with the perspiration…"

As I stood there, shaking my head in disbelief, I wondered how loathsome it would be to grab the bottle and empty it while she spoke.

"…and then there's my private parts— "

"Yes, I think I've heard enough," I said.

"Do you think I'm possessed?"

"How old did you say you were?"

"I didn't, but I reckon I'm in my late fifties, maybe early sixties."

"You're not sure how old you are?"

"I reckon not. Do you think you can rid this here demon fer me?"

"Well, it will take some doing, but I believe I can cleanse the evil spirit."

"Praise be!" she said clasping her hands over her heart.

"My fee for performing a standard rite of exorcism is five dollars."

"Five dollars? What the hell? I haven't that kind of money?"

"You haven't?"

"No. What do I look like? I struck oil or something?"

"Sure. Hasn't everyone in this town?"

"No, not everyone. Some of us are dirt poor, and I happen to be one of 'em."

"Well, then, how much money do you have?"

"I ain't got any."

"You haven't—" I stopped mid-sentence to wipe more perspiration from my forehead. I wish I could have a word with Lucy right about now. "You haven't got any money?" I continued.

"Nope, but perhaps we could make some other arrangement?"

Miss Ethel cocked her head to one side and smiled. Her yellow teeth resembled an old fence with most of its posts crooked or completely missing. She batted her eyelashes in a come-hither fashion that made me wish I wasn't alone in the room with her.

"No, no," I said raising my hands in protest. "We'll just make this free of charge."

"Are ya sure? Cause I—"

"No, no. That's fine. We'll call it pro bono."

"Pro what?"

"Let's say it's for the common good."

"Oh, okay. What should I do now, take off my clothes?"

"What? Good God, woman. No. no, and hell no!"

"Well I don't know. I've never done an exorcism before."

"Why don't you just have a seat at the edge of the bed? No. Strike that. Take a seat at the table while I fetch my bag."

I retrieved my bag and my Bible and placed both items on the table next to her. I pulled out the cross and held it up to Ethel's face; the sun reflected from its shiny surface and back into her eyes causing her to blink repeatedly and avert her gaze.

"Does this bother you?" I said.

"Damn sure it bothers me," she said. "You're near blinding me."

"Oh, sorry," I said lowering the cross. "I meant, are you frightened by it?"

"Should I be?"

"Well, a common sign of demonic possession is a fear of religious artifacts—crosses and such."

Miss Ethel let out a loud squeal that pricked my ears. "Get that thing away from me," she said. "It frightens me."

"Yes," I said nodding my head. "That's the Devil talking."

"Tis? Do you think you can exorcise him for me?"

"Madam, I have been exorcising demons all my life. Trust me, this little devil has no chance against the great Dexter James, demonologist extraordinaire."

Ethel laughed and clapped her hands together repeatedly. "Oh boy," she said. "We're going to get that bugger good. What are you fixin' to do?"

"I'm a fixin' to cleanse the demonic spirit with the ancient rite of exorcism."

"What is that?"

"Well, it's sort of a ceremony. Kind of like a baptism, only with a different purpose."

"What do I have to do?"

"Nothing. You just remain still and have courage while I work. Are you up to it?"

Miss Ethel's eyes grew wide. "Will it hurt?"

I nodded my head and stroked my beard. "It may," I said.

"Has anyone ever died from the ritual?"

"Yes."

"What?" she said with some alarm.

"Oh," I said chuckling. "Hardly any of my customers die. It's me I worry about mostly."

"You? What fer?"

I locked eyes with Ethel and said, "Ma'am, when the demon comes out of you, it will be looking for another soul to take possession of. Who do you think it will be coming after?"

Ethel pointed a bony finger at me.

I nodded my head solemnly. "That's right," I said. "Me."

"Oh dear. I hope everything will be okay."

I carefully removed the purple stole from my bag, kissed it and then placed it around my neck. "What's that?" Miss Ethel asked.

"This is my ceremonial stole," I said. "It's been blessed by the Cardinal of St. Louis. Think of it as my armor against the evil forces."

Next, I took the cross and hung it carefully around my neck. I kissed it and made sure it sat centered and true.

"Let us pray," I said.

Ethel clasped her hands together and closed her eyes as we recited the Lord's prayer together: "Our Father, who art in heaven, hallowed be thy name; thy kingdom come; thy will be done on earth as it is in heaven. Give us this day our daily bread; and forgive us our trespasses as we forgive those who trespass against us; and lead us not into temptation but deliver us from evil. Amen."

"Amen," she said.

Ethel opened her eyes. They sparkled grey and with a youthful spirit that contradicted her physical appearance. I imagined what she had looked like as a young lady; perhaps she was attractive, almost fetching at one time. I wondered what her life had been like as a young girl. I wondered what her life was like now, here in Titusville. It made me sad to think the years robbed her of her youth as it does all of us in the end. Why do I think of things that make me sad? Focus, Dex. A child of God needs you.

I placed my hand on Ethel's forehead, and she instinctively closed her eyes as I prayed over her: "Oh, Dear Lord. We ask your mercy. We pray for forgiveness for our sins, Father in the name of Jesus we repent on behalf of your servant, Ethel, who had sexual relations with an incubus spirit. We renounce and break any covenant or dedications to evil. We renounce all forms of evil. I ask you cleanse this child of God and command this demon to leave this pure vessel at once. Lord, I repent for all those who had night husbands and night wives. Lord forgive us for rejecting You. Forgive our unfaithfulness towards You. Forgive us for finding pleasure from these spirits and for looking to them to fulfill our desires and needs. We choose to rely and trust in You for everything we need. Please restore our joy and faithfulness to the Bridegroom. Amen."

"Amen."

"Ethel, do you renounce the devil, and his demonic spirits?"

"I do."

"And do you renounce all evil, and sin?"

"I do."

"Do you renounce your dedication Nephilim, Baal and Belial and all unholy spirits?"

"I do. I do."

"And do you repent for your fornication and sexual perversions?"
Ethel remained silent.

"Ethel, answer the call, please."

Ethel did not say anything.

"Please respond, Ethel."

I felt Ethel's cool clammy skin grow hot, and when I opened my eyes, I was startled by the black, vacant pupils staring back at me. The old woman was no longer present. Something else had taken her place.

"Who are you?" I said. The corner of Ethel's lip curled upward into a contemptuous smirk. "I command you in the name of Jesus Christ to identify yourself."

Ethel's face broke into a wide, forced grin. Then, a man's baritone rose from deep within her gut. It shocked me and made the small hairs on the back of my neck stand on end.

"I am Glad," the voice calmy announced.

"What? You are Glad? That is your name, or the way you feel?"

"A little of both I should think."

"Whatever your name is, you are not welcome here. This is a child of God and I command you to leave her body at once and never return."

Glad tilted his head back and laughed with a chorus straight from Hell. When Glad fell silent, he stared back at me with unblinking eyes. The room, once stifling hot, had suddenly grown cold. I felt it, but I saw it too in the white, frosty clouds that floated from my mouth with each outbreath.

"Did you hear me?" I said. "I beseech you to leave this child of God in the name of our Lord, Jesus Christ."

With a deplorable grin, Glad shook his head and in a singsong voice said, "No, no, no, no. I do not think so. I like it here, and here I will stay."

I suspected Glad was a minor entity, long on stubbornness and short on brains, but I had to test him to be sure.

"Quod hodie est?" I said. Glad cocked his head to the side and squinted. "What's wrong? You don't speak Latin? How about Español? Tu madre huele a queso."

Glad's expression went blank.

"Francais? Tu sens la viande pourrie."

"What is this?" Glad said. "So, you know some phrases in a few languages and you toss them about to make yourself look superior."

"Yes, I know a few phrases, but you don't. You're not worldly, are you?"

"And you are?"

"I wonder if you could do me a favor," I said ignoring his attempt to draw me into an argument. "See the bottle?"

Glad shifted his eyes towards the whiskey bottle sitting on the table. "What about it?" he said.

"Would you be good enough to move it for me? Just an inch or two will do."

Glad looked at me with suspicious eyes, then reached out for the bottle.

"No, no," I said. "Without touching it."

Glad thought a moment. "If anyone in this room can move a whiskey bottle without touching it, it would be you," he said with a satisfied smile.

I had faced the likes of Glad before, a nuisance to be sure, capable of disrupting the nervous system, causing bouts of depression, anxiety, and heightened—often times—perverse sexual expressions. However, he was a minor demon with limited intelligence and very little preternatural power if any. I relaxed, confident we both knew who was in charge.

Glad watched me intently as I reached into my demon-fighting bag. I had an audience, and I was determined to give him a show.

"What is that?" he asked, his once arrogant tone wavering.

"This?" I said lifting the bottle out in plain sight. "Oh, I think you know what this is. You're not that stupid; are you?"

Glad shook his head back and forth. "No. Put it away. I'll leave."

I smiled and shook my head. "No. You had your chance."

I slowly removed the cap from the bottle as I watched the blood drain from Glad's face. He covered his eyes with both arms, but it was to no avail. The holy water splashed over his arms with a sizzle like cold rain falling on a hot rail. Glad contorted his body as if suffering from an epileptic fit, and he growled like a mad dog as a final protest before exiting the body. After a few seconds, Glad fell silent leaving Ethel behind, slumped in her chair.

"Ethel?" I said. "Miss Ethel, are you in there?"

Ethel lowered her arms and my spirits lifted with the return of her placid face. "When do we begin?" she said.

"Begin? Why, we've finished. We're done."

"Done? I don't remember anything."

"That's probably for the best."

"Was it hard?"

"He was pesky, but he won't bother you anymore."

Ethel stood up, raised her hands over her head and circled in-place. "Saints be, I'm cured. Thank you. Thank you."

"Ah, wasn't nothing," I assured her.

Ethel stopped dancing her jig, and I saw tears in her eyes. "May—may I kiss you? Just a peck on the cheek?" she said.

I was hesitant but offered my right cheek anyway. She touched her lips gently to my skin. It was a long time since my last kiss, if you can call it a real kiss. I normally would not, but in my present state, I counted it as such.

CHAPTER 3

Main Street stirred with the urgency of a beehive. It reminded me of New York City on any ordinary day. Of course, there weren't nearly as many people, nor horses; the buildings were smaller and spaced farther apart and the smell of urine didn't permeate the air as it did in New York. It did, however, remind me of home, and for this, I was grateful.

My first stop this morning was the town clerk's office to secure a vendor's permit. In my travels, I've learned it's best to have a license to avoid trouble with the law. It makes things more official and adds legitimacy to my endeavors. However, when I arrived at the clerk's office and told them what I wanted, I was met with blank stares.

"This here is Titusville, Pennsylvania," the tiny man with the glasses said.

"Yeah," I said. "So what?"

"We sell licenses for business purposes. You want a permit to drill a well or to sell liquor, you come here. You want to cast out demons, you go somewhere else."

"And where do I go for that?"

"I don't know. The church?"

The tiny man and his bald, brawny sidekick started laughing. I think they were laughing at me and not with me; seeing how I wasn't laughing only confirmed my suspicions.

"So," I said. "What you're telling me is I don't need a license to hawk my services from a soapbox, not in Titusville anyway?"

The two idiots stopped laughing and the bald one said, "Do you got any money?"

"That's rather personal," I said.

"How much money you got?"

"Fifty cents," I lied.

They looked at each other and the tiny spectacled man produced a sheet of parchment from behind the counter and started scribbling on it.

"That will be fifty cents," the bald one said holding out his palm.

I walked out of there with a greater contempt for bureaucracy and an official business license from the municipality of Titusville, Pa. However, I wasn't sure if I had gotten a bargain, or if I had just wasted my money.

My next stop was the carpenter's place. It was an easy ten-minute walk following Lucy's directions. When I arrived, a burly man with a thick, dark beard greeted me and I did my best to explain what I wanted.

"A soapbox?" he said after listening to my description. "I got a bunch of them out back. Heck, you can probably find one on the side of the road. People toss them things out."

"No, no. You don't understand. I don't want just any soapbox. I want a platform?"

"A platform?"

"Yes. Like a stage in the theater, and painted with big bold letters, red letters with black shadows to give it dimension and sitting against a gold background. It's got to be sturdy to hold my weight, but light, too, so I can carry it from place-to-place without hurting my back. I'm getting up in years and it's not easy to lug these things around."

"Hmm. Two weeks," he barked at me.

"Two weeks?" I shot back. "I can't wait that long. Can't you do it sooner?"

"How soon?"

"Like by the end of the day?"

For the second time in less than an hour, I heard the barbed strains of laughter aimed at me. It was a hearty laugh; impressive, actually, if it weren't so damn annoying. "You know I'm busy as hell with this oil business," he said after regaining control. "Every day, new people arrive, derricks go up, platforms, oil houses. People need things, furniture, barrels, wagons—"

"I get it," I said cutting him off. "But I need a soapbox right away. My last one was smashed in an unfortunate accident. Would it make a difference if I told you I'm employed in the Lord's work?"

The carpenter ran his hands through his beard and squinted at me. "You a preacher?" he said.

"Well, no, not exactly. I'm a Demonologist specializing in the exorcism of demons and evil minions."

The carpenter squinted harder. "Is there much call for that?"

"Well, I'm assuming there is. In a town like this, you never know what evil lurks about; do you?"

"Uh, huh," the carpenter said. Then he spit a wad of tobacco juice onto the dirt floor mere inches from my boots. "Even so, I'm backed up. Take me at least a week."

I stroked my beard as was my custom while deep in thought.

"I understand," I said. "Perhaps we could make some arrangement. To bump me to the top of your long list?"

"What kind of arrangement?"

"Let's see now. Perhaps we could work a trade. I could offer you my services in exchange for the expedited delivery of my soapbox."

"What do you mean? What kind of services?"

"Like I said, I'm in the demon removal business. Perhaps I could perform an exorcism for you?" The carpenter laughed again. I was a bit ruffled, but undeterred. "What's so funny?" I said. "Lot of people are possessed. They just don't know it."

"Is that right, Mister? What you say your name was?"

"Beg my pardon. My name is Dexter James, demonologist extraordinaire, at your service."

"Woohee," he replied with a big grin. "That is a fancy name, Dexter. You're not from these parts, are you, Dexter?"

"No. I'm originally from New York City, but I've been all around this great country of ours, Chicago, St. Louis, Pittsburgh—"

The Carpenter's face lit up. "Pittsburgh, you say? I got kin up in Pittsburgh."

"Oh, Pittsburgh is a fine city. I performed a lot of exorcisms there."

"My name is John," he said extending his hand toward me.

"I'm glad to meet you, John," I said shaking his hand. He was warming up to me. I could tell.

"Yeah, John is a lot shorter and less fancy than your name."

"It's a good stout name, sorta fits you. Now, John, what do you think about doing a little trade? I need it by tomorrow at the latest. That's when I want to start. I can rest today."

John shook his head. "I just don't know if I can get it done that quick. Besides, I told you, I don't need no exorcism."

I sized Carpenter John up from head to toe and within seconds, I knew just what questions to ask.

"Well," I said. "Don't be so sure about that. How old are you?"

John gave me a suspicious look and said, "I reckon, I'm fifty-three."

"You reckon?"

"Something like that, fifty-three or fifty-four. No more than fifty-five."

I began to wonder if anyone in this town knew their real age. Between Ethel and Carpenter John, it seemed more of a guessing game than an exact measurement. It didn't matter. He was close enough to my age and that told me enough.

"Tell me, John; are you married?"

"Yeah, I reckon so."

"Okay. Do you find you're less amorous with your wife?" Carpenter John scrunched his face. "Are you less interested in, you know, relations?"

"Christ, man. That's kind of personal don't ya think?"

"Just answer my question. Your secrets are safe with me."

Carpenter John looked to his left and his right and then nodded his head sheepishly.

"Ah, now we're getting some place. And how about your body? Do you have nagging aches and pains and is it getting harder to do your work?"

"Well, of course, but that's because I'm fifty-three or fifty-four or something. Everyone goes through that. Got nothing to do with no demons."

I locked eyes with John and slowly shook my head. "Yeah, that's what you think, and that's what I thought when I was your age, but it turned out I was possessed and that was the real reason for my aches and pains and lack of enthusiasm for the female kind."

"It was?"

"Aye, it was. A good friend of mine, a priest, chased the devil spirit away and now—"

"And now?"

I smiled broadly and winked. "Let's just say I have no trouble rising to the occasion."

John's eyebrows arched, and he and I exchanged knowing smiles.

"How old did you say you were?" John said.

"Me? Oh, I'm fifty...I mean I'm sixty-six," I said.

John let out a long, shrill whistle. "Wow," he said. "And you say you can perform this exorcism on me?"

"I could do it right now, if you promise me delivery by the end of the day tomorrow."

John lowered his eyes. "I just don't know," he said. "I tell you I'm backed up."

"I tell you what. You look like a good man, maybe a little rough around the edges, but I can tell you need an exorcism in the worse way. I'll go ahead and perform the exorcism and lower my ten-dollar fee to five dollars, and you deliver the soapbox to me by the end of the day tomorrow."

"Five dollars?" Carpenter John said. "That's crazy."

"Just take it from what I'll owe you."

"I'll be doing the work for free."

"Oh, well, if you insist."

"What the hell?"

"Think of it as an exchange. You're trading your services for mine."

"Yeah, but—"

"You want to please the misses, don't you?"

"Yeah, sure, but—"

"And if she's happy, you'll be happy; am I right?"

"Yeah, I know, but—"

"I'll guarantee my work. If you're not satisfied with the results, I'll pay you whatever I owe you for the soapbox. You can find me at Clem's boarding house. That's where I'm staying."

I could see the wheels spinning.

"You got nothing to lose," I added.

"And you say you can perform this exorcism right here and right now? I'm a busy man, ya know."

"I got my little black bag," I said. "I never leave home without it."

Carpenter John nodded his head, and I performed the rite of exorcism then and there on the dirt floor of his workshop. It didn't take long. Like Ethel, John was infected by an entity which entered his body for sexual purposes, only his was a female spirit instead of a male. The succubus—as the spirit is known—succumbed to a quick prayer and a healthy splash of holy water. The entire cleansing took less than five minutes.

"Is that it?" John said.

"That's it," I said.

"Well, I don't feel much different."

"Oh, there's one thing I forgot." I reached into my bag and fumbled through a half dozen vials until I found the right one. "Here you go," I said handing him the blue pill. "Take one tonight before you have relations with the misses. It's important to take it about an hour before."

John's eyes grew wide, and he stared at the pill as if he had never seen one. "What's this?" he said.

"It's just a little concoction I made up. It has some citrus extracts, some herbs, some more herbs and vitamins. It will restore the energy the succubus drained from you."

"You made this?"

My chest swelled. "Yes, I did. Call it a hobby of mine. I've studied Apothecary, chemistry, herbology, medicine, among other things."

"And you say I take this an hour before—"

"Yes, yes. It takes about an hour to reach its full potential, but you have about a five-hour window." John stared at the blue pill and rolled it between his chubby fingertips. "We good?" I said.

"Yes. I'll get to work on your soapbox. Oh, what did you say you wanted painted on it?"

I spread my hands wide and above my head and said, "Dexter James. Demonologist Extraordinaire. Exorcisms performed. Five dollars."

John's confused expression told me I needed to shorten things up a bit.

"Okay, okay," I said. "How about Exorcisms? Five Dollars?"

"Okay, I'll see what I can do. Wait a minute! Five Dollars? You told me it was ten Dollars and you were giving me a—"

"How are you feeling?" I said, cutting him off.

"You know, I have to admit, I thought you were full of bull crap about this whole business, but I do feel better now that you exorcised me."

"Uh, huh, uh, huh," I said stroking my beard.

"Yeah, I'm less devilish, if that's a word."

"Of course you do. You were infected by a minor demon, but a demon she was. I got rid of her. She won't bother you anymore."

"How did she get inside of me?"

"Oh, well, hard to say. Why just this morning, I exorcised a demon from a woman who had sex with a chicken."

"You mean Ethel?"

"Oh, you know Ethel?"

"Yeah, I know her. Everybody knows her. We all thought she was crazy."

"No, no," I assured him. "She wasn't crazy. She was demon possessed. I cleansed the demon, and now she's just fine."

John scrunched his face and scratched the back of his head. "You don't say."

"Well, I must be off. Now remember, take the pill about an hour before relations, and I hope to see you soon with my order."

"Will do, Dexter."

"Dex. Call me Dex."

✝

On my way back to the boarding house, I saw a woman saunter towards me. She wore a pink dress and twirled a pink parasol over her right shoulder. She wasn't just any woman; anyone could plainly see. There was something different about her, the way she dressed, the way she moved. She flowed like an Impressionist painting next to her Realism contemporaries.

There was something familiar about her too. It took me a moment, but then I remembered. She was the buxom beauty I admired earlier from my balcony window. Her wonderous hair gave her away. It was wild and gold colored like summer wheat. It moved in all directions at once and corkscrewed down her face like an ornate picture frame. It was wonderful and magical and moved with a life all its own, dancing and bobbing as she came closer. It was like nothing I've ever seen before; a blonde chaotic storm, I thought, and I meant this in the nicest way.

She caught me staring. Now, my heart beat faster and my breathing shallowed.

And though I tried to avert my gaze, it was too late; I was caught red handed. Our eyes met, and I fell into a dream-state, in which she appeared to horde all the color and light while everything else faded to black. Her smile invited me in. It was a wonderful smile; straight, white, ordered teeth like perfect kernels on the cob. Normally, I'm never so bold, but I forgot myself and strode up to her without a single plan.

"Hello," I said, removing my hat.

"Hello," she replied in a southern drawl reminiscent of a kitten's purr.

"Hello," I repeated.

27

Normally, I never know when to shut up, but now, when it mattered most, I couldn't put two words together. I wondered why I had approached her in the first place.

"Hello," she said again. "May I help you?"

I tried keeping my eyes above the neckline, but my God, I am a man after all, and I couldn't resist the vision before me. For the sake of modesty, I'll spare the description. Let's just say God had made her a woman in all the right places.

"May I help you?" she repeated.

"Oh, yes," I said snapping out of my trance. "I'm Dex. I mean I'm Dexter James. I mean my friends call me Dex. It's short for Dexter, or decks as in a deck of playing cards as I do have a reputation up and down the East Coast, but only some of which is earned. At any rate, you can call me Dex, if you wish. My mom, she always called me Dexter, though I never knew why."

Her soft, blue eyes glazed over as I spoke.

"Oh well," I continued. "What's your name?"

The pretty blonde pulled her shoulders back and gave her curls a playful toss across her cheeks. "My name?" she said. "My name is Leslie Reed."

"Leslie Reed," I repeated. I said it again, and then again for good measure. Her name rolled off the tongue like a sonnet on a summer's night. I thought it was beautiful and I told her so.

"Ah," she blushed. "I don't like it much."

"But it's a lovely name. Why don't you like it?"

"I don't know. It's kind of ordinary, I guess. Not like your name. Yours is fancy. You're not from around here, are ya?"

"No Ma'am. I'm originally from Brooklyn, New York, a place called Hell's Kitchen."

"Oh, I've heard of Hell's Kitchen."

"It's ironic because it goes along with my line of work. You see, I'm a Demonologist. Do you know what that is?"

Leslie smiled broadly and nodded her head as if she understood. "No," she replied.

"Allow me to enlighten you. A demonologist studies demons and casts them out of people."

"Ooh," she said twirling her parasol. "That sounds fascinating."

"Well," I shrugged. "I've spent the last two years traveling this fair country of ours, casting out demons, and playing poker now and then. I assure you; you're in good hands with me."

Leslie's laugh made her body jiggle in the most seductive way. I swear I tried to not look, but she was so, well, she was so damned there, and I was, at that very moment, in my own private heaven.

"Well," I said laughing. "Perhaps that came out wrong."

"Oh Dex, you're so funny."

"Ah, you are laughing at me, my Dear?"

"Why, Dex, of course not. I'm laughing with you."

"But I'm not laughing."

"Oh Dex," she said placing her hand on my elbow. "You are hilarious."

My heart raced, and I felt warm from the inside out. Miss Leslie, Miss Leslie, Miss Leslie. I repeated her name in my mind while I smiled at her and she smiled back at me. That's all we did for the next several seconds; we just smiled at each other. The butterflies churned in my stomach, and my body clenched with anticipation while I braced for the question I was about to ask.

"So, Leslie Reed," I said. "Is there—is there a Mr. Reed?"

Leslie's smile evaporated. "No," she said. "Not anymore."

"That's good. I—I mean, I'm so sorry."

I felt like the biggest horse's ass as I farted my response. I couldn't take it back, but Miss Leslie was so gracious.

"That's all right," she said.

Summoning all my courage, I dare to speak again. "So, Miss Leslie—"

"Well, I best be off to my appointment," she said cutting me off. "It was nice meeting you."

I was caught off guard by this sudden turn. I wanted to talk, to find out more.

"Wait!" I said.

"Yes?"

"Uh, well I'd like to...I mean perhaps we could do business together. I brought my black bag with me."

Miss Leslie looked at my bag and smiled nervously. "Yes," she said. "Perhaps."

"Oh, that would be great. I'm free all afternoon. You could come to my place. I have a room at Clem's boarding house."

"The one here on Main Street?"

"Yes, that's right. Just down the boardwalk a spell. Are you familiar with it?"

Miss Leslie smiled and blushed. "Yes," she said. "I've been there before. Um—I'm booked all day today. How about tomorrow at seven?"

"Seven A.M.? That's awfully early."

"No, silly. Seven at night. I do my best work in the evening."

"You do?"

"Well, I must be off. Clem's at seven tomorrow?"

"Yes, that's right."

Miss Leslie extended a delicate, white-gloved hand. I took it and placed my lips on her fingers, and in doing so, inhaled her lilac scent. Let me tell you, I've never smelled anything as sweet. I closed my eyes and imagined my arms wrapped around her waist, pulling her close until her face was a scant breath from mine. The vision was sublime and sent a shiver down my spine. It would have been so easy to—well—I held fast against my temptation.

"I'll see you tomorrow, Honey," she said.

I went dumb. Did she call me, Honey? Speak, you fool. Say something.

"Oh, yes, yes," I said. "Till it be morrow, then."

I watched Miss Leslie saunter off, her hips swaying back and forth as she floated down Main Street; her pink dress rustled by a summer breeze, and her matching pink parasol twirling behind her like a carnation. My imagination was in full bloom, and I pictured me and her living in a house outside of town with a white picket fence and surrounded by oil baron neighbors. I saw her lying next to me, my face pressed against her nude back as I listened to her rhythmic breathing. The daydream brought with it a tingly sensation; I felt embarrassed when I finally snapped out of it, but I didn't care. For the first time in a long time, it felt good to be Dexter James.

✝

I arrived at the boarding house wearing my heart on my sleeve. I didn't mean to, but I must have been. Lucy recognized something different in me.

"You must have met a lady," she said before I had a chance to speak.

"How do you know?"

"When you left here this morning, you looked different, like you were carrying the weight of the world on your shoulders, sort of a lonely looking fellow."

"Is that right?"

"Yep and now look at ya. You look like you swallowed the sun."

"Maybe I have. Miss Lucy, may I ask your opinion?"

"Ask away."

"By a chance encounter, I did meet someone, a lovely vision I must say. I have no idea why she'd give me the time of day, but she has. However, I think I'm a lot older than her. Do you think that matters?"

"Naw," Lucy said waving her hand dismissively. "Love is all that matters, Dex. Love is what matters."

Her counsel reminded me of what the Monsignor always told me: "Love conquers all." Between the two of them, I prayed they were right.

"Are you hungry?" Lucy said.

"Oh, yes, very hungry. I'm famished."

"Good. I have some Irish stew on the stove."

"Oh, that sounds like heaven."

"By the way. I talked to my cousin, Ethel." Miss Lucy clasped her hands in front of her chest. "Dex, you must be very good at what you do," she said.

"Is that so?"

"Yes. Cousin Ethel's a new woman. The demon that took hold of her heart, well, he's gone. You got rid of him good."

My chest swelled with pride. I knew I was skillful, but all the same, it's still nice to hear a kind word.

"Well, that's what I do," I said tipping my hat. "I'm glad to be of service."

"Oh, and Dex, don't worry about paying your bill this week. Ethel told me what you did for her, that pro bone thing."

"Thank you very much. I think I'll retire to my room and read my bible for a spell."

"Would you like me to bring up your food?"

"Yes please."

Lucy was kind enough to bring a bottle of whiskey along with the meal. I offered to pay her, but she still gushed about what I had done for Ethel and would have none of it. Who was I to argue? Besides, it was the perfect complement to Irish stew and cornbread.

After supper, I lay in my bed and read from Leviticus, but my eyes soon grew warm and wet, as they strained against the fading light. I put my Bible down and rested. My breathing turned slow and rhythmic; my chest rose and fell in step with my breath as I recounted the day's events. A new town, a fresh start and perhaps a sweetheart were all exciting, but scary too. Don't fret so much Dexter James. Today was a good day.

CHAPTER 4

It was the best night's sleep I've had in a long time, since I was a boy at any rate. No spirits disturbed me, just a few wistful dreams, that I barely recalled. When I awoke, I turned my face to the glorious sunshine flooding my room. I surrendered to its warming rays; it felt good on my cheeks.

I rose from the bed, hobbled to the double doors, and stepped out onto the balcony overlooking town. It was another beautiful day in Titusville. The streets were alive with a fervent energy; a mini Hell's Kitchen, I thought as I looked out over the bobbing heads—all those souls, and all those demons they carry inside—drunks, misfits and thieves and that's just the men. The women are as bad, if not worse. Yesterday, I saw them—let's call them ladies of ill-repute. They were out and strutting about seemingly on every corner. Paint caked their faces and their pronounced cleavage threatened to bust a seam at the slightest breath. There was enough flesh protruding to make any decent man blush. Oh, I didn't ogle their blessings mind you, but it was impossible not to see. Still, I do not judge them too harshly for they are possessed, just as I am.

As I looked down from my balcony, I hoped against hope to catch a glimpse of Miss Leslie out on her morning stroll, but she was nowhere in sight. I remember seeing her for the first time yesterday morning from this same perch. To meet her on the streets, hours later was a small miracle seemingly sanctioned by God, as if he wanted the two of us to meet. I do not subscribe to happenstance; it was, in my heart-of-hearts, meant to be.

The thought of Miss Leslie brought a smile to my face. At the same time, it jogged a memory that sent me head-long into a panic. What have I done? What am I going to do? What do I wear, and why do I place myself in these predicaments? I'm an old man, a rather distinguished-looking old man if I do say so myself, but old, nonetheless. And Miss Leslie—well, she is—she is Miss Leslie, a young and fair woman who can have anyone she wants. She probably has to beat the men aside with that pink parasol of hers. That's why she carries it with her. It's not just a fashion accessory. Even so, she'll be with one man this evening. She will be with me.

She needed an exorcism. She said as much, didn't she? Well, I reckon it's a minor demon. I will dispose of it quickly and waive my fee of course. Then what? Perhaps tea in the parlor. That will be nice. I'll tell Lucy to make plans for us this evening. It wouldn't be fitting for a nice girl like her to be alone with me or any man for that matter. Miss Leslie would never have it even though I would not mind. Perhaps she'll want to kiss me, like Ethel did. If she wants to, I will let her, or perhaps it's better to move slow. I don't know. It's been so long.

It is clear to me I won't make noon let alone into the evening hours. I was already a train wreck. Sweat poured off me like a pig at a roast. I'm not a novice when it comes to the opposite sex. I've had plenty of women in my day, but they were the whorish kind, and I don't use the term loosely. I never had a real sweetheart before, no one that compares to Miss Leslie's kind anyway; she is special, a fine woman, the kind of woman a man thinks about settling down with. I could tell as much in our brief encounter.

Settling down? At my age? Man, the spill from the train must have done some real harm. Only a brain-damaged fool would think such a thing.

"C'mon," I said to myself. "We have work to do."

After washing up, I walked downstairs, and was greeted by Lucy's smiling face.

"Ah, Lucy," I said tipping my hat. "Top of the morning."

"Sleep well?" she said.

"Never better. Never better. It was like the angels watched over me in my slumber."

"Oh, glory be. I'm sure they were."

"I'm hungry, Lucy. Can I get some breakfast?"

"You sure can."

"Great. How about steak and eggs benedict? And don't skimp on the Hollandaise sauce, oh and toast; perhaps a nice rye bread with freshly churned butter. Do you happen to have honey butter?"

Lucy flashed a bemused smile. "I'll have Clem cook up some grits and eggs."

"Wait, what?"

"Hey, Clem," she yelled out over her shoulder. "Fix some grub for Dex, will ya?"

"Uh, huh," a gruff voice called out from the back room.

"Oh, I almost forgot," Lucy said. "The carpenter dropped something off for ya."

"What?" I replied. "I wasn't expecting anything just yet."

"Yeah, he come in this morning smiling from ear-to-ear. He told me he woke up early just to finish it fer ya. I've never seen a man so happy. He said you fixed a demon good for him yesterday, and he's never felt better in his life, and his missus, well, she was pleased too. Kept talking about a blue pill you gave him. He said he wanted more and would be happy to pay you."

"Where is it, Miss Lucy?"

"I told him to leave it on the boardwalk. It's waiting outside fer ya. Hey, what is this about a blue pill? Maybe Clem could use some."

"Sorry. I don't have any at this time. Have to make some more."

I walked out the front door and saw the soapbox sitting on the boardwalk. It was just as I pictured, better actually. Carpenter John had lightly stained the yellow wood. It practically glowed with a golden hue as its dew-covered surface reflected the morning sun. There were a few dark knots, but they only added character. The signage was brilliant too, painted with bold, red letters and black trim like I asked for. They were big enough to be seen from a distance: DEMONS CAST OUT - $5. Carpenter John was kind enough to letter both the front and back, so it could be read coming or going.

I picked it up and found it was light; not feather light mind you for it had to support my weight, but lighter than the old monstrosity, which nearly nicked my head two days ago. I think the conductor did me a favor by smashing the blasted thing. This new box was a work of art, a real gem, and I almost felt guilty for cutting such a hard bargain. Almost.

My heart beat through my chest as I mounted the platform for the first time. Though I was just a few inches off the ground, I felt like a giant up there. At six feet, one inch, I suppose I must have looked like one too. I got some rather strange looks from the few pedestrians who walked past.

I closed my eyes and imagined a queue lining up with cash in hand, waiting to be exorcised. The humiliation of being tossed from a train was long gone. I had a new start in Titusville, Pa.

I allowed myself a brief moment on my box, then I stepped down and hurried back into the boarding house where I met with Lucy.

"Miss, Lucy," I said. "I have a favor to ask you. Since you have a prime location on Main Street, I'd wonder if you'd mind me doing business outside your establishment? I have procured a license."

"Business? What kinda business?"

"The carpenter has delivered my soapbox and it's a dandy piece, a real work of art. Soon, I'll have paying customers lined up for exorcisms. Some of them will spill into the boarding house I'm sure. You can sell ice-cold lemonade. We both win."

Missy Lucy gave me a smirk. "Suit yourself, but I don't think you'll drum up any business that a way."

"What do ya mean?" I said.

"Soapbox is for snake-oil salesmen, not Demons."

"I told you; I'm not a—"

"You've done this before have you, selling demon chasing from a soapbox?"

"I have."

"And it's worked well for you?"

"Well enough. If you get the right crowd, it can be very lucrative. Besides, did you see the beauty sitting outside?"

"That ugly thing? Yeah, I seen it."

"Isn't it magnificent? How can I miss?"

"Well—"

"Perhaps," I interrupted. "You'll need to talk it over with Clem?"

"What fer? I run the show round here. Not Clem."

"Oh yes. Yes of course."

"Clem," She yelled. "Where's breakfast? Dex is hungry."

Miss Lucy smiled and winked at me, and I responded in kind—more from fear than anything else.

✝

It was the busiest part of the Main street; stores, saloons, and restaurants as far as I could see. There was a church too, Saint Titus, just down the road. All those desperate souls in need of my services. It was the perfect location. I held my own destiny, and what more can a man ask for?

I drew a deep breath, said a prayer, and stepped onto the box. Immediately, I sensed their eyes upon me. It was intoxicating. The people, well, they knew something big was about to happen. They were in for a show.

"Here ye! Here ye!" I shouted while raising my hands to the sky. "Listen up, all of you…you lost souls, you who are tired and worn to the nub. I have your salvation at hand and for a mere five dollars, I will cast out your demons."

I was a tad nervous; a new town full of strangers always brought with it a sense of nakedness. However, my voice was strong, deep, and resonant. I was young again. I felt alive. My heart thumped; my blood coursed through my veins. I felt the pump in my ears.

Some people kept walking, paying me no mind. Men on horses turned their heads and smirked as they rode off. There were a few people, however, who ventured in. They shuffled lightly and slowly, but that's all I needed. I had my audience.

"You sir. The one with the daft bowler cap," I said pointing to a diminutive man in the front row. "You look like you need help."

The short man with the bowler looked around and pointed at himself. "Me?" he said.

"Yes, sir. Are you tired, depressed, lonely? Perhaps you have problems with relations, are prone to fits of anger, or take our Lord's name in vain, or perhaps you suffer all these maladies and even more?" The man cast his eyes downward. "That's what I thought," I said. "Do not despair. Your salvation is here and nigh."

The man with the bowler produced a dollar bill and held it out for me. "Okay," he said. "I'll take a bottle."

"A bottle of what?"

"Whatever it is you're selling."

"Oh, my dear, good man," I laughed. "I am not selling anything that comes from a bottle. No, what I'm selling is salvation."

A deep and despondent groan rose from the crowd. Some turned and started to walk away.

"Wait," I pleaded. "The ills of which I speak are not what you think. They are the Devil's work, and for the low, low price of five dollars, I will rid you of your demons."

"Demons?" a woman said.

"Yes, Ma'am. Most people don't know they are so inflicted. Some have as many as two or three evil scoundrels lurking within. In our great capital of Washington, I had to cast out as many as six from one body alone."

Some of the women gasped and I heard a few chuckles sprinkled in.

"I bet it was a politician," a voice cackled.

Everyone laughed, and I felt the sweat dripping from beneath my hat.

"Go ahead and laugh," I said. "You have been forewarned. Many of you walk around possessed and don't even know you are so inflicted. Just yesterday morning, I cleansed the demon from a woman, who's soul had been seized by a chicken."

"You mean, Ethel?" someone from the crowd shouted.

"What? You know her?" I said cringing.

"Yeah, everyone knows her," the voice said. "She's crazy."

The crowd once again erupted with laughter. I pulled out my handkerchief, removed my hat and mopped my brow. It was mid-morning, already stifling hot and getting hotter by the second.

"Well, never mind that," I said. "The devil lurks among us. When you see a man drinking his life away and losing his money in games of chance, that's the work of a demon."

"A demon?" a woman in the crowd said.

"Yes, ma'am," I said pointing to her. "God has made us pure and wholesome vessels, and it's the devil's task to tear us apart and lead us astray from God's plan. Surely, as you see the drunkard walking the street at night, wobbling from side-to-side, I will tell you there's a demon at work inside of him and the only thing that will return him to a life of sobriety is a cleansing—from me."

I panned the crowd trying to read their faces. They returned blank stares and wide eyes. They were on the fence. I had my work cut out.

"And when you see a woman of ill repute, thieves, avarice, greed, and loneliness, I tell you there is a demon behind this too. Good people of Titusville, Satan has come to your town. He has taken root. Heed me now; he will not leave of his own bequest. You will need me for only I can make things right again. Only I can make it happen."

I stopped for dramatic affect as a murmur traveled the crowd; people looked from side-to-side. I had them. All they needed was a final push.

"Now, which brave soul will come forth? Who will be the first?"

Another murmur grew from the audience as they turned their heads looking for support.

"You sir in the daft, bowler cap." The man in the bowler shook his head. "My good man. You like the nip of the bottle, don't you? Perhaps you visit certain establishments in the middle of the night—places the missus wouldn't be too happy about. Am I right?"

The people snickered and the man's cheeks turned bright red. "Now, you wait a minute," he said shaking a finger at me.

Another man shouted, "Hey, Charlie, he got you figured out."

The crowd which had grown to a substantial size by now, erupted in a chorus of laughter. I laughed, too. They were on my side. I felt at home, like a conductor conducting his orchestra; but as quickly as the feeling came, it vanished. People started shuffling their feet, dispersing, turning their backs and walking away.

"Wait," I said. "Where are you going?"

A gruff voice rose above the din. "We're all filled up with demons. We're going to get us some liquor and women."

Alone and discouraged I stepped down, sat on my soapbox and placed my head in my hands. *Tough crowd*, I thought. Maybe it was me; my delivery was off. Perhaps it was the new town. New towns take a while to get used to, especially a place like Titusville where most people are from someplace else.

I felt lonely and sorry for myself, but that's the way life is I reasoned. One moment you're on top of a mountain; the next moment, you're buried in it. I sat there for a full minute, trying to figure what went wrong when a shadow crossed my path. I looked up and saw a boy standing in front of me. He couldn't have been more than twelve. He had dark hair, his face was dirty, and his black-stained clothes screamed oil.

"Hey Mister," he said. "What's your box say?"

"Can't you read?" I snapped.

"No," he said shaking his head. "I cannot."

"Oh. I'm sorry. I didn't know."

"Now you know."

I thought the boy was being a wise ass, but his placid, innocent countenance told me different.

39

"Indeed," I said standing up. I towered over the boy and he looked up at me with confident, unflinching eyes. "Now I know. Let me help you, young man. My box reads, demons cast out. Five dollars."

The boy looked unimpressed.

"Tell me young man. Do you know anyone who may be in need of my services?"

The boy cocked his head, squinted and said, "Maybe. What do you do?"

"What do you mean? I just told you. I'm an exorcist." The boy stared blankly. "I exorcise demons," I continued. He looked positively bewildered. "I cast demons out of people."

"Oh," he replied as if a light had just been switched on in his brain. "I still don't know what that means."

"Do you know anyone in this town who may be possessed?"

"Possessed?"

"Oh, for crying out loud. What are they teaching the youth of Titusville?"

"I don't know what they're teaching, but they should be teaching happiness."

The boy's comment struck me as both ludicrous and brilliant at once.

"Well, never mind that," I said. "I'm here to exorcise the town of Titusville, rid the populace of its demons."

"Demons? What kind of demons?"

"Well," I said stroking my beard. "There's the demon of drink where people are made to drink themselves into a stupor, and there's the demon of wager where people are forced to gamble their life savings playing craps, poker and other games of chance. Then, there's the demon of lust where, oh well, you're too young for that. My point is that demonic possession takes many forms and my job is to rid the frail souls of their dark spirits and return the citizenry to a happy and normal life."

"You talk funny."

"I do not talk funny," I argued. The boy's stare was positively accusatory. "Okay, maybe I do talk funny, but the point is do you know anyone who may need my services?"

The boy looked at me thoughtfully and said, "Mister, I think the entire town needs you somehow or another, especially after they struck oil here. It's like the whole town's gone crazy."

The boy's observation was clever and astute. I felt my ill temper melt with every drop of his accidental charm. Besides, at that very moment, he was the only friend I had in this world.

"Ah," I replied. "That is what I thought, but alas, I have no customers. Do you think you can help an old man out? Do you know of anyone who can use my services and more importantly, can pay for them? I charge five dollars for a demon cleansing."

The boy's eyes lit up. "Five dollars, mister? You crazy?"

"Why do you say this? This town struck oil. Simple farmers and landowners, well, they're rich now. They can afford to send their sons and daughters to the finest colleges in the east: Harvard, Princeton, Yale; they sleep wrapped tight in the finest linens and ride the best carriages. Have you seen the mansions? Five dollars should be of no bother to them."

The boy cast his eyes to the ground and spread the dust with the tip of his big toe. "Well, I reckon," he said. "But regular folks, the one's that haven't struck oil, don't have that kind of money."

"I see," I said stroking my beard. "Perhaps you and I can come to some arrangement."

The boy gave me questioning look. "Arrangement?" he said. "What sort of arrangement?"

"I often enter into business arrangements with people. You know, you help me, and I'll help you?"

"Yes?"

"Well, let us say you bring me a paying customer. I'll pay you twenty-five cents for every one you bring to me."

The boy's eyes lit up. "A whole quarter? That's a lot of money."

"Yes, of course. What was I thinking? How about ten cents? I'll give you a dime for every paying customer you bring to me."

"That's still a lot, but okay, I'll take it."

"Smart, smart boy."

"I don't how smart I am," he lamented. "I started out with twenty-five cents and now I'm down to a dime."

I chuckled and held my hand out to him. "My name is Dexter James," I said. "Friends and business partners call me Dex for short."

He shook my hand and said, "May I call you Dex?"

"I was hoping you would. And your name, lad?"

"People call me Boo. You can call me Boo."

"Well, Boo, pleasure to meet you. I'm sure there's a colorful story behind your nickname."

"Oh, there is. When I was—"

"Yeah, well, save it," I said. "I have lots of work to do, many corners to explore, the backways and the side streets."

"Oh, okay. I'll leave you be," Boo said.

"I'm staying at Clem's. You can find me there and bring the customers too."

I watched Boo walk away slowly and solemnly with his head hung low. Then he stopped, turned around and walked back. "Hey, I think I got a customer for ya."

"Oh, well, that's great. Who is it?"

"Well, he can't exactly pay ya."

"Remember, the deal was for paying customers."

"Yes, I know, but I was wondering if you might be able to help him anyhow. You don't have to pay me the dime or nothing."

"Who is it?"

"Me."

"You?" I said. "Well, what on earth for? What demon possesses a lad like yourself?"

"Is there a demon of dumbness?"

"Dumb?" I said. "What fool told you that?"

"I reckon I do."

"That's ridiculous. You're a bright young lad; a very astute judge of the human condition. I can see that plainly enough."

"Well, I don't likely know what all that means but thank you."

"It simply means you're smart and you have a lot of common sense too."

"Yeah, but I don't know how to read. Most everybody in my school knows how to read, but me."

"Well, there can be other reasons for that. Things unrelated to intelligence or are related, but in inverse proportion." Boo cocked his head to the side and squinted. "Yes, well," I continued. "Perhaps I could get you a reader, and I can help you learn to read and write."

"You'd do that?"

"I'll see what I can do."

"So, you reckon I don't need to be excised?"

"The word is exorcised. Commit it to memory, and no, based on what you've told me, I do not believe you are demon possessed."

Boo's face lit up and then he turned and walked away. He was a good lad. I could tell by our brief conversation.

CHAPTER 5

I ran around the room like a chicken with its head cut off, scurrying about with no intent of purpose. Sweat rained off me like a sinner at a sermon in spite of my cold, clammy skin. It took a moment to realize what I was doing. My God, what was I doing? The worry lords had me by the throat, and I was so anxious.

She is a flower blooming in the weeds, sophisticated and intelligent. Our conversation was brief but illuminating, and in those few moments, her light cast its warm glow upon my heart. I liked how it felt and I'm not ashamed to admit as much. I'm just, you know, frightened. Funny, I hear the irony in my thoughts. Demons do not scare me half as much as a pretty face or the sweet purr of a woman's voice.

I knew little about her; my imagination had to fill in the rest. She may be the daughter of a newly minted oil baron. They abound in droves like flies on a carcass. Maybe she comes from old money for it takes time to develop refinement, and she is clearly refined and well learned. I imagined she went to college in the East, perhaps Ivy League: Harvard, Penn, or maybe Yale.

And the way she smelled—oh, I can close my eyes and inhale her sweet lilac scent right now as if she stood right here beside me. And her face, so soft and pure, would make angels blush. She could have modeled for Titian or Michelangelo for she has just a touch of the cherub in her essence.

I know a beautiful woman when I see one. I had a few in my day. It may be hard to believe for I am nothing to look at, old, grey haired and weathered skin. My wrinkles do me no favors. Who am I kidding? I was never handsome, not even in my youth, but somehow, I've managed to do well for myself. I was never married, never could be, and at fifty-three, time is running short. How does the poem go? *Age is like a crushing weight as twilight nears, and the prospects grow slimmer as the light grows dimmer*—something like that. Miss Leslie, well, she is a sliver of hope, a sliver I desperately cling too, my last chance. Demon fighting is a lonely calling, very lonely.

Ah, she'll be here soon. I must find a new shirt. The one I'm wearing is soaked through.

I checked my pocket watch. The time is near, so I did what only seemed logical at the time. I paced the room like a caged tiger as I waited for those final moments to pass. The minute hand could not circle fast enough for my liking. I took a seat at the edge of my bed, held my head in my hands and started thinking. As it turned out, this was a mistake because all sorts of black thoughts entered my head. I worried about what we'd talk about; I worried if she would remember our meeting, which, if this were the case, would make my worrying all that more useless, and this caused me to worry even more. As soon as one thought would enter, another more insidious one took its place. Perhaps she had no real serious intent of meeting with me. She was younger than me. Oh, she was no spring chicken—I guessed she was in her forties—but perhaps she thought I was nothing more than a foolish old man. Perhaps she was right.

I blew out a breath of hot air. What time is it? It's after seven and she's still not here. Did we agree on seven? Yes, I think we did. She's not coming.

But then, a knock on the door brought me to attention; I sat upright and ran my hands through my hair as a makeshift comb.

"Hello?" I said. "Come in."

To my disappointment and relief, it was Lucy. She opened the door and stepped in. Her face was stern and her manner cold. "Mr. James," she said. "I brought you the McGuffey Readers you asked for."

"Oh, thank you," I said standing up and taking the books from Lucy. I shuffled through them; the memories came pouring back and made me smile. "How much do I owe you?"

"Oh, it's nothing. They belonged to my children, but they're grown now."

"Boo will love them. Do you know him?"

"The Johnson boy? Yeah, he's always running around asking for odd jobs he can do. Sometimes I give him two bits to help me and Clem out."

"He's a good lad. Imagine a boy his age not knowing how to read."

Lucy looked around the room as if something were bothering her. "Mr. James," she said in a stern voice.

"Yes?"

"There's something else I need to talk to you about."

"Go ahead."

"There's a...well...there's a lady waiting in the foyer for you."

"Brilliant. Send her up, Lucy. Would you be so kind?"

"Mr. James," she snapped. "Need I remind you we have rules in our establishment?"

"What?"

"Unmarried couples in the same room together are not permitted. What kind of a boarding house do you think I'm running here? I thought you were a man of God."

I had to admit in my fevered state I had never thought of such decorum. I felt like a cad.

"Oh—oh, yes, of course," I stammered. "There's no need to worry about that. We're not having relations. We're friends; I just met her yesterday. I'm performing a service for her. I mean to say an exorcism. Like I did with your cousin Ethel yesterday."

Miss Lucy's glare reminded me of my mother's face when I had done something wrong. She shook her head and made disapproving clicking sounds with her tongue too.

"Mr. James," she said. "I'm surprised at you."

I could tell by the tone in her voice the surprise was not a good one. For the life of me, I keep forgetting I'm not in a big city, but in the backwoods of the backwoods where tradition and moralism still rule the day. I thought it charming, but highly unnecessary at my advanced age, and so I persisted.

"Yes," I said. "Can you send her up? I can assure you there will be no impropriety. I promise."

"Mr. James, do you know—"

Lucy's sentence was cut short by a sweet, southern drawl that sang like a purring kitten. It was Leslie Reed standing behind Lucy.

"Hello," Miss Leslie said. "Here I am."

I tell you, I watched on with a slack jaw as those two women stared each other down like it was the making of a hen fight. In one corner, Lucy's eyes spat daggers as she scowled like a mad dog. In the other corner, Miss Leslie called her scowl and raised with the sweetest smile I'd ever seen. The tension was palpable. Goosebumps filled my arms. The two women squared off, and I felt the perspiration run down the back of my neck. I was about to crack waiting for one of them to back down. It was exciting in a perverse sort-of-way, but as quickly as it started, it ended with one quick parry by Miss Leslie's sharp tongue.

"Shoo now," Miss Leslie said waving the back of her hand in front of Lucy's face. "I'll take it from here."

Lucy looked at me and Leslie with a scorn normally reserved for the most wicked sinners. Finally, she jerked her chin in the air before turning and exiting the room.

"Gosh," I said. "I wonder what got into her. She was so friendly before."

"Well," Miss Leslie replied. "Some people are just set in their ways you know?"

"I tried explaining to her our meeting was innocent."

Miss Leslie laughed, causing the flesh on her upper chest to jiggle in the most glorious manner. I tried averting my eyes, or not be so conspicuous about it anyway, but Lord knows I am a man.

"Oh dear," she said catching her breath. "You are too funny, Dex."

She thinks I'm funny? That's a good sign, but for the life of me, I wasn't trying to be. Maybe that's a good sign too. I don't have to try so hard with this one.

"Miss Leslie," I said in my most beguiling voice. "Are you laughing at me or with me?"

"Mr. Dexter, of course, I'm laughing _at_ you."

I must have looked confused because for the second time in as many moments, Miss Leslie burst out laughing. I laughed too and for the first time since we met, I drew in a deep breath. I knew we would be okay. Just keep her laughing, I thought. The sight and the sound intoxicated the mind and soothed the soul.

"Well, Dexter, shall we get to business?"

I liked her direct, no-nonsense approach. "Yes," I said reaching for my bag. "Let us get down to business."

"We haven't discussed a price."

"Oh, well, I usually charge five dollars for my services, but there's no need for that. I'll waive my fee."

Miss Leslie frowned. "What?" she said. "Waive _your_ fee?"

"Yes, of course. Just the other day, I waived the fee for Miss Lucy's cousin. She became possessed after having relations with a chicken you know."

The wrinkles on Miss Leslie's forehead grew deep and then she burst out laughing again. I did the same though I had no idea what we were laughing at this time. Still, it felt good, so I played along.

After we had both settled down, Miss Leslie waved her hand dismissively and said, "We can talk money after."

Now I've been around the block once or twice, had my fair share of women, drink, adventure and misadventure. Let's just say I've seen a few things in my time. But what happened next caused the hair on the back of my neck and arms to stand straight on end.

This gorgeous creature—the same one I just met and barely knew—began to undress right there in front of me. She started with the top button of her blouse, undid it and worked her way down in a methodical, unhurried manner that could not be more seductive if she had tried to be. Each button revealed more-and-more of that white, milky flesh of hers. I mean, it practically spilled from her neckline like rising dough escaping the edge of its confines. My eyes nearly popped from my skull and I felt tingly sensations in my—well, let just say there was a lot going on in my nether regions. I shook my head once and then again and then once more for good measure but sure enough, the image in front of me was very much real.

I would be lying if I told you I had not hoped for as much. However, I was thinking weeks into the future, after a proper courtship, maybe a nice dinner or two (at my expense), maybe a fine wine, a few more laughs, and some more wine or something stronger. Sure, I'm as red-blooded and healthy as any man and maybe more so, but this woman was moving faster than a runaway locomotive over ice-covered rails.

"Uh, uh," I stammered. Miss Leslie stopped and looked at me. "What are you doing?" I said.

"I'm removing my dress," she replied in a tone that suggested she was doing the most natural thing in the world. In fact, I felt a little foolish for asking.

"Wa—Why?" I stammered.

She smiled. "Well, dear Dex, it does make things go a little—well, a little smoother."

I like to think of myself as a smart man, an enlightened man, a well learned man, but I had no idea what in the Hell this woman was talking about. Maybe I was right about her. Maybe she was too smart and too sophisticated for me. At the risk of sounding ignorant—nay, stupid—I proceeded.

"Make what go smoother?" I said. "The exorcism?"

"The exorcism?" she said making a funny face. "No! I'm talking about—well, you know what I'm talking about."

"Miss Leslie, I'm going to be honest with you. I have no idea what you're talking about woman."

"Really? You have no idea what I'm talking about? It's the reason you asked me to visit you tonight."

I looked at her and she at me and we stared into each other's eyes for what seemed like the longest time. A warm smile waxed across her face. Then, as if a sledgehammer were laid harshly across my cheek, I suddenly became enlightened.

"Oh," I said dragging the vowel out for several seconds. "I see."

"Do you?" she said.

I was struck dumb and averted my eyes. Miss Leslie quickly buttoned her dress, once again concealing her alabaster skin.

"I'm sorry," I said. "I had no idea. I thought you were a nice girl. I meant—"

"No," Miss Leslie said shaking her curls. "I'm not a nice girl. I mean I am a nice girl, but I'm not nice because of what I do. Oh, you know what I mean. You got me all flustery."

"Oh, dear God."

"Tell me something, Dex. How could you not know? Everyone around here knows what I do."

"I told you. I'm not from around here."

"Yes, but you said you're from New York City. That place must be crawling with women like me. I ain't never been there, but I can imagine."

I had to think a moment. It had been a long time since I was back there.

"Yes, you're right," I concluded. "The place is crawling with them but not a single one looks like you, Miss Leslie."

Miss Leslie stopped. Her face grew soft and her lips curled into a warm smile. "Is that so?" she said.

"Yes, that is so."

"Tell me, Dex. What do they look like?"

I wrinkled my nose and conjured an image in my mind. "Well," I said. "They look like—they look like what they are. Heavily made up, smeared red lipstick and dark eyes with a rat's nest sitting on their heads."

"And what do I look like?"

I looked into her eyes, and my vision turned blurry. "Miss Leslie," I said softly. "You look like, well, you look like a lady; a fine one at that."

Miss Leslie beamed from ear-to-ear. "Why did you ask me up here, Dex?"

"I'm quite embarrassed," I said. "I thought you might be in need of my services. I cast out devils and demons and I thought I might be of some help to you."

"Is that the real reason?"

"Well, I don't know—"

"Do you think I do this, because I have a demon inside me?"

"Miss Leslie, I had no idea what you do or what you don't do. To be frank, I just wanted you to visit me. I just thought…"

"Go on. What did you think?"

"Oh, it doesn't matter. I'm an old fool."

"No, you're not. Tell me."

Miss Leslie looked at me expectantly, but all I could manage was a shrug.

"Well, Dex, I'm sorry to have disappointed you. I am embarrassed for all of this."

I didn't want her to go, not like this. "Wait," I said. "Don't leave. Stay. Are you hungry?" Leslie shook her head. "You see, this was just a big misunderstanding. I'm a demonologist. I cast the Devil and his minions out of people."

"Oh," she said as if she understood. I could tell she didn't. "Is there much call for that around here?"

"To be honest, I thought there would be more of a need in a town like Titusville, with all the sinners, drunkards and prosti—"

I tried to quash the last word, but she heard enough. Leslie's face fell along with my heart. To think I caused her grief made me sick to my stomach. I do that sometimes—cause people grief. I seem to be good at it.

"You know, you're right about one thing," she said. "I'm not like those women in New York. Men do pay me for my company, but sometimes, quite often actually, they just want to talk; they are lonely and sad. They want a female friend to listen to their problems, to understand."

"Yes, yes. I see that now. You're kind of like a counselor."

"That's right."

Miss Leslie's smile returned and for this, I was grateful.

"Listen to me, Leslie. I'm so sorry for all of this. I'm new in town. I had no idea."

"It's okay, Dex. I'm flattered you didn't know."

"You are?"

"Yes. It shows I'm different from all of the rest, right?"

"Oh yes, right, right? You are different. Very different. Please don't go. The night is young. I'll pay you. I'll pay you for your time."

"No," she said shaking her head. "We're friends, right? Friends don't pay for company."

"Then you'll stay?"

Miss Leslie thought a moment, then shook her head. "I really need to go. I have other appointments to keep."

"When will I see you again?"

"Come visit me. I have a place just outside of town. It's small, but cozy. Just ask around, anyone can tell you where I live."

"Okay, I will."

"And good luck with your demon fighting."

"Thank you. I'll need luck at the rate I'm going."

"Well, maybe you just need to go where the sinners are."

I smiled and nodded my head. "Go where the sinners are," I repeated. "Beauty and brains."

Miss Leslie walked up to me and kissed me lightly on the cheek. The scent of lilac flooded my senses and for a moment, my mind escaped my body. "You come and visit me you hear?" she whispered. "During the day."

Miss Leslie left, and I felt like the loneliest man on earth. I reached into my black bag and pulled out my Bible but thought better of it. I still had some whiskey left in the bottle.

CHAPTER 6

Boo skipped, almost ran, as he led the way down a long, winding path. I was jealous. I remember a time when my body was young, and I could float along the ground in this weightless manner. The muggy air didn't do my lungs any favors either, but the cool breath that kicked up the trees every now and then made the long journey more bearable.

"Sorry, I couldn't bring Whiskey," Boo said. "But he threw a shoe."

"That's all right," I said. "Just slow down."

As we made our way through down the path, I basked in the flora and the fauna. I loved the sound of birds singing from above. A church choir could not hold a candle to Mother Nature's psalm. I was born in a big city, but the years I spent in the Ohio sticks made me appreciate the countryside's measured pace, the dew on the long-tangled grass, and the smell of manure. I took deep breaths every so often and turned my face to the sun whenever it broke through the clouds. My senses tingled and my heart warmed.

We didn't see many people, just a few farmers on horseback, tipping their hat in a friendly manner as they strode past. They appeared to know Boo; they exchanged smiles and waved to him and he waved back. I was impressed how such a simple lad who couldn't even write nor read his own name would earn such favor with adults. But that was Boo Johnson, a good kid with a kind heart and a soul well beyond his years. I liked Boo. He reminded me of me when I was his age, so full of life, a thirst for knowledge and a bit of the wise ass in him.

It felt good to be alive and watching Boo with his boundless energy and infectious enthusiasm made me a tad younger.

"Hey, there, slow down," I said. "I'm old."

Boo stopped and turned around. "You don't look that old," he said.

"God bless you child. How old would you say I am?"

Boo twisted his lips and squinted. "I reckon you're about a hundred and something."

I expected Boo to start laughing, but he never did. His deadpan expression told me he wasn't joking. "Just slow down, will ya?" I said. "O'le Dex is about to have a heart attack trying to keep up with you."

Boo, thinking he might have a corpse on his hands, finally heeded my plea. The slower pace suited me fine; it gave me time to take in more scenery and breathe deeply the smell of damp, morning air. We came to a clearing and off in the distance, I saw oil derricks and shanty houses spread across the side of a hill where grazing cattle should have been. The structures formed an alien city that seemed to sprout from the earth as organic plant matter. I squinted hard and could make out the shapes of men milling about, oil workers I presumed. They moved slowly and their drooped shoulders conveyed a sense of sadness. There was something mechanical in their movements as if they were not human at all, but just part of the bigger machine; this made me wonder. Are we all moving away from our humanity?

I squinted harder and concentrated on the oil derricks. They were nothing more than frames grounded by four legs, broad at their base and narrow at the top like wooden, mis-formed pyramids stretching towards the heavens. Their centers had poles, which ran their full length and then set into the ground. For the life of me, I could not figure out how they worked to pull oil from the ground. They were strange and wondrous architectural pieces; a kind of modern art.

Boo's black stained overalls reminded me of something.

"What's it like?" I said. "Working in those fields?"

Boo didn't answer right away, but I could tell by his thoughtful expression, he was thinking hard.

"It's all right," he finally said.

"You make good money?"

"Yes. I usually make ten cents, but the other day, one of the men gave me a whole quarter. He said I worked hard. I'm a good worker."

I let out a shrill whistle. "A whole quarter," I said. "That's good money for a boy your age, and your parents don't mind you working there?"

"No, they don't mind. Momma complains she can't get the oil out my britches, but I give them half. They let me keep the other half. I buy candy sometimes. I'm saving the rest to buy a BB gun, but they cost a lot. I don't know if I'll ever have enough."

"What about the town, Boo? Has it changed much since they found oil?"

"It's different."

I waited for Boo to expound but he never did.

"Different how?"

"I don't know. Lots of strange people in town, people I don't know."

"Do you think I'm strange?"

"You're about the strangest person there is," Boo said laughing.

"Hmm. And your ma and pa don't mind you hanging out with a strange person like me?"

"Naw. I told them, Dex is okay. They're pleased to meet you, especially Ma. She wants you to excise Pa real good."

"The term is exorcise, not excise. Excise is a type of tax."

Boo's lips turned up into a mischievous smile. "Oh, that's right. I keep forgetting."

"You know something young man. I think you know more than what you let on."

Boo didn't say anything. He was too busy trying to stifle a laugh and failing miserably.

We walked another quarter mile or so. My legs felt their age; in fact; my whole body did.

"How much farther?" I said.

"Just up here a spell," Boo said.

"Ah, just up here a spell. Can you be more vague?"

We rounded a bend and the dirt road opened into a spacious yard littered with chickens pecking the ground. Straight ahead was a small farmhouse. Off to the right, there was an old, rickety barn. The aroma of farm animals permeated the air, a not so unpleasant smell.

Boo mounted the steps leading into the house, then he stopped and turned around and called out to me. "Well, come on," he said.

I stopped at the bottom step clutching my demon-fighting bag to my chest.

"Now, you're sure this is okay with your ma and pa?" I said.

"Sure, I'm sure. They told me I should bring ya."

"And your parents, you said they can pay my fee?"

"No," Boo said shaking his head. "I never said that."

"What?"

"The oil men didn't find any oil on our property. They looked and all, but they didn't find any. My Pa will probably pay you in pork."

Pork? I thought. I wondered what the going exchange rate is for that.

"Do you think you can help Pa?" Boo said.

"How bad is it, Boo?"

Boo twisted his mouth and looked at me through squinted eyes. "It's not good," he announced. "You reckon he's got a demon inside him?"

"I reckon so, and I reckon it's time to chase that demon out."

"Now, don't forget our agreement. I get a quarter. For every customer I bring ya."

"A quarter?" I said. "I thought I had you down to a dime."

Ray Johnson was a large man with meaty hands and a firm handshake that could inadvertently crush a man's hand. The bright white of his eyes stood in stark contrast to his weathered, dark skin. He wore a pleasant smile that took the edge off of an otherwise intimidating face. In some ways, he looked a lot like Boo.

Ray sat at his kitchen table across from me. His wife, a small, pretty woman named Sarah, sat next to him. She smiled tentatively at me and I smiled back. Boo was fidgeting next to me and we all just sat around smiling awkwardly at each other until Mr. Johnson decide to speak up.

"Mr. Dexter," Ray said. "I'm sure pleased you're here, sir."

"Dex," I said. "Just call me Dex."

"Yes sir, Mr. Dex. I reckon my boy Boo, told you about me?"

"He did, Mr. Johnson. I've brought my black bag," I said lifting it up for him to see.

"Like a regular doctor," he laughed.

"Boo said you can afford to pay me fifty cents and some pork?"

"No to the fifty cents. Yes to the pork."

I let out a big sigh. "That's all right," I said. "We can settle up when we're done."

Ray hung his head and started washing his hands with imaginary soap.

"It's okay," I assured him. "Hardly anyone dies during my exorcisms."

I waited for him to laugh. Instead, he just stared at me with his dark eyes looking scared out of his wits

"Just relax," I told Ray. "I was merely joking."

"Sorry, Mister Dex, but I ain't in no mood for jokes."

"Yes, of course. Maybe you can tell me a little more about your situation. I understand you may have a problem with the bottle. Is that so?"

Ray looked over at his wife and she nodded at him. "Yes sir, Mr. Dex. I reckon I do."

"Raymond is a good man," Sarah said. "He works hard."

"Yes ma'am," I said.

"Yes," she continued. "It's just that sometimes he drinks too much. Gets all mean on me."

I looked at Ray for confirmation. His head hung low like a scolded puppy.

"I understand," I said.

"I never thought it was no demon," Ray said shaking his head. "I just thought I was no good, but Boo here told me it might be just that, and you could fix it for me."

"Yes. That's exactly right. You've heard of the seven deadly sins: pride, greed, lust, envy, gluttony, wrath, and sloth. Each sin is ascribed to a hierarchy of seven archdemons: Lucifer (pride); Mammon (greed); Asmodeus (Lust); Leviathan (Envy); Beelzebub (Gluttony); Satan (Wrath); and Belphegor (Sloth). Besides tempting humans to sin, these seven princes of Hell are responsible for various types of calamities, both natural and accidental. Do you understand?"

Ray's mouth hung wide open and I detected a small bit of drool dangling from the corner of his mouth.

"Tell me something, Mr. Johnson. Are you a church-going man?"

Ray looked at his wife. "Well, not exactly," he said.

Sarah put a hand on Ray's shoulder and said, "I told him he should go to church, get right with God, but he don't listen. He's a good man, but something just ain't right."

"That's true," Ray agreed. "I ain't right. Can you help?"

"I've tangled with Beelzebub before. He's the demon of gluttony, which includes drinking to excess. I dare say he's been a thorn in my own side for some years. I shouldn't have any trouble with him. Do you trust me?"

Ray looked at me with his big, dark eyes. He looked at his wife and then at Boo. He nodded his head and said, "I trust you."

"Good," I said. "I like to start out with a brief blessing before we begin the actual ceremony. Shall we bow our heads?"

We closed our eyes and the room went quiet like a church. I prayed: "In nomine Patris, et Filii, et Spiritus Sancti. Amen."

"Amen."

"What's that you're saying?" Boo said.

"It's Latin, my boy."

I reached into my bag and pulled out the cross, the Holy Bible and my purple stole. I laid the Bible and the cross on the table. Then I kissed my stole and placed it gently around my neck. Everyone watched me carefully and in total silence. Ray looked as pale as death.

"Let us bow our heads," I said.

"Saint Michael the Archangel, defend us in our battle against principalities and powers, against the rulers of this world of darkness, against the spirits of wickedness in the high places."

I paused to catch my breath and when I did, I opened my eyes. All heads were bowed in reverence except for Rays. He was staring at me with an absent, far off look.

I closed my eyes and continued to pray, but I spoke only a few words before I was interrupted by a loud noise which reverberated throughout the kitchen like the clamor of a church bell. It gave everyone a start. A large metallic bowl had fallen from its perch and bounced off of the stone floor. It danced in a circle before finally coming to rest and ending the calamity.

Sarah and Boo looked petrified, but Raymond wore a slight smirk on his face. I looked into his eyes. There was no color that I could discern, just two coal pieces staring vacantly back at me. It was as though I had a window into his soul, and what I saw sent a chill through my body.

"Identify yourself." I said.

The demon didn't answer right away. Instead, it lifted its chin as if it were analyzing me, sizing me up.

"I am Ray Johnson," the demon said.

"No," I answered. "Who's inside of Ray, making him drink, to be so mean and angry to his wife?"

"What do you mean? It's me talking, Ray. There are no demons here."

"Hmm," I said stroking my beard. "There are demons in there, Raymond Johnson. To be sure."

Ray looked to his wife for support. She offered him nothing, but a confused look, so he laughed in a way intended to make <u>me</u> look like the crazy one.

"Mrs. Johnson," I said keeping my eyes fixed on Ray. "Leave and take Boo with you. Now."

"I'm not going anywhere," Boo said.

"Neither am I," said Mrs. Johnson.

I turned to Mrs. Johnson and commanded her attention with my eyes. "Did you hear me?" I told her. "Take the boy and leave now. Go to the room, lock the door behind you. Wait until I come get you."

Sarah recognized the urgency in my voice. She stood quickly. Grabbed a protesting, sullen Boo and left me alone with the demon.

"Let's try this again," I said. "Identify yourself."

"I'm Ray Johns—"

"Ray, let me ask you something. Why do you think you drink?"

"My pa," he said after several seconds. "He drank. You think he may have been demon possessed too?"

"Yes. I do. This form of possession can carry on from one generation to the next." Ray swallowed hard and nodded his head. "Ray, this has to stop. The drinking, the abuse. The curse of the Johnson family stops with Raymond Johnson."

"I know, but how? Aren't you supposed to be exorcising me?"

"I'll continue the prayers. I'll place my hand on your forehead. You will close your eyes and concentrate the entire time. Do you understand?"

"I know but—."

"Good. Let us pray."

I placed my hand on Ray's hot, sweaty head and said the prayer to Michael, the archangel.

"Saint Michael the Archangel, defend us in our battle against principalities and powers, against the rulers of this world of darkness, against the spirits of wickedness in the high place…"

"How will praying help?" Ray interrupted.

"…come to the aid of men, whom God created immortal, made in his own image and likeness and redeemed at a great price from the tyranny of the devil."

"Do you think your fancy praying is going to make me stop drinking?"

I recited louder and more fervently to drown out Ray's voice.

"Fight this day the battle of the Lord, together with the holy angels, as already thou hast fought the leader of the proud angels, Lucifer, and his apostate host, who were powerless to resist thee, nor was there a place for them any longer in Heaven. But that cruel, that ancient serpent, who is called the devil or Satan, who seduces the whole world, was cast into the abyss with all his angels. Behold—"

"I ain't never going to stop. I'll be drinking till the day I die."

My patience, already worn thin by his insolence, had completely vanished.

"Look, you rube prick," I said. "You want to drink yourself to death and take the rest of your family with you, then fine, go right ahead. But if you want to shut up for five seconds, you might be surprised how little you actually know."

"What are you getting so sore for?"

"Because there are good people out there, people who need my help, want my help, and have the humility to accept it without question. This is charity work—more for Boo's sake than anyone else. He's a good lad."

"Hey, that's quality pork you're getting; worth more than what you're asking for."

"And what am I supposed to do with it? I haven't an icebox."

"I'll have it delivered to the boarding house. I bet they have a big one. I'll fill it up."

"If I am to help you, you have to want my help. Without that, there's no point in going any further."

Ray looked over at the empty chairs where his wife and Boo once sat, then he turned back to me and said, "All right. I'll keep my big mouth shut."

"No."

"Oh come on. I said I'm sorry. Don't be a stubborn, old mule."

"You never did say you were sorry and I'm not a stubborn, old mule, but you're right about one thing. You're beyond a simple prayer. Beelzebub has a firm grip over your heart and soul."

I reached down, picked up my demon fighting bag and pulled out a piece of parchment from the secret inner compartment.

"What's that?" said Ray.

"This here is a plan," I said holding it up for him to see. "I call it Dexter's twelve phases to the demon drink recovery."

I slid the paper toward Raymond; he stared at it like it was a rotting fish.

"Can you read?" I said. Ray's eyes told me he could not. "That's okay. Have Mrs. Johnson help you. Follow each phase like a prescription. Begin with step one. Do not vary from the course."

"But how is this supposed to help? You said I had a demon inside of me."

"You do, a very powerful one; this will help you remove the demon or at the very least, keep tight hold of it."

"This makes no sense."

"Here. I'll help you with the first one. Phase one says to admit you have no power over the demon drink and your life has become a living hell. Do you admit as much?"

"Well, sure, but—"

"No buts. Admit it to me, confess it to your wife, your child and most importantly to God. Now say it."

"What, you mean, now?"

"Yes. Right now. It's only me and God listening. Do it Raymond." I saw the sweat form on Ray's upper lip, and he kept looking from side-to-side. "Stop looking around," I scolded. "Your wife's not here. Boo is not here. There's just you and me."

Ray closed his eyes and clasped his hands together. Then, he lowered his head and offered a prayer to the heavens. It was a made-up prayer, a bit rough, but I could tell he was sincere.

"Dear God. I—I don't know what to say. I'm not used to talking to you like this. You know me. Hell, you know me better than I know me. Well, anyway, I just want to say I'm right sorry about the things I done."

Ray opened his eyes and gave me a questioning look.

"Go ahead," I told him. "You're doing fine; just admit you're powerless over the bottle."

Ray nodded his head and continued. "And Lord, you know I'm weak. I have no power over this need to drink."

When he finished, he looked and me and said, "How's that?"

"Good, good," I said. "That was nice."

"Now, do I have to pray to you and my wife?"

"No. That won't be necessary. God heard you, I've heard you. You just need to tell your wife and your son how sorry you are and admit to them you are powerless."

"That ain't easy for a man to do."

"I know. I never said it would be easy."

I reached into my secret compartment once more and pulled out a piece of one inch-by-one-inch parchment. This one had my initials on it along with a drawing I made: two dots for eyes and an arching line meant to represent a smiling face.

"Here," I said handing it to Ray.

"What's this?"

"If you feel the need to drink, I want you to deliver this parchment to me. Send Boo on horseback if need be. That will be my signal to come at once."

"What if it's three in the morning?"

"Well, for God's sake. I should hope you'd be asleep at that hour," I said. I drew a deep breath and let the air out slowly. "But, yes. Any hour. Any day."

"And what are you going to do once you get here?"

"We'll talk. We'll pray. I'll slap you upside the head if need be, anything to keep you from drinking."

Ray looked at the parchment and laughed. "You're not much of an artist," he said.

"Well, I suppose not."

"So, are we done?"

"Wait. I almost forgot." I reached into my demon-fighting bag and pulled out the books. "Take these," I said handing them to Ray. "They are for Boo."

"Boo can't read. He's dumb like me."

"Boo is not dumb," I said shaking my head emphatically. "On the contrary, he's very bright. I believe he's just mixing up the letters. I procured these readers special for him. Inside are my personal notes that will help him make more sense of the words. Have his mother work with him every night and when he's done with these, I'll get more."

Ray looked at the books and scratched his head. "What does he need with books?" he said. "He got the farm."

"Mr. Johnson," I said. "Books are, well, books are wonderful. They teach; they show us the world and allow the discovery of new ones. They talk to us and soothe our souls when need be. They make us laugh and cry." I picked up the Bible and held it up. "Mr. Johnson, I want your son to read this book. Wouldn't do you any harm neither."

"But I told you already. I can't read."

I didn't say anything. I just nodded at the readers in his hands.

Ray smiled and shook his head. "You know, you're a real pain in the ass."

"I know," I said laughing. "But sometimes you need a real pain in the ass to get to where you're going."

CHAPTER 7

Boo wanted to tag along, but I told him no. I needed alone time, some privacy. The look on his face told me he did not understand. More likely, he did, but he just wanted to be a pest.

"You like her?" he said.

It seemed like an odd question because I never thought about it in such a direct manner. I liked a lot of women; they're soft and they smell good, but this felt different. Leslie did things to me, lighting up parts of my brain I never knew existed. I did possess the capacity to feel this way once, but the embers have cooled in recent years. Now, the flames seemed to have been stoked once more.

"Sure," I said. "What's not to like?"

Boo twisted his mouth as he was in the habit of doing. Then he swept a wide arc in the dirt with his big toe. "Momma don't like her."

This revelation came as no surprise to me.

"Well, maybe she hasn't gotten to know her."

"Oh, she knows her. They used to be friends."

"Miss Leslie, and your Ma?"

Boo nodded his head, and now I was surprised, a little shocked even. I keep forgetting in a small town like this, everyone knows everyone. I imagined Leslie's professional choices must have been the talk of the town; still is.

"I like her, though," Boo said.

"You've talked to her?"

"Yeah, she used to come over before they found oil, before she started doing bad things."

This was a delicate topic, not one I was eager to broach with a twelve-year-old, but my curiosity insisted on answers.

"Do you think she's a bad person, Boo?"

Boo immediately shook his head and his voice rose with excitement. "Oh, no, Dex. She ain't. She's about the nicest lady I know. Sometimes, I do errands for her. She pays me. But don't tell Ma. Pa don't mind so much."

"Is Miss Leslie nicer than your Ma?"

"Well, yes," he answered without hesitation. "Ma can be kind of ornery. We had this pig named, Doris. She was kind of mean and—"

"Uh, Boo," I said cutting him off. "For the sake of your survival, you may want to refrain from making comparisons between a pig named Doris and your Ma."

"It's okay. Ma and Doris got along real good."

"Whatever became of Doris?"

"Pa is sending parts of her to the boarding house because he didn't have money to pay you."

I cringed at the thought of a dismembered Doris resting inside of Clem's icebox. I pictured an apple in her mouth, and I had to shake my head hard to clear the image from my brain.

"Tell me something, Boo. What happened? I mean why did Miss Leslie start doing, well, bad things for lack of a better term?"

Boo shrugged. "Don't know. Maybe you should ask her when you see her."

"Yes, well, it's not the kind of thing you go asking a lady. Is it?"

"It ain't the kinda of thing you go asking a boy, is it?"

"How old did you say you were?" Boo opened his mouth, but I cut him off. "Never mind. Be a good lad and point the direction."

"Follow the path till you get to the creek, then follow the creek. Miss Leslie's the first shack you'll come to. Creek run right behind her yard. Tell her I said, hey."

As I walked, chirping birds serenaded me. Leaves rustled in the warm breeze. The sun was setting, but I felt its warm rays on my cheeks whenever it broke through the trees. My chest swelled, and I strode with a sense of purpose. I felt good, alive, more alive than I've been in a long time. I fought another demon today and won another battle. Raymond Johnson's clear, determined eyes were my spoils—the money sure wasn't. I had one other thought on my mind, a woman as sweet as Miss Leslie, and I was about to call on her.

As I approached her door, the familiar lump in my throat reappeared. It hurt to swallow. My heart beat faster, and my once confident stride had slowed to the shuffle of a condemned man facing the gallows. What if she wasn't home, or worse, what if she was? I saw the glow of a lamp shining through a window. Perhaps she was, ahem, busy? Have I taken leave of my senses? I felt naked and about to swan dive from a four-hundred-foot cliff as I knocked on her door.

An eternity passed. I pressed my ear to the door and listened for the sound of feet. Nothing. I knocked again, and still nothing. With a sense of relief, I turned to walk away, but a sound from inside stopped me; the door swung open. Miss Leslie's high-pitched twang greeted me.

"Well, hello, Dex," she said.

A new kind of panic fell over me. My God she was stunning. I mean she was gorgeous before, but her hair, it was matted down and straighter than I've seen it before, like she just woke up from a nap. There was something wild and unkept about her that spoke to an inner animal that dwelled somewhere deep inside of me.

"Oh, Miss Leslie," I said. "Are you alone?" I whispered delicately.

"Of course I'm alone. Would you like to come in?"

"Come in?"

"Yes, as in come into my house? Or would you rather stand outside like a mule that doesn't have sense to get out of the rain?"

"A mule?"

Miss Leslie laughed. "I swear Dex, you are the funniest man I've ever met."

There it was again. She thinks I'm funny. I swear I wasn't trying to be. But if she thinks so, I'll not be the one to persuade her otherwise.

"Oh, yes," I said. "I'm funny, very funny."

Miss Leslie laughed again, and now I cared less if she were laughing with me or at me. Just to see that beautiful smile of hers. Her teeth were as white as fine china, and her face lit up like a thousand fireflies in the night sky.

"Would you get in here?" she said. "I got some coffee on the stove."

I walked into her house and noticed how small but incredibly well kept it was. It was bright...cheerful, even. Everything had its place; nothing was in disarray. It was the home of a wholesome woman, not a lady of ill repute. It wasn't what I expected though I didn't know what to expect. Not this. It didn't make any sense to me. Her face, her dress, and her impeccable manner painted a picture that contrasted greatly with her profession.

Miss Leslie gestured toward a chair at the table and I took a seat. She poured us steaming cups of coffee, then she sat down across from me and crossed her legs at the ankles like ladies do.

"To what do I owe the pleasure?" she said, smiling.

"You—you said I should visit you," I said. "Well, here I am."

"Here you are."

"Yes, here I am."

I must have sounded like a fool because I certainly felt like one and her giggling only confirmed my suspicions. This lovely vision in front of me must be in cahoots with the devil, I thought. She's cast a spell and bewitched my tongue. Why else do my words flow like molasses and get stuck in the back of my throat?

"I was afraid I might be interrupting you," I said.

"No. This is my home." Miss Leslie looked around with more than just a hint of pride. "I live alone."

"It's lovely," I said. "You have style, refinement and taste."

"Why thank you, Dex. Coming from you, that means a lot to me. So you were in my neck of the woods and decided to stop by and pay me a visit?"

"Well, I was actually conducting business. Just up the road at the Johnson place."

"Oh, I know the Johnsons. Good people. Boo is just the cutest thing."

"Oh, Boo says hi."

"Oh, Boo. He's adorable. His momma and me we used to be friends, but she don't like me anymore on the account of what I do."

"Well, people can be closed minded."

"What business did you have at the Johnson's?"

"I think that information is privileged."

"I understand. I wouldn't—"

"Mr. Johnson was possessed," I interrupted.

"He was? You know I always thought that man looked a little bewitched."

"Yes, by the demon of drink."

"The demon of what?"

"The demon of drink as in he drinks too much. Beelzebub."

"Beelze what?"

"Beelzebub, the demon of gluttony, which includes hard drink. It had taken over Ray Johnson's heart, darkened it, made it hard."

Miss Leslie pressed her lips against her cup as she took a sip of coffee. A red stain marked the rim when she pulled her lips away. "Oh well," she said. "I could have told you that. Did you run that demon off?"

I smiled, and said, "Yep. I sure did."

Leslie's voice grew soft like a whisper. "Were you scared?" she said.

"Scared? What me? Heavens no; I wasn't scared. Oh, don't get me wrong, most mortal men would be scared out of their wits. Demonic spirits thrive on fear. They sense it; they eat it up. They search the depths of our souls and tear the fear from our throat like a gardener yanking weeds from the ground. They hold it up in exhibition for you and all to see. That is their weapon of choice, fear and lies."

"Oh, my. What did you do, Dex?"

"Well, fortunately, I've had plenty of practice. I've dealt with such malevolent forces all my life, ever since I was a child it seems. I remember them at my crib. Hovering, floating, waiting for my mother to leave me alone, vulnerable, and helpless."

"You poor thing."

"It's okay. There were other spirits too. They were kind and sought to protect me, and they did. I sense them around to this day."

"Is that why you got into this business?"

I stared into my mug and saw my reflection in the dark liquid; I was startled by the old man with the wrinkled face staring back at me. I remember myself a young man, walking through the darkened nave, admiring the stained glass, stopping at votive candle altar to make a prayer to the Virgin. For a moment, I missed it so very much, even the god-awful confessions and their miserable confessors. I never thought I'd miss them.

I looked up and gazed into Miss Leslie's pale blue eyes. *It's okay*, I thought. Everything happens for a reason. Everything happens for a reason, Dex.

"Yes," I said. "You can say that."

"It sounds fascinating. I don't believe I've ever met someone like you before."

"Yes. I dare say you'll never meet another like me."

Miss Leslie giggled. Her laugh was infectious, and so I laughed too. Then we settled down, sat quietly and sipped our coffee; neither one of us spoke, but it was a comfortable quiet. I was content to stare into her eyes, and study her marvelous face, and she seemed content to smile and bat her eyes at me.

"A real live demon fighter," Miss Leslie said finally breaking the silence. "Right here in Titusville. Who would've ever thought?"

"Well, I'm more than just a demon fighter. I've made a life's work of studying theology, spirituality, and other things too, apothecary, chemistry, biology, science."

"Wow," Miss Leslie said clasping her hands to her chest. "You are a remarkable man."

"Ah," I said. "Not so remarkable."

"And modest too."

We fell into another bout of silence which gave me time to think. This next topic had to be broached with some caution, and arguably, shouldn't be brought up at all. However, I could never be accused of decorum, so I went ahead.

"Miss Leslie," I said. "Forgive, but I must ask about your husband. Did he abandon you?"

"Abandon me?" Leslie laughed and shook her head. "I finally got enough sense and kicked him out. He left town after that. I don't know where he's at. Probably drunk or dead in a cornfield someplace."

"I'm so sorry."

"You know, after all that, I still pray for him."

"Pray?"

"Yes. You may not believe this, but I'm a good Christian woman. Attended church every Sunday before St. Titus kicked me out."

"The church kicked you out?"

"Well, they said I wasn't welcomed on the account of what I do."

"But that doesn't make sense. Jesus himself befriended a prostitute."

"He that is without sin among you, let him cast the first stone at her."

She recited the verse nearly flawlessly. Then, she smiled and nodded her head emphatically at me.

"Perhaps they didn't read that part," I said.

"They're priests. They should have read <u>all</u> them parts."

Her comment, with its thought and insight, rung true in a way that pained me. I thought about the Church, and the hypocrisy that festered deep like a fevered wound. For what? There was no reason, none I could comprehend.

"You know something?" I said.

"What's that?"

"You're wise, Miss Leslie. Very wise."

"It's just common sense that's all."

I gripped the mug tighter and took another sip. I looked around the kitchen and once again admired the tidiness. Then, I noticed an inordinate number of roosters, I counted nine in all. They were bright, colorful birds wearing red and purple plumage for crowns.

"What's with the roosters?" I said pointing to the large ceramic bird next to the sink. Its beak opened up into a spout and its tail formed a handle.

Leslie threw her shoulders back and raised her chin. "You might say I collect them," she answered with pride.

I scanned the kitchen again and envisioned Leslie baking bread, maybe there would be a child or two pulling at her apron. She looked so, well, normal, a bit proper, and even god-fearing. It made no sense.

I know them. I'm not proud to say, but I was acquainted with many—shall we say—in the biblical sense. I know what they look like, and how they act. They're hard women, with hard lives hidden by clownish faces. They wear dresses hiked to the waist, showing off their tight fitting, striped-stocking legs—displaying their wares you might say. They live in squalor with strong armed sadistic men in the seediest neighborhoods in the seediest apartment houses. They do not glow. They have no charm, no personality. They certainly do not collect roosters, nor do they lovingly maintain shanty homes in the sticks. They do not smile like Leslie. Their spirits do not shine like hers. They don't smell like her, and I venture to guess, they do not taste like her. They possess none of her charm, her wit. They are not her and she, not them.

"May I ask you something personal, Miss Leslie?"

Leslie, as if psychically divining the question before I asked, closed her eyes and shook her head no. She was smiling all the time.

"But you don't even know what I was going to ask," I protested.

"I do know what you were going to ask."

"Why Leslie? It doesn't make sense. You could have any man you want."

"Who says I want a man?"

"Don't you?"

"I do not."

"But why? You can't be happy doing—"

"You're wrong, Dex. I don't need a man to make me happy. I answer to no one."

I wanted to argue with her. Correct her. Tell her she answers to every two-bit, drunk oilman lucky enough to have a sawbuck in his pocket and thirty minutes to spare. But I stopped short. I saw the conviction in her eyes, and the pride on her sleeve and the pride she took in decorating her kitchen—all those damned roosters. I simply smiled at her and raised my mug.

"Do you perhaps have something a wee stronger?" I said.

"Stronger?"

"Yes. You know. Stronger,"

Leslies winked and flashed a devilish smile that conveyed what a thousand words could not.

"I got just the thing for you, Sweetie. I'll make us some lemonade; that'll perk you up."

I didn't hear a damn thing after, Sweetie. There was something about lemonade. I'm not sure.

Miss Leslie sauntered off and I watched intently as she fixed our refreshments. She took out two large jars, the kind used for preserving jams and pickles; then she filled them from a pitcher containing a yellow liquid—which I presumed was lemonade. Next, she opened a cupboard and retrieved a large brown jug, capped by a cork. The light was dim, so I couldn't be sure, but it looked like there was a crude impression of a skull and cross bones etched into the jug's side. She poured copious amounts of this clear liquid into the jars until they both nearly overflowed. Then she returned to the table and placed one of the sloppy jars in front of me while she took a sip from hers.

"Drink up," she said taking her seat. "It'll put hair on your chest."

"What is it?"

"Oh, ya know."

There was a sparkle in her eye; it made me a little apprehensive, but as they say, you only live once, and I was not about to turn down some good ole' country shine, especially set before me by a pretty woman who was practically coercing me to partake. I raised my glass and smiled, and Leslie did the same. I took a sip.

The cool liquid traveled smoothly down my throat and into my gullet before it suddenly reversed direction and exited my mouth. I turned my head quickly to avoid dousing Leslie with her own concoction of lemonade and whatever ghastly fluid she added to it. Did she make this with distilled crude oil, I wondered? I looked at her with pleading eyes.

"You'll get used to it," she said. "Drink up."

I took another swig. This time, it tasted better; mildly so, but better all the same, and I was able to hold it down.

"Come on now," she said. "I feel like I'm drinking alone."

I saw she was right. This beauty was drinking me under the table, and so I tipped the jar back once and once more for good measure. It tasted sweet like honey and felt warm and soothing as it whisked down my throat. The room turned hazy; it swirled, and the soft glow around Miss Leslie intensified. She was laughing at me or with me; I couldn't tell, nor did I care. Her teeth were perfect, and her laugh infectious. It was the best dream ever, yet it was very real.

I placed my empty jar on the table and said, "More."

Miss Leslie filled my cup to overflowing, and she did the same for hers. We drank and we talked, and we drank some more, and as time passed, I became more intoxicated and my heart fell down a path I wish it would not go. I now saw two Leslies not just one. In fact, there were two of everything. Two mouths, two noses, two sets of eyes, two pairs of...well, you get the idea.

"You know, Dex," she said. "I may have a customer fer ya."

"A what?" I said trying to remember what we were talking about.

"My friend Jenny. She's bewitched."

"Bewitched? Hey, are you even drinking?"

"Yeah, I'm drinking. You're the one falling behind."

Miss Leslie laughed again. The room spun, and my heart raced. I found myself sitting close to her though I don't remember moving my chair. Fueled by intoxication, I held her hands; they were small and feminine and caused my own hands to tremble. Then, I made the mistake of looking into her eyes. They were the color of the night sky, and I saw the lamp's flicker dancing in her pupils; my eyes watered and in a moment of clarity, I realized what I was doing. I apologized to her, but I did not let go.

"It's okay," she said in a sympathetic tone. "It's nice to hold hands."

Oh, God. I was high, but I remember so clearly, so vividly, her warm, soft skin and the energy that seemed to pass between us like the sun's rays. I was far from home, but in that very moment, I found a new home.

She smiled at me and I at her, and I don't know what came over me exactly, but it seemed the right thing to do. I leaned in and kissed her, softly, on the lips, and when I pulled back, I read the reaction in her face. She didn't seem to mind.

The rest of the evening, well, it was a blur. Truly it was. I don't remember much after that, I just know, it was the best time I ever had—ever.

CHAPTER 8

Leslie and I floated down the river in a rowboat. It was bright and sunny, and a cool breeze swept over the water. Her pink parasol rested over her shoulder; she wore a pink dress, and she flashed that slightly devilish smile. Her smile sent shivers down my spine and lit a fire in my heart.

I leaned in; she leaned in; I closed my eyes and she closed hers, and just before our lips met, an infuriating knock racked my brain. It sounded like someone pounding my skull from the inside out.

"Go away," I said in a raspy, voice. I heard the door squeak open and looked up to see Lucy's scowling face. "Damn it," I said. "I need to remember to lock that door."

"There ain't no lock on the door," Lucy shot back.

"Well, why don't you tell Clem to put one on?"

"That'll be extra."

"Of course it will. Could you leave me be? I was having the nicest dream before you spoiled it."

"Where were you last night?" Lucy demanded. "I heard you stumbling in late like a drunken polecat in the moonlight."

I had to think for a moment. My head hurt and Lucy's voice grated like nails on a blackboard. Where was I? Oh yes, I remember; then I made the mistake of being honest about it.

"I went calling on Miss Leslie," I said.

There was a delay, couldn't have been more than a second or two where all was calm, quiet and peaceful. Lucy's face grew soft and placid, so I thought it no harm in laying my head back down, melting into the pillow and dozing off. Leslie will be waiting for me. She wants me with a capital want.

My eyes closed for a moment, then I felt something, a blow to my head. It scared the *bejesus* out of me and made me bolt straight up in bed. I looked up and saw Miss Lucy standing over me, holding a pillow over my head. She didn't look happy. Her face was not soft, nor was it placid. It was a red, angry mass, wrinkled and contorted.

"It's time to get up," she said.

"Woman," I said. "Have you gone stark raving—"

Before I could finish my sentence, another blow caught me flush; this one landed across my face. I wasn't expecting it, or else I could have stopped it. After all, I was twice her size; I must have had a hundred pounds on her, maybe more. However, in my present hungover state, I was probably no match for her. She was a little woman, but very surly.

"I thought you told me you were a man of God," she bellowed. "What kind of godly man calls on a woman like that?"

"First of all, I never suggested I was a godly man, and secondly, even a Godly man is still a man."

Miss Lucy cocked the pillow high above her head, but this time I was wise to her. "Ah, ah, ah," I said pointing a long, spindly finger toward her nose. "I wouldn't press my luck if I were you."

She recognized I meant business and lowered the pillow to her side. "Honestly," she said. "I expected more from you, not like the other roughnecks around here."

"What's the problem? We didn't do anything."

"You didn't?"

I had to pause and think about it. Did we do anything? I don't think we did, but if I'm being honest, I don't remember. Now, that's a ghastly thought, not to remember something like that. That damned devil's drink she gave me.

"No," I said with a confident tone. "We did not."

"What was the matter? You didn't have any money to pay her?"

"What? No that wasn't it."

Lucy's face took on a sympathetic shine. "Oh," she said drawing out the vowel to exaggerated lengths. "Well, it's okay. Ya know Clem is getting up there in years too and he hasn't—"

"Miss Lucy," I interrupted. "Would you mind closing the door?"

"Oh sure."

"On your way out?"

"But I ain't going nowhere."

"No," I corrected her. "You are going somewhere, somewhere far away from me."

Miss Lucy laid the pillow down on my bed. The fight in her had subsided. "I'll go fetch you some breakfast," she said.

"That will be fine. Steak, and eggs, and hash browns."

Lucy smiled and said, "Clem is making grits."

✝

There's an art to drawing a crowd. It's a performance. My soapbox is my stage and I am the main character. Hell, I'm the only character, a show of one, and this show was bombing.

I was hungover from last night, or still drunk for that matter. I spoke the words, but I didn't feel them. They sounded odd and forced to my own ears. I could only imagine what my audience thought. Judging by their reaction, it wasn't good. People stared at me with confusion, some smiled, and some pointed and laughed. A few would stop and gawk but would leave before I had a chance to reel them in.

Despite the general disinterest, there were two curious onlookers off to my side. Priests—I could tell by their dress, but mostly I recognized them by the judgmental scowls etched on their faces. One was big and flabby. He looked like he had been gorging on the communion wafers and helping himself to the wine on a regular basis between masses. The other was a small, thin, pasty-looking man with a hint of a smile daring to break through a serious face. I tried my best to ignore them both, but they made me nervous with their staring and hand-over-mouth conversations. I couldn't hear what they were saying, but I have a good imagination, and I imagined it was nothing complimentary. They weren't doing anything wrong per se, but their mere presence annoyed me, and besides, I was way too hungover for religion this morning.

I turned my back to the priests and continued my pitch, but it was useless. The only person to approach me was a woman and her dog—I had to shoo both away when the stupid dog lifted its leg on my soapbox.

"Damn you, woman! Mind your dog!" I shouted at her.

My head throbbed after that, so I sat on my box to rest a spell. That's when I saw the collars approach me. Oh no, I thought. I was in no mood for these earthly fathers, never was, but especially not now. I felt their contempt glow thick and hot as they neared.

One of them—I'll call him The Fat One because the other one was skinny and he was, well, fat—approached me with a big grin on his face like he thought he was special. The skinny one was grinning too, but his was more of a friendly grin. I wanted to punch them both in the face. God help me. I pictured the blood running down their holy faces, and this brought me some comfort. I admit, I was a little ornery.

The fat one said to me, "Good morning. I am Father O'Brien, and this is Father De la Cruz."

"Hello," Father De la Cruz said. "My name is Francisco, but you may call me Paco. All my friends call me Paco, or Father Paco. But you may call me whatever you wish."

"Charmed," I snorted.

"We were wondering," O'Brien said. "What is it you're doing?"

"Well, what's it look like I'm doing?" I said. "I'm scaring away half the town."

The priests smirked. "Yes, we see that," Father Paco said. "But why?"

"I was making fun. I'm not really trying to scare them. Haven't you been listening?"

"Well," O'Brien said. "Perhaps this is where the confusion lies. We've been trying to make sense of what you were saying, but frankly, it didn't make any sense at all. Something about Satan and drinking and there was something else about the Devil's drink and uh, lemonade? Were you perhaps poisoned?"

I stared at Father O'Brien for what seemed like the longest time.

"Really?" I said. "That's all you got from it. No wonder I'm terrifying folks. Please accept my apologies for the rambling."

"Well, never mind that," Father Paco said. "What is it you're selling?"

"Selling?" I said. "I'm selling me."

"Oh, dear God," Father O'Brien said in a hushed voice.

"Interesting," said Father Paco.

The two priests hastily made the sign of the cross.

"Now hold on; wait a minute," I said. "It's not what you're thinking."

"How do you know what we're thinking?" said Father O'Brien.

"Well, I don't, but whatever it is, it's not that. I'm a demonologist, I exorcise demons from people and sometimes from places. I'm selling my services to these woeful town folks."

This time there was no reaction from the Fathers, just blank stares. Then, in choreographed unison, they made the sign of the cross, very slowly and very deliberately. In the name of the Father, The Son, and the Holy Ghost, I wanted to run, like sprint out of there as fast as my old legs would carry me, but I had the box to carry. I'd be flat on my face in two steps, so I stayed and braced myself.

"Oh dear," said Father Paco. "It's worse than what I thought."

Father O'Brien turned red. "By whose authority do you do this?" he said.

The question seemed hostile, so I answered back in kind. "By my authority," I said.

Father O'Brien, well, I swear he did a jig. He twisted his big frame left and right as if looking for a witness to my insolence. There were no witnesses except for his skinny friend, Paco.

"You have no such authority," Father O'Brien said. "Only the Holy Roman Catholic Church can perform the rite of exorcism, and only by the Church's decree and by a qualified exorcist trained by the Holy Roman Catholic Church. Who here needs to be exorcised, anyway?"

"Who needs to be exorcised?" I laughed. "Hell, Padre, this whole damn town needs exorcising; take a look around."

I meant that as a figure of speech, but the fat priest took it as my word and did as I asked, searching the dusty road as if he could spot a demon-possessed person then and there.

"Where?" he said. "I don't see anyone who shows signs of demon-possession."

"And how would you know what those signs are?"

Father O'Brien's jowls shook. "Because," he answered in a flabbergasted tone. "I'm a priest. I've studied demonology as part of my training and so has Father De la Cruz."

I stood on my feet and found myself looming over the portly priest by nearly five inches. It felt good to look down at him.

Oh yeah?" I said pressing my thumb against my chest. "I was a..."

"You were a what?" Father O'Brien said.

I thought a moment and quickly altered course. "There's more to possession than what you think," I said.

"Perhaps you will enlighten us," Father Paco said.

"I'm just saying there's more to possession than supernatural phenomena."

"No there's not," Father O'Brien said. "That is by its very nature what demonic possession is all about."

"Father O'Brien is right," said Father Paco.

"Look," I said. "All I'm saying is there's different types of demons. Some people are possessed by the demon of drink, others by the demon of lust, gluttony, and adultery. I help people get rid of those demons."

The two Fathers gave each other a strange look.

"I'm sorry," Father Paco said. "I didn't catch the name. Who did you say you were?"

"I didn't," I said. "But my name is Dexter James. My friends call me Dex. You may call me Mr. James."

Father Paco held out his hand, and I shook it out of habit.

"Well, Dex. I'm afraid you're wrong about that. Those evils you mentioned, while sinful and deeply troubling to God, they are not caused by demonic possession, but are merely the product of man's sinful nature."

"Well, Father, you believe what you believe, and I'll believe what I believe."

"This is outrageous," said Father O'Brien. "You're nothing more than an imposter, a swindler robbing people of their hard-earned cash."

"Listen here," I said taking a step closer toward the chubby priest. "I'm no thief. I provide people a needed service and if they're not happy with the results, they can have their money back."

"Really?" Father O'Brien said with a raised eyebrow. "You'll refund their money if they're not happy?"

"Yeah, okay," I said.

"Come on Father," Father O'Brien said. "We're wasting our time. This is a matter for the sheriff."

"The sheriff? What's he got to do with this?"

"Well, I think he'd like to know there's a crook on the loose. He'll have a place ready for you to spend the night."

"Ah, ah, ah," I said pulling out my license. I always kept it on hand in such cases. "I'm fully legal. sheriff has no cause to run me in."

"I'm not so sure about that," Father O'Brien said.

"Father O'Brien," Paco said. "Let's go. I don't believe Dexter is doing any harm."

"No harm? He's moving in on our business, not to mention he's polluting the minds of these innocent folks."

"Yes, but he does have a business license, and it looks real."

Father O'Brien scowled and held a shaky finger up to me. "I'm keeping my eye on you," he said before turning and walking away hurriedly.

Father Paco smiled at me and then followed Father O'Brien down Main Street. The two priests kicked-up a dusty trail behind them as they walked out of sight.

I sat back down on my box and rested my head in my hands. The sweat streamed down my face providing much-needed relief from the summer heat. It felt good. The streets were near empty now, so I sat, staring at the ground while trying to empty my mind of all its negativity. After a few minutes, a shadow broke my concentration and made me look up.

An elderly woman stood over me. She had grey hair of which several strands flowed from either side of her blue bonnet.

"Sorry, about my dog," the woman said. "He doesn't mind his manners. I should have been paying him more mind."

I smiled at the little dog, and it wagged its tail furiously at me. Its mouth hung open and its tongue spilled from the side in a wonderfully, stupid grin.

"That's okay," I said. "What's his name?"

"Runt," she said. Given the dog's diminutive size, there was no need for further explanation. "What is it you're selling?" she asked.

"Salvation," I said flippantly.

"Oh?"

"Well, not really," I said standing up and tipping my hat. "I'm a demonologist. I exorcise demonic spirits from people."

"Oh, how interesting. I've always thought I've been troubled by spirits."

"What makes you think that?"

The women's face turned sad. "I don't know," she said shaking her head. "Just seems—just seems like I had my share of troubles, loneliness, heartache. My husband, he left me a long time ago, left me to raise my daughter all by myself. I did the best I could you know, but it was hard."

"I'm so sorry to hear that. Perhaps I could perform an exorcism for you?"

"How much do you charge?"

I looked her over carefully and could tell by her faded and mended dress, that she was not a woman of means.

"Well, I normally charge five dollars for my services," I said. "But for you, we'll say two dollars."

"I'm sorry," she said. "But I don't have any money."

"You don't have any money? Well, then why did you ask me...oh never mind; we'll just call it pro bono?"

"Pro what?"

"Let us say it's for the common good. In other words, no charge."

The old woman's face lit up like a candle. "Oh, I'd like that," she said.

"I'm sorry, Miss. I don't believe I caught your name."

"I'm Lois and you already know Runt."

"It's nice to meet you Lois. My name is Dexter James, but my friends call me Dex. You may call me Dex."

"Pleased to meet you, Dex."

My first and only customer that day turned out to be another broke one. It didn't matter. Lois and Runt were good company and they helped me forget the unpleasant encounter with the local clergy.

I spent the next ten minutes praying over Lois. I exorcised Runt too. He had beady eyes, which pointed to a possible demonic possession, and well, I had the holy water out anyway. There was no harm in splashing him even though he lapped up most of the droplets with his tongue.

When we finished, I could tell the ceremony had done some good. Lois looked different, more spirited and less troubled than before. She appeared to glow. Before leaving, she asked permission to kiss me on the cheek, and I said yes. I bent down; she rose on her tippy toes and planted the softest kiss on my cheek. I couldn't even feel it.

I watched Lois and Runt stroll off as they appeared to fade into the dust, then I gathered my belongings, hoisted my soapbox on my shoulders and headed back to Clem's. It was getting late, and I was thirsty.

CHAPTER 9

The bottle came compliments of Lucy. She saw I was melancholy and thought it would lift my spirits. For a moment, I considered kindly turning it down, but the brown liquid, well, it was so inviting, and in my present, miserable state, I could not refuse. I carried the bottle upstairs to my room where I could be alone with it. My hands trembled as I poured the first sip. I drank a glass and then another and soon, its warm, medicinal effects made my eyes droop. I watched nightfall from my balcony perch as I reflected.

I don't understand. This town is filled with more demon-possessed souls per capita than any place I've seen. Yet, I was getting nowhere. So far, I've performed three exorcisms and have hardly anything to show of it except for two kisses (both on the cheek) and parts of a pig named Doris cooling in the icebox. Lucy happily agreed to take Doris in exchange for this week's room and board. I suppose I ought to be grateful as I am short on funds and unless business picks up, I'll be forced to make other living arrangements. That would be a shame because even though it's overpriced—for God's sake, the door doesn't even lock—and Lucy can be a real pain in my ass, I've grown fond of the place. It's comfortable and conveniently located on the busy side of Main Street. Besides, I've developed a taste for Clem's grits.

Sometimes, I miss my home away from home. Westerville was a pleasant little town in Ohio, not far from my parish and filled with many possessed souls. I would have stayed if it weren't for the banishment of alcohol. The town's female population hung posters that read: Bread Not Booze, and this stirred up sentiment on the evils of drink. Sure, it's evil, but what were those fools thinking? An entire town without alcohol?

Well, after that miserable campaign, it was impossible to find safe hooch within a twenty-mile radius of town. This was bad enough, but the inebriated college students from the local university were some of my best customers—they were wealthy protestants (pious except for their excessive drinking) and gladly shelled out their parent's cash for a demonic cleansing. When the town dried up, so did my business.

A breeze raised goosebumps on my arms. Summer was about over, and despite the heat of day, I sensed the chill of Autumn in the night air. Soon, the leaves would turn color in a magnificent fiery display. I heard winters can be brutal in these parts of Pennsylvania. I might have another month, maybe two if I were lucky and then I'd have to work my way south. If things don't get better, I might leave sooner than later. I probably should. I probably would, if it were not for Miss Leslie. God, Miss Leslie— a part of me was still delusional. Maybe we have a future together; the thought brought a smile to my face.

I picked up my bottle and glass and closed the balcony doors behind me. The relative warmth of the room felt good. I looked around and noted how stark it was, empty and lonely looking. I had one last swig left, so I polished off the bottle. I saw my Bible laying on the nightstand and took it to bed with me. With the back of my head resting on the pillow, and my Bible held out in front of me at arms-length, I slowly thumbed through Samuel, to Kings, and from Kings to Chronicles. As I turned the pages, an old, worn piece of parchment floated out like a wounded duck before landing on my chest. It had some writing on it. I almost forgot it was there. I almost forgot what it said:

My Dearest Son:

I believed in you when no one else did. Now, I can tell them, he is a man of God. Keep this Bible with you always.

God Bless,

Ma

I wiped my eyes and shook my head. "A man of God," I laughed.

I heard a soft voice.

"Dex," it said. "Dex. Wake up."

My body gently shook. I opened my eyes and wiped the drool from my cheek. My vision was blurred, but I saw—glory be—not one woman, but two. Was I dead? All that drinking must have caught up to me, or maybe the Shylocks had finally got me and struck me down in the middle of the night. By God's grace, I was in heaven.

I closed my eyes again—it was only for a moment—but the same voice, this time with annoyance, implored me to wake up and so I did. As it turned out, I wasn't dead after all. I was merely half-awake. In actuality, there were two—very real—women standing over me as I lay in my bed. I immediately recognized Miss Leslie; I smiled at her and she smiled back. The other woman stood off of Miss Leslie's shoulder. She was a heavily made up brunette with a rather impressive bosom, more impressive than Miss Leslie's I dare say.

"Miss Leslie?" I said rubbing the sleep from my eyes. "Who's that with you?"

"This is my friend Jenny," Leslie said. "Jenny, this is Dex. Say hi to Dex."

"Hi," said Jenny.

"Charmed," I replied tipping an imaginary hat. "How did you get in here?"

"The door was unlocked," Leslie said.

"I mean, how did you get past Lucy?"

"Oh, that. It wasn't easy. She's real mad. You may want to look for a new place to live."

"Wait, what? I don't want to—"

"Never mind that," Leslie interrupted. "We're here for business purposes."

My eyes veered toward the ceiling as I offered up a prayer to the heavens. "Thank you," I whispered.

Miss Leslie frowned and wrinkled her forehead. "It's not what you think," she said. "Jenny is possessed. She wants to get unpossessed."

I looked at Jenny and she smiled. She had a pretty smile, not as nice as Miss Leslie's, but pretty all the same.

"And what seems to be the source of your possession?" I said to Jenny.

"Well, I was playing around, you know with the spirit board, and well, strange things started happening."

I cringed when I heard spirit board. "You mean the Devil's board?" I shouted at her. I bolted upright in bed. "I'd like to burn every one of them blasted things."

I was fully awake now and stood on my feet. Thank goodness I had fallen asleep fully clothed, or this might have been more awkward than it already was.

"What on earth possessed you to play around with that thing?" I said.

"I thought it would be fun?" Jenny said raising her voice to make it sound like a question.

"Fun? Fun? And tell me how much fun are you having now?"

Jenny cast her eyes towards the floor without saying a word.

"Yes. Just as I thought. And what fool did you rope into playing the Devil's board with you?"

Jenny and Miss Leslie exchanged glances.

"Oh, no, Miss Leslie," I said. "Tell me it's not so. I thought you were more sensible. Okay. I can do both of you at the same time. Where is my black bag? Have you seen my black bag?"

"What are you talking about?" Miss Leslie said, shaking her head. "It wasn't me. Jenny was playing with herself; I meant she was playing with the board by herself. Oh, you know what I mean."

I knew what she meant, and this revelation sent a shiver down my spine. I locked eyes with Jenny. "Dear, child," I said. "You got the planchette to move...on your own...without the help of another?"

Jenny nodded her head slowly. "Is that bad?"

I covered my face with my hands.

"What is it, Dex?" Miss Leslie said. "You can help her, right?"

"Of course I can help her, but you should never play with the spirit board, and you should never, ever, under no circumstances, play it alone. It uses the energy of two or more people, but when there's only one person, the circle must be completed by an outside force, a malevolent force, one that is bent on occupying your body and using it as a host, feeding off of your soul for the sole purpose of committing evil. By playing with the Devil's board, you're offering the spirit an invitation and it's only by this invitation that it can enter into your being."

Miss Leslie and Jenny looked pale and stricken. Jenny held her hand over her heart and Miss Leslie wrapped her arm around Jenny's shoulders.

"It's okay," I told them. "You've come to the right place."

"I don't have much money," Jenny said. "I'll have more by this evening, or perhaps we can work out some other arrangement?" This last part, she said with a bit of mischief in her eye.

"I've got this," Leslie said as she pulled out a wad of dollar bills from her bosom.

"Wait a minute," I said. "I want to hear about this other arrangement."

Miss Leslie slapped my chest. "Shut up," she said. "You do not."

"Actually, I do." I should've expected the second blow, but I was surprised at how hard this smallish woman could hit. "Ouch," I said. "Would you stop doing that?"

"Mind yourself," Leslie said. "Jenny needs your help."

"Put your money away, Leslie. She's a friend of yours. I'll not charge for my services."

Leslie stepped up and kissed me on the cheek. It was payment in full and then some.

"When can we start?" Jenny said.

"We'll start now. Tell me what's going on."

"Like I said, I was playing with the spirit board and I made contact with a man from the spirit world. Said his name was Lucas."

"Really?" Leslie said with a sharp, indignant jerk of her head. "Lucas? You wouldn't happen to notice that Lucas sounds a lot like Lucifer?"

"Oh my God!" Jenny said. "It does."

"Calm down," I said. "Lucas is probably not its real name anyway. Tell me, Jenny, what happened after you made contact with Lucas?"

"You know, it was fun at first. I'd ask Lucas questions, and he'd answer yes or no. You know, silly questions like am I ever going to be rich?"

"Then what happened?"

Jenny's eyes narrowed. "Then—uh—things changed."

"Changed? How?"

"I don't know exactly. Lucas began spelling things out, not just moving to the yes or no. After a while, the little pointer was moving across the board really fast. I could barely keep up with it. I'm not that fast a reader."

"You felt it? I mean the energy in the planchette?"

Jenny's eyes looked off into the distance as if she were reliving the event. "Yes," she said. "The pointer vibrated when it moved; like it was full of lightning. I felt it all right."

"Yes, that's common," I said stroking my beard. "That's the demonic. What happened next?"

Jenny played with a strand of hair, twirling it around her index finger like a ribbon around a maypole. "I don't know," she said. "Lucas spelled things out, things I didn't like. You know, bad things."

"What sorts of bad things?"

"He told me improper things; things you don't tell a lady. It's like he knew what I did for a living."

"Incubus," I said nodding my head.

"What's that?"

"It's a male spirit that invades the female body to experience relations." Jenny's jaw fell open and her face turned pale. "It's okay," I assured her. "It's probably a minor spirit. Nothing to worry about, but it's good you came to me. You didn't invite the spirit in, did you?"

"No, never."

"And the board? What did you with it?"

"I threw it away."

"No!" I said. "You never throw a spirit board away. They must be burned."

"I'm sorry. I didn't know."

"Where did you throw it out?"

"I wrapped it in burlap and tossed in the briar near one of them derricks. Someone else's problem now."

"Someone else's problem?" I said shaking my head.

"She didn't know," Leslie said wrapping her arm around her friend's shoulder. "She thought it was harmless...like a game."

"Let me assure you, the Devil's Board is not a game. The spirit world is not a game. Do you understand me?"

The two women joined hands and nodded their heads in unison. They looked like misbehaved schoolgirls.

"Well, good," I said. "I suppose there's nothing that can be done about the board now. Let's just hope the next person has the sense enough to destroy the blasted thing."

"I'm so sorry," Jenny said. "I really didn't know."

"It's okay child. Tell me; is there anything else I should know?"

Jenny looked at her friend and Leslie nodded her head. "I've been having dreams," Jenny said. "Scary dreams, strange dreams."

I know enough about the Incubus to know the nature of her dreams, how awful and tormenting they must have been. I had all the information I needed.

"We will perform the ancient rite of exorcism at once," I said.

"Do you think you can exorcise this demon?" Leslie said.

"Do I think? I know so."

I located my demon-fighting bag, Then, I pulled out the tools of my trade and laid them carefully on the table while the women looked on. Jenny looked scared, so I did my best to comfort her with a warm smile. This was grave business to be sure, but I did not want her to know how high the stakes were. As they say, ignorance is bliss.

With my weaponry laid out, I prepared myself for battle. First, I placed the purple embroidered stole around my neck. Miss Leslie helped me so that it laid even and flat against my shirt. Next, I kissed the cross and hung it too around my neck. Finally, I removed the bottle of holy water from my bag and placed it on the table in front of me. I was ready now; ready for whatever darkness may come my way.

"Let us pray," I said.

All of us bowed our heads, and I spoke a simple prayer from the heart. I asked God for his mercy and our protection. I thanked him and when I finished, I looked up and saw the two women's eyes. They were wet and glistened in the light of the morning sun.

"Well then," I said. "Shall we proceed?"

The two ladies studied me, marking my every move. I was especially aware of Miss Leslie. Her big, blue eyes watched keenly and there was a slight, nearly imperceptible smile etched on her face. Her fascination fascinated me; so youthful she looked and how she glowed in the soft light. It was all I could do to maintain my concentration with the task at hand.

"Is there anything I can do?" said Miss Leslie.

"Yes. Sit. Do not show fear and pray."

"What should I pray?"

"The Lord's prayer. Do you know it?"

"Of course."

"Good. Begin praying now. Do so quietly."

I was surprised to see Miss Leslie produce a strand of rosary beads from her dress pocket. They were black, well-worn and had a small crucifix dangling from one end. Miss Leslie closed her eyes and prayed. "Our Father…"

While Leslie's gentle drawl filled the room, I held the silver cross to Jenny's face. Illuminous flecks bounced off the metal and danced on her cheeks in a spectacular light show. As I suspected, Jenny's reaction was swift and troubled. She squinted and threw her head to one side as if the soft glow was painful. I've seen this before, many times, too many to count.

I let go of the cross and allowed it to dangle from my neck. This seemed to appease Jenny as she returned her gaze on me. I looked deep into her eyes and saw something different than before. Their color was completely drained. I was looking at two dark pieces of coal, lifeless and without emotion. The fear, once clearly etched on Jenny's face, was gone. She now stared at me with an air of certainty boarding on maniacal arrogance.

I did not dare take my eyes off of the demon, so I felt for the holy water and when my hands found the bottle, I immediately uncapped it. Then, I paused a moment and listened to Leslie's prayer.

"…give us this day our daily bread and forgive…"

"Pray louder," I commanded.

"…as we forgive those who trespass…"

"Who are you?" I asked the demon.

The demon picked up his index finger and scraped Jenny's chin with the sharp point of its nail. He did not answer me. Instead, he locked eyes with mine as his mouth curled into a slight, sinister smile. This went on for several seconds as I waited for an answer.

My patience, already thin, was near its end, and I reacted at the sight of blood now oozing from the poor women's flesh. It was a harsh move, but something had to be done to avoid further injury. I reached out and grabbed Jenny's wrist. I was much bigger than her, and my fingers easily wrapped around until my thumb and middle finger touched. I had a firm grip, but when I tried to pull her arm away, I was met with a resistance that contradicted Jenny's diminutive size. I had almost forgotten. It was not Jenny I was holding, but a demonic force that had taken control of her body.

I remembered the holy water in my free hand and raised the bottle high above my head as if I were about to plunge a knife into its heart. Then, with a downward, slashing motion, I made the sign of the cross as water flew and splashed onto the demon's skin. I held fast to the demon's wrist—I did not dare let go—while the demon tossed and protested with pain. I watched in satisfaction as the arrogant smirk melted from its face. I had the demon by its ball sack. I knew it and more importantly, he knew it too.

Now, when I pulled Jenny's wrist, it came away easily revealing a bright, red raspberry stain on her chin. I slammed the bottle down on the table and then I covered Jenny's forehead with my palm. I was about to exorcise the demon when I noticed something. Leslie had stopped praying. I looked over at her and saw her holding her Rosary beads in front of her as if they were a shield. Her eyes were wide, and her skin paler than I remembered. There was something else too. The demon stared at Miss Leslie, seemingly transfixed by the wooden cross.

"Who told you to stop praying?" I demanded. "Recite the Hail Mary."

"…Hail Mary, full of grace…"

"Keep praying. Don't stop."

The strains of Leslie's sweet voice were comforting, and I turned my attention back to Jenny. This time, when I looked into her eyes, I saw fear. I took this as a very good sign, and I prayed over her.

"In the Name of the Father, and of the Son, and of the Holy Ghost. Amen. Most glorious Prince of the heavenly armies, Saint Michael the Archangel, defend us in our battle against principalities and powers, against the rulers of this world of darkness, against the spirits of wickedness in the high places…"

We were lucky. As far as demons go, this was a relatively minor one. Some exorcisms last weeks. Some even kill the host, the exorcist or both. The exorcism of Jennifer Millspaugh lasted but an hour. When we had finished, her sweet countenance had returned, and the faint aroma of roses filled the room. And though I had vanquished the demon, Miss Leslie kept praying. I did not try to stop her.

CHAPTER 10

People gawked at me. They must have thought I was a lunatic, an escapee from the asylum. They may have been right; I wasn't sure anymore. My only real audience was Lois and her dog, Runt. They stood in front of my soapbox and watched my miserable efforts unfold for the train wreck it was. Lois smiled at me, and Runt appeared to wince with sympathy pain. I had a raging headache that made my stomach churn and threatened to deposit Clem's grits all over my boots. Runt didn't piss on my soapbox. He tried, but Lois scolded him before he got the chance, so there was that.

"What am I doing wrong?" I said to Lois.

Lois shrugged. "I don't know," she said. "You sound all right to me."

She was lying. I actually skunked up the place, but this misguided, old woman was apparently sweet on me. I hadn't paid much attention before, but this time, I looked her over good. I could tell she was attractive in her youth, a natural beauty, no paint and a pretty smile faintly reminiscent of Miss Leslie's. In fact, she looked like an older version of Leslie.

"You need an exorcism?" I said stepping down from my box.

Lois shook her head. "You already exorcised me, remember?"

"Oh, that's right. How 'bout Runt? He looks like he's demon possessed. Look at them eyes."

Runt looked up at me with his thoughtful, blue eyes.

"See there?" I said. "That's a demon possessed canine if I ever seen one."

Lois laughed. "Little Runt here ain't possessed. He's a little rambunctious now and then, but he's a good, dog. Ain't you Runt?"

Runt's tongue fell out of his mouth, and his tail wagged viciously. He looked like he was smiling.

"Oh, I don't know. He looks demon possessed to me."

"Can an animal even be demon possessed?"

"Sure. Animals, dolls, people, places...I once performed an exorcism on a cat. People thought the cat was crazy cause it snarled and batted the air as if something was there even though there wasn't. Turns out the cat was possessed as the day is long. After I performed an exorcism, she turned out to be the sweetest little kitten you ever saw, purring and happy—just as normal as can be."

"Well, Runt here ain't like that. He's a good little puppy." We watched Runt playfully roll in the dirt, jerking his body one way and then twisting it the other. "Besides, I don't have the money to pay you."

"Yeah, well there's that I suppose."

"But I do thank you, Mr. James, for the prayer you said over me the other day. It sure did help. I feel much better now."

"Hey, you remembered my name."

"Of course I did. Besides, how can I forget. The entire town's talking about you."

"They are? What have they been saying?"

"Oh, well, you know, that you're a trickster, a phony, a snake oil salesman. Some people think you're crazy."

"Yes, but do they have anything bad to say about me?"

"Pay them no mind," Lois laughed. "People around here are suspicious. You know, with all the new folks in town. They see you as another slickster trying to cash in on the oil business. They don't know you; they don't see the good you can do, or the kindness in your heart. But I've seen it."

"Maybe you can tell them I'm okay. I could sure use the business."

"I will. I'll tell them, Mr. James is a fine man."

"I'd appreciate that."

Lois smiled and nodded her head. "Well, me and Runt better be moving on. Wouldn't be proper to talk to a man in public for so long. You know; people talk."

"Oh yes, of course."

I nodded my head and tipped my hat, then I watched Lois and Runt saunter down Main street before they melted into a cloud of dust.

When they were out of sight, I turned around and noticed a man staring at me in the most peculiar way. When I asked him what he was looking at, he turned and hurried off without saying a word. *What a strange place this Titusville is*, I thought.

I turned and looked at my soapbox, then kicked it hard with my right boot. It was like kicking a rock and made my toe hurt like Hell. I hopped on one leg, clutched my foot in my hands and howled like a banshee as I spun in circles. I'm sure my dance only served to confirm people's suspicions about my sanity.

I heard the sound of laughter and I stopped to find Father, O'Brien and Father, Paco laughing at me. They were cackling their fool heads off. Father, Paco, at least, tried to stifle his laugh. Father, O'Brien, however, slapped his knee over and over as if it were the funniest thing he had ever witnessed. I hated Father O'Brien.

"Don't you have some coffers to plunder?" I yelled at them.

My arrow was true and struck like a bolt from the sky. The Fathers turned and left in a huff, and that pleased me to no end.

With the last ounce of dignity sucked from me, I sat on my box and buried my head deep in my hands. The sweat washed over my forehead and face. It was late September, but I'd swear it was the middle of August judging by the hot, stifling air. I listened to my labored breathing and thought about what Lois had said: people called me a fraud, a phony, and a snake oil salesman. That pissed me off. What did they know? I was the educated one, not them. I've trained for years to learn my craft, just as a painter, a writer, or any other artist; Only my art was a mix of performance, theology, and psychology. Anyone could see, if they looked close enough.

"What you thinking about?" a soft voice said.

I looked up and was pleased to see Miss Leslie looking down at me.

"I'm thinking what a failure I am," I said.

"Aw, Dex, why would you think something like that? You're not a failure."

"Look at me. I'm old, broke, lonely."

Miss Leslie told me to move over and took a seat next to me.

"You shouldn't do that," I said. "People talk."

Miss Leslie leaned in close as if she were about to share a secret. "Do you think there are people in this town that aren't already talking about me?" she said.

"Well, it will give them one more reason."

"Let them."

"Do you know what people are saying about me, Leslie? They're calling me a fraud and a phony. They walk past me and laugh and gawk and whisper behind my back. My only customers are ones that can't afford to pay; dogs stop and piss on my box. They piss on my box while I'm standing on it. Sorry, I'm dealing with a lot right now."

Leslie placed a hand on my shoulder. "And what about you, Dex? Who do you think you are?"

I shook my head and said, "A fool?"

"Well then, you are a fool."

"What?"

"If you think you're a fool, you really are one. Dex, you're about the smartest man I know, smarter than these other clodhoppers around here. And you're no fraud. Those people should talk to Jenny."

"Jenny? How is she?"

"Well, let me tell you, I've never seen her so happy. It's like a weight has been lifted from her. That exorcism, worked. Those words you spoke were powerful. I even think I got exorcised just by being in the same room."

"The ancient rite of exorcism, yes, it does work, doesn't it?"

"Of course it does. You just need to get the word out. Jenny and I will tell everyone we know, and in our line of work, we know a lot of people who need their demons exorcised."

"That's right. I am providing a valuable service. I am good."

"Yes sir. You just need a little luck. That's all."

We talked some more, smiled, laughed, and every so often, our shoulders would touch, or she'd place a hand on my elbow. Women walked past us and smirked. The men, well, they were envious. I saw it in their faces. I'd smile at them, gave them a wink, and they returned a knowing smile. Let them talk; let them think what they want. Nothing else seemed to matter when I was with Miss Leslie.

I didn't want our time alone together to end, but of course, nothing good ever lasts. We were interrupted by a boy approaching from a distance. He ran hard and straight toward us, and I prayed it wasn't so, but as he neared, I saw it was Boo. He had a silly grin plastered on his face, and he was panting like a dog.

"Hey, Dex," Boo said gasping for breath. "Hello, Miss Reed."

"Hello, Boo," Miss Leslie said. "How's your ma?"

"She's good. She says hi and that you should come over for dinner."

"Now, don't you lie to me boy," she said in mock anger. "I'm likely to take a switch to you."

"Yes, Ma'am," Boo said smiling. "Hey, Dex. I got someone for you. She's real demon possessed."

"Does she have money?"

"No," Boo said shaking his head. "She's only twelve."

"Oh, well, do her parents have money?"

"By the looks of it, they don't. The oil men tried, but they didn't find oil on their farm."

"Who is it?" said Leslie.

"It's Rebecca Radley. She's demon possessed. I come to fetch, Dex."

"Rebecca? That sweet, little thing. How can she be possessed?"

"She can't walk," Boo said.

"Oh no," Leslie said shaking her head. "Becca's not possessed."

"What is this?" I said. "Who's Becca, and why can't she walk?"

"I told you," Boo said. "She's demon possessed. She wears these funny shoes with two sticks going up the side and tied down by pieces of leather."

Boo's crude description conjured up images of children in the ward where I used to visit. The little angels, their innocent faces and sweet temperaments, they could barely walk. Some couldn't do that much. It was enough to soften the most hardened heart. It just about broke mine.

"She's not possessed," I scolded, Boo. " She has Infantile Paralysis."

"What's that?" Boo said.

"Well, it's a disease; also known as polio."

"You shouldn't say she's possessed," Leslie said. "Becca is sick."

"But I was just up there talking to Mr. Radley. I told him all about Dex, about how he can chase demons away. He wants Dex to come to his farm and perform an exorcism right away."

I admired Boo's thirst for business. Lord knows I could use the money. However, the notion was preposterous. Only Christ could make the lame walk, and I was not him.

"Look," I said to Boo. "I know you meant well, but you shouldn't have done that. Rebecca isn't possessed. She has a disease. An awful disease. I can't do anything for her. No one can. There is no cure."

"But, Dex, you told me—you told me that demons come inside of people and make them sick. They make them do bad things and they make them sick. Isn't that what you said?"

"I know what I said, but I'm telling you now, this isn't one of those times. She has a disease. She needs a doctor."

"But she's been to the doctors. You're the only one that can help her."

"In that case, the best thing to do is make her comfortable."

"But, Dex, I told—"

"Shut up!"

I hadn't meant to snap but sometimes the boy is insufferable, and his talk about healing a sick girl, made me uncomfortable. The tears streaming down Boo cheeks made me feel that much worse. Leslie stood, walked towards Boo and wrapped her arms around him in a motherly fashion. Then, she turned to me and scowled. I looked around, but there was nowhere to hide.

"It's okay," Leslie said still glaring at me. "He didn't mean to yell."

"I ain't crying because he yelled," Boo told her. "Lots of people yell at me."

"Then why are you so upset?"

"I know—I know Dex can help her. He's the best demon fighter in town."

"Oh, Boo," Leslie said shaking her head and smiling. "He's the only demon fighter in town, but she's not troubled by a demon. She has a disease."

"I don't care what you call it. Demon still a demon. Besides, the Radleys tried all the doctors. Ain't got no use for them anymore. Mr. Radley told me to fetch, Dex. He'd pay him the five dollars just for trying."

I was out in the sun for a long time, tired and a little hung over. The prospect of walking a distance was daunting, but I could use the five dollars and if I could convince Miss Leslie to come along, well, that would convince me.

"How far is the Radley house?" I said.

"Just up the road a spell," Boo answered.

"Yes, that's quite descriptive and exact."

"It's not far," Leslie said. "Just half-mile past my place."

Boo and Leslie looked at me, waiting for me to say something. "Fetch me my demon-fighting bag," I finally told Boo.

"What are you doing?" Miss Leslie said.

"I'm going to pay a visit to the Radleys."

Boo's face broke into a wide grin, and he quickly retrieved my demon-fighting bag. "You carry it," I told him. "I'm old and it's hot."

"Dex, are you sure?" Leslie said.

"It won't hurt to pay a visit, maybe pray over the child. Never hurts to pray." Then, I added, "Oh, and you're coming with us."

Miss Leslie's face turned somber and she shook her head back and forth. "Oh, no, Dex. That's not a good idea."

"It is a good idea. You're my assistant, a valuable member of my demon-fighting posse—you and Boo here." Boo smiled.

"No, Dex. They wouldn't take kindly to me being there. Maybe Mr. Radley would be okay with it, but certainly not Mrs. Radley."

"Fine. I'll not go."

My poker bluff worked better than planned because I had an ally in Boo. He grabbed Miss Leslie's arm and tugged on her arm. "But you gotta go Miss Reed. If Dex don't go, they'll make me give back the fifty cents."

"See there," I said. "You gotta go. You don't want to take money from the boy's coffers, would you? That would be akin to stealing."

Boo looked at me. I mimed a frowny face for him, and he in turn flashed Miss Leslie his sad face. I admit; the boy's devious nature made my chest swell with pride. We had Miss Leslie surrounded, me on one side, and Boo on the other, looking like we were about to cry.

"Really?" she said crossing her arms over her chest. "You really think those puppy dog eyes and those pouty lips are going to persuade me?"

I nodded my head and offered Leslie my arm. To my relief, she took it.

"What do we have to lose?" I said.

The Radley home was a modest one, but its ordered appearance spoke of the care and love that went into its maintenance. The kitchen was full, but every utensil had its place; many hung from the wall above the sink. It reminded me of Miss Leslie's kitchen. I could close my eyes and almost smell the warm bread baking and the meals cooking on the stovetop. I imagined they were delicious.

They looked like a typical farm family in a typical farmhouse. Mr. Radley's overalls were dirty and patched in several spots. Mrs. Radley's dress was clean, but it too showed much wear. The little girl, well, she was made up like a life-sized doll and when she flashed me the sweetest smile, my heart melted just a little. She could have had the decency to scowl or spit. It would have made the leg braces more tolerable.

Her parents smiled too and offered me a warm welcome. Mrs. Radley asked if I wanted cold lemonade, but I waved her off. However, she didn't seem fond of Miss Leslie and made her displeasure known with pursing lips and scornful countenance. She responded to Leslie's friendly greeting with a sound rather than a word: "hmm."

Mr. Radley, on the other hand, looked pleased to see Leslie. I caught him stealing glances at her curvaceous figure. Unfortunately, so did Mrs. Radley.

"What is she doing here?" Mrs. Radley demanded.

Miss Leslie turned and headed towards the door. "I was just leaving."

"Wait a minute," I said.

"I told you this was a bad idea, Dex."

"You're staying."

"No she's not," Mrs. Radley said. "This is a Christian home and we're Christian folk. How dare you bring her to my house?"

"Fine," I said. "She goes. I go."

I stared down Mrs. Radley and waited on her to call my bluff, but I had her. I knew it and more importantly, she knew it too. To me, it was only money. To Mrs. Radley, it was her ill child, her world. I felt a little ashamed, but only a little. The battle was won when, Mrs. Radley lowered her eyes in surrender.

"Good," I said. "Now that's settled, let's get started. Boo, open my bag. Fetch my stole. Mr. Radley, let's make something clear before we begin. I tried telling Boo. He's a good lad. He means well, but your daughter suffers from infantile paralysis. Is that right?"

"Rebecca," Mrs. Radley said. "Her name is Rebecca and yes. Boo told us you might be able to help. He said you were, well, special—like a man of God."

Some man of God, I thought. "Well, I just mean to say, I'll do my best, but don't expect miracles."

"Understood," Mr. Radley said. "It's all we ask."

"Good. Now, my standard fee, is—"

Before I could finish, Mr. Radley turned and picked up a jar sitting next to the kitchen sink. I watched intently as he opened it, reached in and pulled out some dollar bills. He reached in a second time and began fishing for the loose change on the bottom.

"Boo said you charge five dollars," he said. "I got about four dollars and some change. Perhaps I can owe you the rest."

I could see Miss Leslie looking at me from my peripheral vision, but I did my best not to meet her stare.

"I reckon four dollars will do," I said. "Don't worry about the change."

I motioned to Mr. Radley, and he handed the bills over to Miss Leslie. With the money counted, folded and safely tucked in her brassiere, I went to work.

I spoke Latin, alternating between bits of real prayer and nonsensical phrases that would have landed me in jail or the asylum if anyone actually understood me. It wasn't my proudest moment, but there were four dollars burning a hole in Miss Leslie's brassiere, and for this, I would give them a show. Devil or no devil, the Radleys were going to get their money's worth, and as for Rebecca, she'd be no worse for it.

The exorcism, well, let's just say it was unlike any I've ever performed. I literally danced around the room and around the Radley girl. I waved my hands above my head, sometimes raising my voice as if I were confronting an unseen entity. Every so often, I'd catch a glimpse of the Radleys, Boo and Miss Leslie. Their dropped jaws and entranced faces reflected the spectacle I was making of myself. Rebecca, however, stood there with a stone-cold expression. The room was spinning alright, but I held that room in my palm.

After a sufficient time had passed, I placed my hand on Rebecca's forehead. Then I mouthed some more gibberish before pushing hard, a little harder than I planned, actually. I forgot about her condition and my own strength. The poor girl. She went flying backwards and landed hard, flat on her back staring up at the kitchen ceiling through wild eyes. My quick thinking saved me from an awkward situation. I pretended this was the intended consequence of the exorcism and I did not show the least bit of surprise or concern.

"It is done," I said holding my palms towards the heavens. "The exorcism is complete."

Rebecca's parents ran to her side.

"I'm fine," she told them.

"Dex, shouldn't you splash some Holy water on her?" Leslie said.

"Oh yes, the holy water. Boo, be a good boy and fetch the water from my bag."

Boo brought me the bottle and I uncapped it.

"Step aside I told the Radley's."

Her parents made room for me, and I doused the girl with water while mumbling some more Latin phrases.

"Is that it?" said Mr. Radley as he helped his daughter to her feet. "Is the exorcism done?"

"It is."

"But how do we know if it worked or not?"

"Oh, it's hard to tell about these things. Could take weeks, months even."

I avoided Leslie's eyes; nonetheless, I felt her hot, disapproving gaze trained directly on me.

"Weeks?" Mr. Radley repeated.

"Or months."

There was a long stretch of silence during which I held my breath.

"Well," Mrs. Radley said. "We sure do thank you for coming out this way."

"My pleasure, Ma'am," I said picking up my bag. "Come along, Boo, Miss Leslie, our work here is done."

"Wait a minute," said Miss Leslie. "Wait just a minute."

Leslie brushed past me without as much as a glance. She made a beeline for Rebecca, knelt down and placed both hands on the girl's shoulders. I was tempted to flee. I wanted to be somewhere else at that moment, but I couldn't move. Besides, Miss Leslie had all my money, so I just stood there.

"Do you feel any different, sweetie?" Miss Leslie said to Rebecca.

Rebecca looked up at me with her questioning eyes, and I nodded my head and smiled. "A little," Rebecca answered.

"A little?" Leslie said looking back at me with a disapproving face. I looked the other way.

"What's that?" Rebecca said pointing to Miss Leslie's neck.

"Oh, this? These are my Rosary beads. My Momma gave them to me when I was a girl no bigger than you."

Without warning, Rebecca threw her arms around Leslie, and pressed her chubby cheek tight against her shoulder. The two embraced for a long time while the rest of us watched on. I swear I saw a glow emanating from the two, but when I looked at the Radleys and Boo, they did not appear alarmed. I decided I was still a little hungover.

"Oh sweetie," Leslie said, her voice cracking. "Oh, sweetie. God bless you."

Yes, I thought. God bless Rebecca Radley.

CHAPTER 11

The saloon buzzed with life: voices and glasses chattered, the women laughed too loud, wore too much makeup and the men were too drunk to care. Miss Leslie and I sat at a table, alone in our own bubble. We drank. We talked. Mostly, I did the talking—and most of the drinking for that matter. I was so excited, I barely stopped for a breath. Leslie smiled and shrugged her shoulders and listened; her eyes glistened, and I could tell she was interested, but she was quiet too, unusually quiet, not her normal, animated self. I could tell something was off since the Radley house, but I didn't want to ask. I was too afraid, but now, an uncomfortable moment had wedged its way between us.

"What's wrong?" I said.

She smiled and took a sip of bourbon. "What was that?" she said.

"What was what?"

"What you did at the Radleys'."

"Oh. That was your standard, run-of-the-mill exorcism," I said trying to sound confident.

Leslie was too smart to fall for my ploy.

"No it wasn't." she said. "What you did for Jenny, that was real. What you did for Rebecca was a performance."

I finished my Bourbon in a gulp and signaled the waitress to bring me another. "Yes, I know, but I told you and Boo and the Radleys. Little Rebecca wasn't demon possessed. There's no point in performing an actual exorcism. Wouldn't do any good."

"Then what were you saying, and why were you prancing about like a show girl?"

"I wasn't prancing?"

"Yes, you were."

"I was offering a prayer in Latin."

"A prayer?"

"Yes, a healing prayer, and, well, some other things."

"But you took their money anyway?"

"You, of all people, are going to judge me for engaging in dubious commerce? Where is that blasted waitress?"

There was a long, awkward moment in which neither of us spoke. When I finally looked up, I saw the pained expression in Leslie's eyes, and I immediately regretted my harsh words.

"I didn't mean anything by that," I said. She smiled and told me it was okay, but I didn't believe her. "I'll return the money if it makes you feel better."

"It's okay," she said. "I think you did some good. Little Rebecca said she felt something different. Besides, I think we drank half of it."

The waitress brought my Bourbon and I drank it. She brought two more after that, and I quickly dispensed with them. I started to relax, and the conversation once again flowed as we returned to our normal, easy manner. My head spun in a whirl of conversation and color. I was intoxicated; that much was clear, but it had nothing to do with the drink as much as it did with Leslie's sweet voice, and her beautiful smile. We were good, and I was good. In fact, I don't remember a time when I felt better.

I ordered food at Leslie's suggestion and we ate and drank some more. We talked for hours, and I lost track of time. It might have been two in the morning, or maybe five. I didn't know, and I didn't care. I wished the night would never end, but like all good things, it had to.

I smelled him before I saw him. He sauntered up to Leslie's side like he owned the goddamned place and he wreaked of booze and cow manure. It was not a good blend. I don't like most people, but I had a particularly bad feeling with this one. He reminded me of Hell's Kitchen, a character straight from the darkest part of town, and he made the hair on the back of my neck stand on end. I could tell by his blackened hands and clothes he was an oil field worker. He looked like he hadn't had a shower in, well, forever.

It was evident he was drunk—drunker than me even—and I immediately sized him up. I was taller than him, maybe by three inches or so, but he was thick with a powerful build and he was much younger than me. I was street tough. I had this going for me, but he looked like he lived a hard life. I shook my head and took another sip of Bourbon, hoping he would just disappear, but I was never so lucky.

"Leslie Reed?" he said. "Is that you? What you doing here?"

Miss Leslie squirmed in her seat and forced a smile. "I'm trying to enjoy an evening with my friend, Hank," she said.

For the first time, the swine looked my way. He ran his eyes up and down me and smirked before turning his attention back to Miss Leslie.

"Oh, sorry," he said. "I didn't realize you were working."

Now, I could have—probably should have—let things be. Hank would likely have walked away, and Leslie and I could return to our conversation. Instead, I found myself standing on my feet. I don't know how I got there, but sure enough, I was there, and once you're there, there's no backing down.

Standing next to him, I immediately noticed an error in my earlier calculation. I was NOT taller than Hank. In fact, he was looking me straight in the eye, and at six feet, one inch, not many men can lay claim to that. And while I miscalculated his height, he was, however, every bit as thick and muscled as I originally thought, maybe even more so.

One might think I'd be nervous or a wee bit scared standing toe-to-toe with this hulking specimen of a man. Perhaps a smarter or less lovesick man would have been. I, on the other hand, had no such fear, just the unsettled rush of blood coursing through my veins causing my ears and cheeks to burn hot as embers.

I'm hardly ever at a loss for words, but I was this time. I continued to stare into his cold, grey eyes, and he returned the favor in kind before finally saying something to me.

"What you want?" he spat. "His breath reeked of booze and tobacco.

It was a reasonable question. What did I want? I wasn't exactly sure, but I was about to find out.

"Listen here," I said trying to sound calm but making poor work of it. "This lady is not working as you so delicately put it. She is—well, we are trying to enjoy a pleasant evening out and your disruption with your ill-informed thoughts are making it impossible to do so."

Hank's mouth fell open and he squinted at me. I could tell he didn't understand a word I said—I'm not sure I understood myself.

"You're not from around here are you boy?"

"I am not, and I'm not a boy. I'm a man."

"Of course you are," he said smiling. Then he finished his sentence. "...boy."

I was about to give him a severe tongue-lashing, but Miss Leslie intervened and was now standing between us; her short, feminine stature contrasted greatly next to our sizeable physiques.

"Now, now, gentlemen," she said. "No need for this. Hank, why don't you move on? You've had too much to drink and your missus is probably waiting at home for you."

Hank turned his head and spit out a disgusting stream of black juice that splattered on the wood floor and across my boots. Then he grinned wide at me and said, "Aw, I didn't mean anything ole, fancy-pants. Where did you say you're from?"

"Originally, I am from New York City," I answered proudly.

"Oh, well, that explains a lot."

"I'm from a place called Hell's Kitchen. Ever hear of it?"

I was hoping my town's reputation would be enough to instill fear into him. It did not.

"Nope," he said shaking his head and laughing. "But if you need to come all this way to get a piece of ass, who am I—"

Call it a reflex or call it what you want, but I insist my next move was purely an involuntary act. I watched in amazement as my left fist sprang forth like a Cobra and punctuated his sentence with a loud crack to his jaw. I got him a good one, a straight left over the top of Miss Leslie's bushy hair that contorted his flesh like a ripple across a still pond. His head jerked backward violently. Brown juice splattered in all directions at once. It landed on his face and shirt and it looked like shit.

The blow would have fell most normal men, but it was soon evident that Hank was no normal man. This brute stood tall acting more pissed off than hurt. His eyes were wide as silver dollars and his jaw hung open as he wiped the blood pooling on his lip. Then, he glared at me. There are moments when time stands still. This was one of those moments.

Hank's eyes turned black and his face went from annoyed to ornery like a bull's. I stole a glance at Miss Leslie. She didn't say a word; she didn't have to. I could read her eyes: *what in the hell did you just do?* I shrugged my response.

I wasn't sure why I just cold-clocked the largest man in the saloon, but I knew there would be hell to pay. I'm quick witted and been in lots of fights in my youth, so I knew enough to duck, but Miss Leslie wasn't so inclined. I heard a crack and I looked down and there she lay in a heap on the floor at my feet. The blow that was meant for me, had glanced off her temple and put her down like a young sapling. I locked eyes with Hank, and though I could tell it was an accident—he had not meant to deck Miss Leslie—I did not care.

With a war whoop that would make an Apache Indian blush, I leapt over Miss Leslie's prone body, and lit into Hank. There was a swirl of light and shadow, and tables and bottles and the color red. Yes, I saw red. I was older, and not as strong as my opponent, but I had hell's fury and righteousness on my side, two powerful allies in any fight.

Let me tell you, it's no exaggeration to say, ole fancy pants lit Hank up. I felt a little sorry for the brute as I thrashed him good, but I knew better not to give an inch. I was in my glory, raining lefts and rights, elbows and knees, pounding him like salt into the dirty floor. I heard the crowd, whooping and hollering. They were on my side. I felt it. Then, something happened. I grew tired, and I remembered how old I was. My arms turned to lead weights and the blows came less frequently; suddenly, they stopped altogether. I could barely lift my hands; I was so tired.

Sensing the opening, Hank turned the tables on me, and I was forced to cover up for dear life. The crowd—once on my side—now seemed to root for Hank as he beat me mercilessly. I tell you, that country boy punched like a mule-kick. I'd cover my gut and he went for my face. I'd cover my face and he'd go for my gut. Every punch stung like a hornet's nest and sucked the wind from my lungs. Blood flew everywhere. I'm not sure who's blood. I just hoped it wasn't mine.

Just when I thought my ribs were going to crack and I was ready to pass out from the searing pain, I remembered how to fight—fight dirty that is. I was on the bottom—not the most enviable position, but still very survivable if you know what you're doing. I wrapped my arms around the back of Hank's sweaty neck and pulled him in close. Then, I wrapped my thighs around his waist like a Python squeezing a rabbit. I had him in a bear hug, and it worked. Well, sort of. He had no leverage and couldn't unleash any more damaging blows, and I got a much-needed break from the ass-whooping. I used this respite to gulp some deep breaths; during which time, I figured out who the blood belonged to. It was mine.

With my cheek pressed tight against Hank's greasy head, I could hear his labored breathing. It mingled with my own heavy breath. I wanted to call off the stalemate. I had gotten my licks in and he certainly got his fair share. I waited for someone to intervene and bring an end to our entanglement, but of course, no one obliged. That's when I whispered into Hank's ear.

"Hey," I said. "Why don't we call a truce? What do ya say?"

His voice was muffled on the account his mouth was mashed against my lapel, but I heard him plain enough. "Yeah, okay."

"All right. I'll let go and you get off me?"

"Okay."

"No funny business, right? If I let go, you won't start wailing on me again?"

"You have my word."

I'm sure how good his word was. I suspected it didn't count for much, but I was tired, and I knew I couldn't keep him tied up for much longer, so I decided to take the chance.

I was about to turn him loose when I saw something loom over Hank's shoulder. It was a big mound of hair, blond hair. *Sweet Jesus*, I thought. No! This can't be happening, but it was.

It was Miss Leslie, but it wasn't. I mean it was her, but her face had metamorphosed into something I didn't recognize. She leapt with the grace of a cougar onto Hank's back. I tried shooing her away with my eyes, but everything happened so fast. She ignored me and started wailing on the back of Hank's head with her walnut-sized fists.

Poor, Miss Leslie, well, she was simply pitiful. There's no other way to describe it. Her punches had as much effect as raindrops falling on a granite slab. That is to say they had no effect at all other than to piss Hank off. I imagined what we must have looked like from a bird's-eye view; three fools intertwined in a life-and-death struggle on the floor of Nate's Saloon.

Time had lost all meaning. It seemed like an eternity had passed, but in reality, it could have only been a minute or two. Miss Leslie was relentless and tireless, raining her less-than-worthless blows on the back of Hank's skull. I had him simmered down and now I could tell he was agitated again, not that I blamed him. For my part, I clung tightly to Hank while I offered up a prayer: *Jesus help us live to see another day*. But Miss Leslie—God bless her—persisted in her assault.

Hank did what most any sane person would have done. He reached up and grabbed the closest thing available—a clump of Miss Leslie's hair. He tugged hard and pulled Miss Leslie off of him. While Hank was preoccupied with the bird's nest of blonde, curly locks, I seized the moment and landed the bony part of my forearm straight across his jaw. It landed with a resounding whack, so I knew I got that peckerwood good.

Fate had turned once more and now Hank rolled onto his back and clutched his jaw as he writhed in pain. I saw Miss Leslie was about to pounce again, so I scrambled to my feet in time to grab her arm. I dragged that fierce woman out of there—kicking and screaming—past the cheering crowd and out the door. Miss Leslie and I laughed as we half-ran, half-limped down the road and through the chilled, night air. I was sure Hank was hobbling after us, but we never stopped to find out. We kept going as fast as we could. My head throbbed and my body ached, but I don't remember a time when I laughed so hard or felt so good.

We walked for several minutes in silence, absentmindedly making our way from town into the sticks and towards her little home in the woods. My heart fluttered at the possibilities which lay ahead.

"I didn't know you had it in you," I said. "You were laying into 'ole Hank pretty good."

Leslie feigned some punches toward my jaw. "I'm a tough gal when I need to be."

"Tough and pretty," I said without thinking. But Miss Leslie pretended not to hear the compliment.

"I like it out here, late at night," she said while casting her gaze to the stars. "It's so pretty, so peaceful. Reminds me of the time I spent outdoors when I was a little girl. We'd have campfires, chase fireflies."

"Simpler times?"

"Much."

"You know, I can picture you as a little girl. You still have that in you, the child, the sweetness, the innocence."

"Thanks," she said shaking her head. "But I'm afraid that's all in the past. Life isn't so simple anymore. I'm not so innocent."

Time passed too quickly when I was with Miss Leslie. I could have walked for hours and talked about everything or nothing at all. However, each step—no matter how slowly I walked—brought us closer to her house and our logical end. I was sad when we arrived at her door; we stopped and faced each other awkwardly neither one of us mustering the courage to speak. She averted her gaze momentarily, but then lifted her eyes to meet mine. I didn't say anything. I was happy to take it all in, those eyes, her smile, that face.

"Well," she finally said. "I had fun, Dexter James. You made me laugh tonight."

"I made you laugh?" I said incredulously. "I nearly got you knocked unconscious."

"I can handle myself."

I turned sappy as I always did in front of beautiful women. "Miss Leslie," I said. "I can't tell you how much fun I had tonight. I hadn't been in a bar room brawl in forever."

"Really? I can't picture you ever being in a fight. You're too sophisticated, so gentile."

"Well," I said sheepishly. "I grew up in a tough town. I've tried, but I'm afraid I've never fully shaken my early influences."

Miss Leslie laid a gentle hand on my elbow. It was a simple gesture, but for this touch-starved, old man, it made my body shiver. She then rose on her toes and planted a kiss on my swollen cheek. It was a small peck, but I felt it everywhere.

"Good night," she whispered softly.

"Wait," I said. "When will I see you again?"

"I have to see Doctor Brown tomorrow. How about the day after?"

"Doctor Brown? I hope there's nothing wrong. You weren't hurt in the fight, were you?"

"It's nothing like that," she said smiling. "I've just been a little—I've been under the weather."

"I see." I wanted to swallow her in my arms, to pull her in close and press my lips hard to hers, but I stood there frozen with awe, and though I wished she'd invite me in, the tired look in her eyes told me it was time to leave. "Good night, Miss Leslie."

Miss Leslie let herself in and then she turned and smiled ever so faintly before closing the door behind her. I walked back to Clem's beneath a blanket of stars. At that moment, in a town filled with wealthy men, I was the richest of them all.

CHAPTER 12

I felt the hard lump where my eye should have been, and it made me wince and laugh at once. Tears streamed down my face; the salty water stung as it rolled past the open wound on my cheek.

Last night was a blur. There was a fight. I remember this, but I'm not sure who won. I am sure, however, I was with the prettiest woman in Titusville. I am sure she kissed me on the lips and that we made passionate love out in the open air beneath the witness of a million twinkling stars. At least that's how I remembered it.

It took a lot of effort to sit up, but when I did, I turned to my left and was startled to see Lucy standing next to my bed sort of looming over me like a hawk over its fallen prey. I had no idea how she got in my room or how long she had been there. Then a terrible thought crossed my mind: *oh God, what in the hell happened last night?*

Lucy scowled at me and in her right hand, she held a steaming pot of coffee just inches above my head. If I didn't know better, I thought she might dump the contents over my head. She looked like she was about to at any rate.

I closed my eyes and shook my head, but when I opened them again, she was still standing there, and this time she spoke, but she really didn't say anything. She made a disapproving clicking sound with her mouth; kind of reminded me of Momma when I was a little boy about to be scolded.

"Lucy?" I said. "That you?"

"Well of course it's me; who else would it be?"

"Damn. I need to remember to lock the door."

"How many times I need to tell you? It ain't got no lock."

"Yes, well, that's a problem."

"What on earth did you do last night? The Sherriff came looking for ya, and the whole town is talking."

"What? The Sheriff came looking for me?"

"Sheriff Tom Coffin was looking for ya this morning."

"What did you tell him?"

"I told him to get lost. Told him you weren't around."

"That's my girl," I said grabbing her free hand and kissing it profusely. She wasn't having any of it and yanked her hand away.

"He said you and another feller got into it at the saloon over a woman. He said you busted up the place good, and from the looks of it, you got busted up good too."

I laughed, but that made the pain flare up, so I quickly stopped.

"You know I still got it," I said nodding my head.

"Sure you do," Lucy scoffed. "Just whatever you got, keep it to yourself. What's the other feller look like?"

"Oh, let's just say he's not feeling any better than me."

Miss Lucy shook her head and poured a cup of coffee into the mug sitting on the nightstand.

"Here, drink this," she said. "We need to tend to your wounds. For goodness sakes, I don't know what to make of you, Dex. When I first met you, I thought you were decent folk, a man of God doing God's work and now look at ya. Hanging out with Jezebels and brawling all over town."

"Wait a minute," I said taking the cup from Lucy. "You keep Miss Leslie out of this. She's a good woman."

"Really? You know what she does for a living, right?"

"She was forced into it."

"Forced my behind. She had a husband. She could have stayed with him."

I felt my cheeks turn red. "Yes, a husband who hit her, who belittled her. She's doing what she has to do to stay alive without the help of a man. Good for her, I say."

"She's got plenty men helping her."

"Why you—"

"Now don't get into such a fuss," Lucy said cutting me off. "You're a grown man. You do what you want. See who you want."

"Exactly. So why do you care?"

Miss Lucy's face softened. "I don't know, Dex," she shrugged. "I like you, that's all. You remind me of a crazy stray cat that needs a helping hand every now and then."

I was at once touched and annoyed by her observation. "What do you mean a stray cat?" I said. "And a crazy one at that? How do I remind you of a crazy, stray cat?"

"I don't know," she said. "You just do."

I waited for her to clarify, but she just stood there shaking her head back and forth, then she abruptly turned and walked out of the room leaving me to wonder.

I was grateful for the coffee and even more grateful for the bottle of whiskey I had purchased earlier. I poured some into my mug and it helped with the pain. I swung my legs over the side of my bed and stumbled to the dresser where I got a good look at my face in the mirror. It wasn't nearly as bad as I thought; judging by the pain, I expected a ghastly, swollen monster would be staring back at me. On the contrary, I didn't look half bad. I had a shiner over my left eye, which was swollen shut. Other than that, I was fine. Still had all my teeth. I bet Hank wasn't looking much better. I got my pokes in.

I washed up, got dressed and quickly went downstairs for breakfast. Clem had made grits again. I didn't even know what grits were before I came to this town and now, I've had it every morning since I got here, but I wasn't in the mood to argue over the fine cuisine at Clem's boarding house. I felt excited and was anxious to get out of there.

"Miss, Lucy," I said. "My compliments to the chef. Another fine culinary experience as usual. Please apply this to my room and board and keep the rest as a tip."

I pulled a crumpled dollar bill from my billfold and tossed it on the table. Then I donned my cap and headed for the door before Lucy's screeching voice stopped me.

"You owe me a lot more than a dollar," she yelled.

"Oh?"

"And where are you going in such a hurry?"

"Not that it's your business—"

"You're going to call on Leslie," Lucy interrupted.

"And what if I am?"

Lucy paused. "I'm just saying, you owe me more than a dollar."

I vaguely remember something about Miss Leslie seeing the doctor, but I hoped she'd still be home. I hadn't gotten fifty paces down the road, when I saw a rider galloping towards me on a black steed. From a distance and through a single eye, it was difficult to make out who it was and for a moment, I was scared. I wondered if it was Hank fixing to run me down. I imagined the rider wielded a big sword over his head and was about to slice my head off like that fellow, Ichabod Crane. But as the horse drew near, I could see the rider was too small to be Hank and in fact, he was unarmed. It was something much worse: Boo.

I don't know what I was thinking. I was on foot and Boo was on a horse, but that didn't stop me from turning in the other direction and trying to make a run for it. I had other plans today and was in no mood for the boy.

"Wait," Boo said. "Dex, I got something to tell ya."

I turned around in time to watch Boo deftly slide down his mount and land softly on two bare feet.

"Well, what is it?" I said.

"It's Rebecca Radley. You have to come see, Dex. You gotta come see what you've done."

Blame it on the whiskey, or blame it on the bump on my head, but I honestly didn't know what Boo was yapping about.

"What have I done? Rebecca Radley?"

"The girl who had infant, infantile…"

"Polio?"

"Yeah, the one you exorcised yesterday."

My body went rigid. "What's wrong with her?"

"Nothing. She's fine."

"Oh, well then, why should I go see her?"

"I mean she's completely fine. She don't have the polio no more. You chased that demon away good."

I fixed my eyes on Boo, but everything was foggy, and grey, and his body swayed from side-to-side like a tree limb. It sounded like he said Rebecca was fine, but I knew better. Sadly, there is no cure for polio, and one could only pray Rebecca would not end up completely paralyzed or worse. I'm not proud to admit as much, but my nonsensical performance last night didn't do anything for her. Then, I remembered I was dealing with a young boy, a somewhat daft young boy at that.

"Ah, Boo," I said. "You're joshing me. I don't have time—"

"Naw, I ain't joshing ya, Dex."

I listened for a hint of deception in his tone, but there was only sincerity in his voice and a serious expression written on his face that I had not seen before now.

"What do you mean?" I said grasping him by both shoulders. "She doesn't have polio? That's impossible."

"It ain't. She's walking. Her poppa threw away her crutches. He told me to come fetch ya. Come on, Dex, let's go."

I pictured Leslies round face, her alabaster skin and warm smile. I wanted to show off my wounds, to talk and laugh with her once more.

"C'mon, Dex. Her Pa says he's got more money for ya."

"More money?" I said. "Okay, Boo. Take me to her."

"I got ole Whiskey here," Boo said, stroking the horse's mane.

I thought for a moment he meant for me to get on the horse. I started to laugh, but I stopped when I realized that's precisely what he meant.

"Oh no," I said shaking my head. Boo stared back blankly. "Oh, no," I repeated several times.

"It's okay," Boo assured me. "Ole Whiskey here won't hurt you."

Just then, the dark-haired beast turned and looked me in the eye. I swear the horse had murder in its heart.

"Ole whiskey has hurt me plenty of times in the past. Can't we just walk? It's not far."

"C'mon, Dex. Quit fooling. The Radleys are waiting."

I had a horrible thought. What if this was a setup, an Ambush at the Radley house? Boo was in on it. He might even be the mastermind. He speaks Latin and knows I was just spouting gibberish last night and now he's outed me as a fraud, and this is an elaborate scheme to get the Radley's money back.

"C'mon, Dex. Are you coming or not?"

"Boy, if you're lying to me…"

"Honest, I'm not. C'mon, Dex. Get on."

I looked at the angry-looking and saddleless beast, then I looked at Boo. Fortunately, he was an understanding lad. He cupped his hands for me, and I stepped into his makeshift stirrup. With his help, I managed to swing my leg over Whiskey's rump. The real miracle was I managed to take a proper seat without pitching myself off the other side. I offered my hand to Boo, but he didn't need it. To my amazement, he grabbed the horse's mane and pulled himself into a seated position in front of me.

"Hold on," Boo said.

He kicked Whiskey's ribs and we went flying; I held on for dear life.

The journey was mercifully short but very taxing on my already throbbing head, not to mention what it did to my queasy stomach. I felt a tad pale, green by the time we reached the Radleys' front porch and when we came to a stop, I didn't so much slide off the horse as much as fell off. It didn't matter. I was so happy to be on the ground, I kissed it while there.

"Don't you have trains in Titusville?" I said.

"Sure," Boo said. "But no trains come out here."

"Well, that's a shame," I said picking myself up off the ground. "I swear, Boo, this better not be a wild goose chase."

The porch door swung open, and out came Mr. and Mrs. Radley, and I knew right away; this was no joke. They looked at me like I was the second coming of Christ. Mrs. Radley clasped her hands over her mouth. Her eyes were wide and wet. Mr. Radley smiled broadly; his eyes were misty too. I took off my hat and held it over my heart because it seemed like the right thing to do.

"Mr. Radley," I said in a soft voice. "Mrs. Radley. Sorry for the intrusion, but Boo told me an incredible story. He said to come quick, that you wanted to see me."

"You did it," Mr. Radley said.

Did what, I thought? What the Hell did I do? Then, I saw Rebecca Radley float easily between her mother and father. She smiled at me, and her mom gently stroked her long, brown locks.

Something was different about Rebecca. She glowed with an angelic light, but there was something else. I noticed her hands; she held a flower and was twirling it back and forth between her fingers. That's when I realized: she held a flower; her hands and arms were free; she had no crutches. My eyes immediately looked down for confirmation. Sure enough, no special shoes with braces, just two, plump legs where I expected to see withered limbs. Suddenly, I felt cold despite the heat. I trembled, and my legs wobbled like a newborn fawn's. I felt like I was about to fall, and I reached out for Boo to support my weight, which he did with some difficulty.

The rest was a blur. I remember feeling dizzy and being whisked into the house and seated at the kitchen table while Boo and Rebecca hovered around me like two pesky flies. Someone, I think it was Mrs. Radley, offered me cold lemonade and I drank it gratefully even though I would've like something stronger.

"Are you okay?" Mrs. Radley asked.

I had to think about my answer. My head was spinning like a top, but I reckon I felt well enough now.

"I—I'm embarrassed," I said.

Boo, acting like a boy coming to the defense of his Pa chimed in. "He's okay," he said. "He was in an awful scrape last night."

"Boo!" I scolded. "How did you know about that?"

"The whole town knows."

I looked at the Radleys for confirmation. Mr. Radley nodded his head and said, "Good news travels fast around here."

"Yes," Mrs. Radley added. "And so will the news about our Rebecca. We'll make sure of that."

Hearing Rebecca's name brought my focus back. "Rebecca?" I said. "What's this about Rebecca?"

"Well, you can see for yourself," said Mr. Radley. "Look, no crutches. No braces. She can walk just like any normal child, just like you and me, better even."

I closed my eyes and shook my head trying to clear my thoughts. "But that's impossible," I said.

"No it ain't," said Boo. "You excised that demon just like you said you would. You did it, Dex."

"I did no such thing," I protested. "I told you; she wasn't possessed. She has polio, and medical science has no cure for polio."

Mr. Radley shook his head. "I hate to disagree with you," he said. "But you did something and whatever you did, worked."

"That's right," Boo said. "Dex here ain't the bragging type. Go ahead, Dex, tell 'em. Tell 'em what you did."

I looked around the room and saw their wide-eyed expectant faces—so innocent, so trusting—staring back at me. I stammered out a reply, "I, uh—the Lord works in mysterious ways I guess."

"That he does," said Mrs. Radley clasping her hands together. "Glory, he does work in mysterious ways." Mr. Radley nodded his head in agreement.

I felt drunk with excitement and confusion. I had never before seen anything so peculiar and I've witnessed some strange things in my lifetime. I looked for an answer, anything that might explain the situation in a way that made sense to my now overtaxed brain.

"Perhaps," I said. "Perhaps there was a misdiagnosis."

Mr. Radley crinkled his forehead. "What ya mean?" he said.

"Oh, I don't know. Sometimes, doctors get things wrong. You did say she saw an actual doctor?"

"Of course," Mr. Radley said. "We took her to Doc Brown; he lives right in town. He said she had the polio, and she was no different than a lot of folks who have it. The only difference is they've never been to you. You're a doctor of the soul and that may be the best kind of doctoring there is. Wait till everyone finds out about you."

"No please. I wish you wouldn't tell anyone. Not just yet."

"Why not?"

"it's too late, anyways," said Mrs. Radley. "We told everyone."

"What?"

"Why sure. Why wouldn't we? This is a true blessing, a real miracle, and we want to give you the credit for it."

"That's right," said Mr. Radley. "You're a man of God. In fact, you're God himself. Ain't that right, Ellie?"

Mrs. Radley smiled warmly at me and said, "Well, the next best thing I suppose." Then, she pushed her daughter forward and I accepted a grateful hug from the girl.

"Rebecca, dear," I said. "May I have a look at your legs?"

Rebecca looked at her parents. They smiled and nodded. I had Rebecca sit at the edge of the kitchen table where I examined her legs. My eyeballs nearly popped from their sockets. Her skin was alabaster white with red patches where the leather straps had been. The most startling thing, however, were the size of her legs. They were thick, fleshy limbs showing no signs of atrophy common to polio victims. Her legs were normal for a twelve-year-old child. In less than twenty-four hours, they had gone from frail hickory sticks to virtual oaks. Either that, or my mind had become possessed with false visions, or false memories.

"That's fine, Rebecca. You can get down now."

"Praise God," said Mrs. Radley. Then she nudged Mr. Radley in the ribs.

"Oh, yes," said Mr. Radley. "Praise God and praise Mr. James too. He's the one that made this happen. Don't think I forgot about you."

Mr. Radley walked over to the kitchen counter and retrieved the glass jar filled with money. Then he walked back and dumped the contents onto the table.

"It's not much," he said. "But it's all we have. We want you to have it."

I felt a small hand pat me on the shoulder. It was Boo, beaming, proud as can be.

CHAPTER 13

Boo and I stepped into Clem's. It's normally quiet lobby bustled with a rather motley crew of men and women, young and old, wealthy and impoverished. They were quite the spectacle, jostling for position, arguing with and cursing at each other. When they spotted me, however, they immediately stopped and swarmed like drones around their queen. I was surrounded.

"We heard what you did for the Radley girl," a woman shouted at me. "I have this awful rheumatism—"

How did they know, I thought? I just found out myself.

I scanned the faces and recognized my only friend in the crowd. Leslie's eyes met mine, and I threw up my hands as if to say what's going on? She smiled and did the same.

Standing off to the side with her arms folded across her chest, was Lucy. She shook her head from side-to-side, and though I couldn't hear her above the crowd, I knew she was making that disapproving, clicking sound.

"My husband drinks too much," a woman said waving what looked to be a ten-dollar bill in front of my face.

"The missus is always tired," another man said. "She always has a headache. Can you lay hands on her?"

The crowd pressed closer. I felt claustrophobic and struggled to get a clear breath. Good God, what have I done? I turned and looked at the door leading back out to Main street. It was tempting. I could bull rush the crowd, run out the door, hop on Whiskey's back, board a train and be out of Titusville by noon. Boo, of course, could fend for himself, so could Leslie for that matter. Then I remembered, I didn't have the money for a ticket to anywhere. I'd have to hop a train and hope I didn't get caught. Besides, I'd likely not survive the horse ride. Fortunately, I had an angelic presence on my side.

"Now, just you hold on everyone," Leslie said her voice rising above the din like a steam whistle. "Dexter will take all your requests, but one at a time. Now everyone form a line."

Miss Leslie clapped her hands sharply as she herded the people like cattle. There were a few grumbles from the crowd, but to my astonishment, they obeyed and formed themselves into a single, somewhat orderly line.

Then I saw Lucy charging towards me. "What's going on here?" she demanded. "What's this nonsense I heard about a miracle?"

"Believe me," I told her. "I'm as shocked as you."

"Look at what you've done to the place. Used to be a respectable boarding house with respectable people. Now look at it. Full of drunks, whores and beggars."

"Hey," a woman shouted at Lucy. "Speak for yourself."

"Y'all are trespassing," Lucy shouted back. "Dex, take your circus out of here."

I'd be happy to leave this mess behind. I especially wanted to get away from Lucy and her judgmental tone, but before I had a chance to tell her as much, Miss Leslie came to my defense.

"Now you hold on," Leslie said pointing a finger at Lucy. "Dex is a hero. He chased that polio demon right out of Titusville. Ain't that right, Dex?"

The room had grown quiet in deference to Leslie's raised voice. My stomach grew queasy and I felt everyone's eyes directly trained on me. I was at a loss for words. I didn't want to lie, but I didn't know what the truth was. I looked at Leslie for guidance, however, she had the same expectant expression as everyone else.

"Yeah, I reckon that's right," I said.

"See there?" Leslie said with an air of satisfaction. "Now, Lucy, I reckon these folks will need something to eat. Go tell Clem to cook up some food."

The anger drained from Lucy's eyes and was replaced with dollar signs. "Food?" she said. "As in paying customers?"

"That's right," Leslie nodded. "I think two dollars is a fair price to pay under the circumstances." Miss Leslie nodded her head at the crowd, and they all nodded back in unison.

"And beer," a man called out from the line."

"Oh you, Jim Patty," Lucy shouted back at him. "You've already had enough to drink and it's still morning. You'd do good to have old Dex exorcise the Demon of drink from ya."

Everyone laughed, and for the first time in a long while, I breathed easy.

Lucy hiked up her dress and ran to the back room calling out Clem's name. I turned to Miss Leslie and asked her how she had heard.

"The same as everyone else," she said. "I was in town for my appointment with Doc Brown. Everyone's talking about it. It's the biggest news since they struck oil."

Boo scanned the long line of restless people. "Gee," he said. "I'm not so good at figuring, but at five dollars a head, we should fetch a sum."

Boo was right. There must have been close to twenty people gathered in the lobby, many holding cash in their fists and wanting me to perform some type of miracle for them. No one was on crutches, either. There wasn't a polio case in the crowd. These were just common folks, with common demons—demons I've exorcised a thousand times before. Twenty people at five dollars a head should buy some nice things, new clothes, and a thick steak—Clem's grits be damned. I could afford to take Leslie out to a fine eating establishment.

I smiled at Boo. "Thank you for the ride," I told him. "You can be off. I'll take it from here."

"Oh, I'm not going anywhere. Did you forget our arrangement, Dex?"

"What arrangement is that?" I said wrinkling my forehead.

"You know. I get fifty cents for every customer I bring you."

"What? You didn't bring me these customers. They came to me of their own accord."

I turned to Leslie, but her stern expression told me she was on the boy's side.

"Fine," I said. "We'll settle up afterwards."

I had Boo run to my room and fetch my demon-fighting bag. Leslie was a Godsend, taking people's money, organizing the crowd, and restoring order when scuffles broke out. Lucy sold sandwiches and beer and gave away coffee, and I was in my glory, performing exorcisms with a verve I haven't known in some time. It was like the good old days. In fact, it was better than that. I've never seen excitement like this before. The crowd was on my side. They looked up to me. They had problems and, well, I held their solutions in the form of a prayer and some holy water.

The first few performances were grand; I cast out their demons left and right—the demon of drink, and lust, and of achy tooth and of broken heart. A few afflicted women dropped to their knees and passed out after I laid hands on them. Boo and Leslie looked troubled by this, but I just laughed. I had seen it all before. As soon as one fainted, I was onto the next. Even Lucy joined in, helping to revive people and offering them lemonade at five cents a glass. Lucy was no longer angry with me. She was all smiles.

A small, frightened woman approached me clutching a five-dollar bill. I snatched it from her and handed it to Leslie for safe keeping in her brassiere.

"Problem?" I asked the woman.

"What?" she replied.

"Your problem? What is the nature of the evil that dwells within?"

The woman looked from side-to-side. She was either too embarrassed or too scared to speak up, but either way, I didn't have time for this. I saw the crowd growing restless and shuffling their feet.

"Never mind," I said. "It doesn't matter. It's probably a minor demon. A standard exorcism should work nicely for you."

I placed my hand on her forehead and in a loud voice that commanded the attention of the room, I prayed over her in Latin. When I finished, I removed my hand and said, "There you go. Next?"

"Wait?" she said grabbing my coat sleeve. "Is that it?"

"Well, yes. You feel better, right?"

"I suppose. Is the demon gone? Is he gone for good?"

"Sure," I said trying to sound convincing.

She smiled and went on her way.

"Okay, who's next?"

I performed around twelve exorcisms in about thirty minutes, but despite the brutal pace, Leslie told me to hurry things up. I looked and saw there was now a long queue snaking out the door. Apparently, word traveled fast about the Radley girl, and more people were starting to file in. Lucy ran around the lobby, frantically trying to keep up with orders. There was no sign of Clem. He must have been slammed in the kitchen fixing sandwiches. Though I had never met the men, I felt a little sorry for him.

At this rate, we'll be here all night, or worse, have to turn people away and if we did that, they may not come back the next day. It's like poker, you play the hot hand, so I kept dealing. I offered short prayers and quick blessings and the turnover was incredible. Patrons would enter as demon-possessed slaves and leave with a renewed soul ready to take on the world less five dollars.

Leslie smiled as she took their money and stuffed it down her dress. Her bosom now overflowed with cash dollars. What a sight, everything a man could ever want in a single place. I was young again, more powerful than I had ever been, and I liked that feeling. A part of me never wanted it to end. Then I'd catch the twinkle in Leslie's eye. She looked at me with admiration, and it wasn't just my imagination. In those moments, I wished everyone would go away and leave us alone; money be damned.

At one point, the holy water ran out, so I handed the bottle to Boo and quietly asked him to fetch some more for me. He gave me a puzzled look and asked me if it didn't have to be a special kind of water. I told him the bottle held the specialness and that anything you put into the bottle became special. He looked at me with some puzzlement but ran the errand anyway.

It was like a dream, but only better because it was very much real—that is until two uninvited guests showed up. They walked in and stood off to the side, surveying the room and staring at me with their judgmental faces. I tried not to pay attention, but I couldn't help it. I saw them from the corner of my eye, shaking their heads in disgust as though I was committing a crime.

It was bad enough just having them there—their energy ruined my flow and disrupted my thoughts—but then they stopped the proceedings as they cut the line and confronted me.

As usual, the fat priest had something to say to me. "What—what is going on here?" Father O'Brien said.

I'm beholding to no man, so at first, I was tempted to ignore the portly priest. However, with every eye on the place now trained directly on me, I saw a response—even a flippant one—was needed.

"I'm churning butter," I said. "What does it look like I'm doing?"

Everyone laughed. Even the skinny priest tried to stifle a smile which infuriated the chubby priest even more. O'Brien's face turned beet red and it looked like the vein on his forehead would pop.

"This man is a fraud," O'Brien said turning to the crowd while shaking his finger at me. "You all should go home, or better still, go to church and ask forgiveness for your sins. We will hold a special mass for your absolution."

For a second, I was worried. Then I remembered, the crowd was on my side, and as the rumbling grew, so did my confidence. I didn't need to defend myself. The people were my advocates.

"Leave him alone," someone said. "This man is a hero."

"That's right," another said. "He drove a demon out of the Radley girl. She can walk."

"Have you all gone mad?" Father O'Brien said. "This man's a liar. Has anyone seen the Radley girl?"

The room went silent and the crowd looked around for confirmation. Then, Boo stepped forth. "I did," he said. "We were at the Radley's this morning. Rebecca walks just fine. No crutches."

The crowd came to life. People crossed themselves and I could hear individuals praising their God above the din.

"Oh great," Father O'Brien said in a loud voice. "You're going to take the word of this—this imbecile?"

Boo's eyes drooped and he put his head down. I swear, if it weren't for the collar around Father O'Brien's neck, I would have dropped him where he stood. I was about to say something, when a flash of pink stormed past me and made a beeline for the chubby priest. It was Leslie. Her hand was cocked as if she would hit him. I thought of stopping her but decided against it. She was in full mother hen mode, and I didn't want to get between her and her unfortunate target.

"Listen here," Leslie said jabbing her finger into Father O'Brien's soft chest. "This boy is no imbecile. In fact, he's smarter than you!"

People shouted and cheered Miss Leslie on, yelling, and waving their fists in the air. I found myself jumping up and down. It reminded me of a prize fight, and I had a front-row seat.

"That's right!" a supporter yelled out. "The boy is smarter than you."

That really got the room going. Everyone laughed at O'Brien. His face turned red, but I was not the least bit sorry for him. He had brought this on himself.

"Wait a minute. Wait a minute!" O'Brien said in a booming voice that silenced his tormentors. "Look at you. You're acting like fools, standing here; waiting in line to hand your hard-earned money over to this charlatan on the word of a boy, and this, this...this prostitute."

The only sound I heard was that of rushing blood through my ears. Collar or no collar, I was ready to take him out. There's no telling what I would have done to O'Brien, probably killed him before they could pull me off. I thank God for the paralysis that kept me planted in my boots. I couldn't move a muscle. It was as if a divine force put a hand on my shoulder and held me firm in place.

The air had been sucked out of the room. Everyone, including Leslie, just stood and stared at O'Brien with an accusatory expression. The tension was palpable. I could see O'Brien sweat. It was worse than any beating he could have taken. He loosened his collar and looked from side-to-side, pleading with his eyes for a friend. Lucky for him, he had one by his side.

Father Paco stepped forward and placed a hand on O'Brien's shoulder. Then he spoke to us in a soothing voice. "What Father O'Brien means is that we should all be careful. Satan comes to us in different forms and that we should be vigilant. Isn't that right, Father O'Brien?"

"Yes. That's right. You know I only want the best for all of you," he said gesturing towards the crowd. "Many of you are my parishioners, my flock, or you were before you stopped coming to church."

"No," Leslie said looking Father O'Brien in the eye. "That's not what you meant at all. I think we all know what you meant. You made yourself quite clear."

"Leslie," Father O'Brien said shaking his head. "Leslie, what has happened to you? I knew your mother and she wouldn't approve of you—"

"You keep my mother out of this," Leslie snapped. "You don't know anything about me or my mother."

I saw Leslie was on the verge of tears, so I walked up behind her and placed my hands on her shoulders. Her body was a coiled, steel spring.

"Why don't you come to Mass this Sunday," Father Paco said.

"Well, I would, but Father O'Brien kicked me out. Remember?"

"We can't have her in our church," O'Brien said. "It wouldn't be proper."

By this time, the crowd had inched forth, closing in on the priests, surrounding them like ravenous wolves salivating over a helpless fawn.

Father O'Brien's eyes darted back and forth in search of a sympathetic face, but the only thing he found was a stone-cold mob staring back at him. For the first time, I felt a twinge of empathy for O'Brien. I knew men like him, spewing the company line whether he believed it or not, whether others liked it or not. Perhaps O'Brien wasn't such a bad fellow. Maybe he couldn't help it. After all, he was schooled by others who were taught the same way, and so on down the line for the past two thousand years. I was once like him.

"Father, O'Brien," I said. "If you're finished, I'll kindly ask you to leave. I still have work left to do. These people need me."

"C'mon. Let's go," Father Paco said to Father O'Brien.

The crowd parted and the priests walked, arm-in-arm towards the door, but before leaving, Father Paco stopped, turned around and walked up to Miss Leslie.

"Miss Reed," Father Paco said. "If you're ever so inclined, stop by the church and confess your sins. I'll be glad to hear them anytime."

There was something gracious and sincere in his offer. I heard it and Miss Leslie heard it too.

"That's kind of you, Father," Leslie said.

Father Paco smiled at her, then he turned around and he and Father O'Brien left.

"All right, all right," said Lucy. "There's nothing more to see here. Let's get back to business. I got sandwiches. Who wants a sandwich? How about a nice cold lemonade?"

CHAPTER 14

The dank interior was illuminated by the soft glow of colored light from a stained-glass window. It took me a moment for my eyes to adjust and when they did, I made out the bookshelf filled with Bibles and Catechism books, old-looking ones; I could practically taste the must. Behind the desk sat Father O'Brien with his usual sourpuss face and behind him, standing just off of O'Brien's shoulder was Paco. He smiled at me.

It was against my better judgment, but I was fond of Paco. He was pleasant enough to me, and he was real fine with Miss Leslie the other day. He had a calming effect, a soothing voice, and a Latin accent that sort of chortled like a bird. He understood what most priests don't: rules are to be damned if need be. The only thing that matters is how we help our fellow man. This is how we will be judged. Nothing more.

Father O'Brien, well, he's everything we'd come to expect from the Roman Catholic Church: stiff, rigid, and quite frankly, a bore. O'Brien looked at me as if I was his mortal enemy, which to him, I probably was. I returned his grim face with a big, sweet smile, which caused him to turn his head away quickly.

Paco spoke first. "Thank you for coming in," he said. "Care for some tea?"

"Naw, I'm good," I said. "Wait. Do you have anything stronger?"

"We have wine."

"We're not giving him the wine," Father O'Brien said.

"Never mind," I said. "Let's get down to business. What do you want as if I don't already know?"

The two priests gave each other hesitant looks before Paco spoke. "Well," he said. "We have concerns."

"Yeah, I know all about your concerns. You told me about them in no uncertain terms. Why don't you leave me alone?"

"Now, listen up," Father O'Brien said. "Have you no Christian in you? What you're doing is wrong. This is work for the Church not an amateur like you. And what is it you're doing anyway, taking people's money, cheating them out of their hard-earned cash?"

"Seems like the Church and I have a lot in common," I said smugly.

I touched a nerve with that one. O'Brien's neck swelled, and his face turned beet red. "Now, now, look here," he said waving a sausage-sized finger at me.

"Well, we are both in the business of serving God," Paco said. "Isn't that what you meant, Mr. James?"

"Sure," I said.

"We talked things over," Father O'Brien said. "We decided it would be best for you to leave town."

"You want me to leave town?" I chuckled. "Gosh, for priests, you sure do have a pair; a rather large pair at that."

"Listen," O'Brien said doing his best to sound calm and compassionate. "It's the Catholic Church's responsibility to cast out demons and dark spirits. Wouldn't you agree?"

"Naw," I said. "I don't agree at all. I think it's all our responsibility to confront evil when we encounter it."

"We both know that's <u>not</u> what you're doing."

"What do you mean?"

"Well come on," O'Brien laughed. "I mean casting out the demon of drink and the demon of lust, or whatever other sorts of demons you think you're casting out?"

"Think I'm casting out? I don't think nothing. I know I'm helping these poor souls, people the church forgot about or never cared about in the first place."

"Hogwash."

"Hogwash? You heard about the Radley girl."

"I heard it," O'Brien acknowledged.

"Well, how do you explain that one?"

Father O'Brien paused and then flashed the biggest eat-shit grin. "How do *you* explain it?" he said.

I wanted so bad to knock the smugness from his face, to come back with a retort that would floor him and shut his mouth for good, but I was speechless. I had no answer for him, the Radleys or anyone else for that matter. I had no idea what happened. Rebecca Radley was sick; she had polio. I knew that much. I also knew I didn't even say a proper prayer over her, let alone perform a proper exorcism. I'm not proud to say, but I was hungover and useless and didn't try very hard. I knew it and so did Miss Leslie. What happened? I don't know. It was a miracle from God. I had nothing to do with it.

"Look," I said. "I don't have to explain anything to you, and I have no intention of leaving this town anytime soon. I kinda like it here; I made a new friend."

"Yes," Father O'Brien nodded. "We know all about your friend."

"Yeah, I bet you do, Fatso," I said aiming a finger at O'Brien's chest. "Miss Leslie told me all about you."

It was a low blow and a lie, but it hit like a locomotive. O'Brien's face melted into a red, angry mass. His body shook and his mouth hung open as if to say something, but nothing came out. I had rendered the man speechless and for this, I believe we were all blessed.

"Mr. James," said Paco. "Please don't take this as a personal attack. We have nothing against you, but it's our job to look after our parishioners, and we take our job seriously. You can understand this, can't you, Mr. James?"

"You can call me, Dex," I said. "Friends call me Dex, and yes, I do understand. In fact, that's the first thing you've said that makes any sense."

"Well, then you understand our concern over the rogue exorcisms by a non-qualified exorcist."

I knew I should have kept my mouth shut and let them believe what they wanted. It would have been wiser. They didn't need to know, and the less they knew, the less they could hurt me, but I'm way too proud and sometimes, too stupid.

"Well, I am a qualified exorcist," I said softly.

I saw the dubious look in O'Brien's eyes. "Oh, yeah?" he said. "By whose authority are you qualified?"

"Ab auctoritate catholica Ecclesia, in Roma, et fama virtutis eius."

O'Brien and Paco looked puzzled. "So what?" O'Brien said. "You learned some Latin. Any nitwit can do that."

"Acta deos numquam mortalia fallunt."

"Wait," Paco said. "I am sorry, my Latin isn't so good as it should be, but did you say you were sanctioned by the Catholic Church?" I closed my eyes and nodded. "But how is this possible? Most exorcists are priests."

I locked eyes with Paco but didn't say anything.

"You're a priest?" he said.

"Was."

"What happened?"

"It's obvious," said O'Brien. "The Church saw him for the scoundrel he is and expelled him."

"Hush, please," Paco scolded. "I want to hear from him."

"It's okay," I said. "O'Brien had it pretty much right."

There was a long, awkward silence before Paco spoke. "Well," he said. "Then you of all people should know there's a process to follow. Evidence of a true demonic possession must be submitted to the archdiocese, and in turn, passed on to the Vatican. Protocols must be followed; permission must be granted to proceed with an exorcism. How else would you know if you're dealing with a true demonic entity as opposed to mental illness? As an ordained, Church exorcist, you must understand this?"

I sat back in my chair and shook my head. The only thing I understood was how sick I was of the Church, its rules and gatekeepers.

"Yes," I said. "I know all about that."

"Well, then. Why do you insist on carrying on, screaming from soapboxes? Go. Leave this town or at least leave the business of the Church to the Church."

"Because. I'm filling a need left by the church."

"This church?" O'Brien said. "St. Titus? What need have we left unfulfilled?"

"Aw, don't get so riled," I said. "It's not just this local parish; it's all the parishes, and it starts at the very top in Rome."

Judging by their expressions, you would have thought I said Jesus was as fake as a three-dollar bill. They didn't say a word, not a thing. They looked at each other and then at me and then at each other again and then back at me. Their jaws hung slack and their eyes begged me for an explanation, but I'd had enough.

"Well," I said putting on my hat. "This has been a real pleasure. We should do this again sometime."

I got up and headed for the door. I was about to leave, but I knew it was too easy.

"Wait, a minute," O'Brien blurted out. "Who are you—who do you think you are coming into our parish and telling us about the Church as if you know anything about it? The nerve."

I turned to face O'Brien. "You're the one that sent for me," I said. "I was an invited guest. Remember?"

"Yes, a guest, so that we could sit down as civilized men, and break bread and talk."

"Ha. What a joke," I said smiling. "You had no intention of talking with me. You wanted to lecture me about what I'm doing wrong, and to impose demands, and penalties for not obeying. That's more like it."

"Gentleman, please," said Paco. "Can't we—"

"Yeah, that's what you do," I interrupted. "You and the Church, you make up rules that never existed before, but you make them up to serve an end. You hold people to a standard they cannot possibly achieve and when they fall short, you cast them into the fires of Hell, or a made-up place called Purgatory."

I marched to the bookcase and picked up a Bible. Then, I walked up to O'Brien and plopped it on his desk where it landed with a resounding thud in the cavernous space.

"Look," I said. "It's the Bible. Open it. Read it."

"I have read it. Thank you very much," O'Brien said.

"Good. Then tell me... where does it say—where does it say you cannot eat meat on Fridays or priests cannot have sex? Where does it say that? Old Testament? New Testament?"

To my own ears, I sounded like a raving lunatic, but I was acting instinctively, running on pure adrenaline.

"We took a vow of chastity," Paco said in a soft voice. "As an ordained priest, you did the same. Why should this bother you?"

"Yes," O'Brien said rubbing his jaw. "Why should this bother you?"

I had almost forgotten. So many memories. Water beneath the bridge as they say.

"Well, I guess it doesn't," I said. "At least not anymore."

I turned toward the door but once again, I was stopped before I could leave.

"I have to warn you," O'Brien said. "We've been in contact with the Sheriff and though we hate to resort to such measures—"

"And what business does the law have with me?" I said wheeling around. "When is it a crime to help people, to cure a little girl?"

"Helping people is not a crime. Swindling people out of money, barroom brawling, and God knows what you're doing with that whore. Well, there's enough there to put you away for months, if not longer."

I heard enough and walked out with Father Joe's voice still ringing in my ears.

"You can't hide in a small town like this. If I were you, I'd pack my bags and leave while you still can."

CHAPTER 15

Her spirit was like a benevolent twister that picks up everything in its path and spits it back out in a way that's better than it ever was. Walking beside her, arm-in-arm down Main Street, I was sucked into her vortex. The feeling was odd, yet wonderful and intoxicating. No, I hadn't touched a drop this morning, but still, I don't remember a time when I was happier or less lonely than now.

I was rich too, or at least it felt that way. My billfold swelled with cash and Miss Leslie would help me spend some of it. We would occasionally stop in front of a shop window and her face would light up as she ogled the expensive merchandise inside. I'd find myself looking at her. I could not be blamed for she was an earthbound angel, ethereal and flawless. When we started walking again, I'd have to turn my head quickly, so she didn't catch me gawking.

The entire town knew about the Radley girl by this time. I saw it in people's faces as we passed them. Folks stopped walking; they covered their mouths and whispered to each other. Some would point and smile at me and I drank in their attention like sweet nectar. We could have been stars of the Broadway Theater. That's what it felt like at any rate. Leslie occasionally drew a look of contempt from the women, but she didn't pay them any mind. It bothered me more than her. I knew what they were thinking, those self-serving hypocrites. In my book, they were all whores. The price and the terms were different, but that was all.

"It's such a nice day," Miss Leslie said.

"It's a glorious day," I replied. "The sun is out."

"Well, it's not actually. The sun is behind the clouds. Maybe that's why I'm so cold."

"Well, my dear Leslie. When I'm with you, the sun is always out."

Leslie laughed nervously and blushed, and it made me feel like an old man trying too hard.

"Are you hungry?" I said. "We could get a bite to eat."

"Not now," she said. "I'm not hungry."

"Are you okay? You look tired. Perhaps we should stop and rest."

"Oh, I'm just fine," she said flashing her disarming smile. "Let's walk a spell."

We strolled past the nameless faces; past shops and saloons as our banter continued without pause. We then came upon a man dressed in black and wearing a top hat. He stood next to a large wooden box sitting on three legs. The contraption had a single, glass eye fixed to its center and a black clothing hanging down its back. From my extensive travels, I recognized the box as a camera obscura. However, the camera—or its owner for that matter—wasn't the most remarkable sight on the boardwalk. On top of the box sat a bouncy, chattering, hairy beast that looked like it was suffering from an acute overdose of strong, black coffee. The miniature ape spun in circles and chased its tail like some sort of deranged cat. I thought it would corkscrew itself right into oblivion until it caught the eye of Miss Leslie and suddenly stopped. Then, the beauty and the beast stared into each other's eyes. It was quite remarkable actually, and if I didn't know better, I'd think they were in love.

"Oh, my God," Leslie gushed while placing her hands over her heart. "Dex, look at that."

"Yes, I'm looking," I said.

"Oh, my God. What is it?"

Obviously, there weren't a lot of primates walking around Titusville other than us humans; but from my travels in South America I immediately identified the scamp for what it was.

"It's a monkey," I said.

"A monkey?" Leslie squealed.

"A Capuchin to be exact, so named after the Friars Minor Capuchin. They wore long, brown hoods, and when the Portuguese came to the Americas, they saw these little apes with brown coloring that resembled the hoods, so they called them little Capuchins."

"His name is Mikey," the man said.

After hearing its name, the little beast jumped up and down and clapped its hands. I'd swear he was smiling. Then, without warning, he leapt into the air like an acrobat and landed on Miss Leslie's—well, let's just say he landed on her female parts. That was bad enough, but then the little beast started kissing Miss Leslie's face. He was practically eating her alive, slobbering over her like the cad he was. Even worse, Miss Leslie seemed to enjoy it. She giggled and hugged the critter in a rather unseemly manner.

I cringed at this display and looked around for some help—a sympathetic soul to share my pain—but the monkey's owner just threw up his hands and said, "What can I tell ya? He's got a way with women."

"Hey," I said to Leslie. "Hey, how do I get some of that?"

"Oh, Dex," she gushed. "Look at him. Isn't he the most darling thing?"

I grunted my response.

"Would you like your picture took with him?" the owner said.

"Let's get our picture taken," I said to Leslie.

"Oh no," Leslie said.

My heart sank. "No? Why?"

"My hair," she said running her hands through her golden mane. "Look at me. I look horrible."

It was true the monkey had ruined her carefully manicured head of hair, but even in this chaotic state, and with a monkey wrapped around her neck like a scarf, she was still the prettiest woman in Titusville.

"My dear, Leslie. If that's horrible, give me some horrible."

"Oh, Dex," Leslie blushed.

"What do you say?" the man said. "Only two dollars."

"Yes. Yes," I said pulling out my billfold.

"Dex, c'mon. I look awful and you know it."

"Miss Leslie," I said taking her hand in mine. "You are as pretty as the sun is warm."

I kissed Leslie's hand, while Mikey chattered his disapproval.

"Now, stand here," the photographer said motioning to a spot in front of the camera obscura.

"Must we have that ragged excuse for a primate in the picture?" I said.

Mikey looked at me with his beady, little eyes and waved his fist at me as he chattered away. It was as though he understood what I said.

"Why of course we'll have Mikey in the picture," Leslie said. "You're such a good little boy, aren't you, Mikey?"

Oh for goodness sakes, I thought. Does this indignation have no end?

Leslie, with Mikey perched on her shoulder, and I took our places in front of the camera obscura. The device looked simple enough, but what it did was remarkable. I heard it described as a light painting and in the hands of a master, the results could be spectacular.

"Are you using Daguerreotype?" I said to the photographer. "I've heard of this process."

"No, no," he said. "I'm using a new process called albumen printing."

"Albumen, as in the egg?"

"Yes, that's right."

"Fascinating."

"Does my hair look all right?" Leslie said. "What about my makeup?"

"Now, does this albumen produce the same quality as the Daguerreotype?" I said. "Money is no object. I want the best."

"Oh," the photographer said. "It's even better than Daguerreotype."

"Even better you say?"

"That's why I switched to albumen. It looks like—well it looks like real life. Real life on a sheet of paper. I think you'll be pleased. Now, you two scooch closer together."

The photographer disappeared behind his black sheet and Leslie and I moved closer until our shoulders pressed together. A warm breeze kicked up and lifted the scent of lilac mixed with the sour smell of monkey breath to my nose. I closed my eyes and imagined the photo in my hands, a little painting of the two of us—well, the three of us—on this perfect fall day. I couldn't help but smile. I wanted to put my arms around Leslie, to pull her in close, but I hadn't the nerve. I was content for now.

When I opened my eyes, I saw the photographer had come out from under his sheet.

"No, no," he said looking directly at me. "That won't do."

"Hey," I said. "I know I'm not as pretty as this fair maiden off to my right, but I'd still like to be in the picture."

I felt a blow on my chest followed by Leslie's high-pitched squeal. She was no doubt laughing at me, but I ignored her.

"It's the hat," the photographer said. "Remove the hat."

"What's wrong with my hat?" I said. "I like my hat."

"It's the sun. It's casting a shadow."

"Yes, but I'm afraid I haven't combed my hair this morning. I would have, but I lost my comb; the only real good comb I—"

Before I could finish my sentence, Leslie's left hand came flying up and smacked me in the head, knocking my hat off and onto the boardwalk. I stared at it for several seconds and then looked at Leslie for an explanation of what just happened.

"You're as beautiful as the sun is warm," she said batting her eyelashes at me.

"Where did you hear that rubbish, I wonder?" Leslie shrugged. "And you really need to stop smacking me like that."

"I'll stop smacking at you when you stop being so ridiculous," she said pointing an accusing finger at me.

"Oh, is that so?"

By this time, the little monster had joined in the argument and was chattering and waving his fist at me. I was clearly outnumbered.

The sound of clapping hands brought our attention back to the photographer.

"Now, now," he said. "Let's focus people. I have lots of pictures to take today."

"See there," Leslie said. "You made the man mad. He's clapping his hands at us."

"I made the photographer mad?"

We could have gone forever, arguing, kibitzing, poking fun, and that would have been fine with me, but the photographer's crossed arms and incessant foot tapping told us it was time to calm down. He turned out to be a real fussbudget, making last-minute adjustments, directing, our stance one inch this way and then one inch that way, so that we arrived at the very point from which we started. Well, I suppose he was taking the time, making sure everything was just so before taking the exposure, and for this, I was grateful. I wanted the photograph to be perfect. I wanted this day to never end.

As we waited for the photographer to make his final adjustments, Leslie, primped like it was her wedding day, bouncing her hair up and down on her palms, puckering her lips and adjusting her corset. Mikey seemed to help by grooming her hair. Then she blew kisses at the camera as if it were capturing her every move. I couldn't help but laugh at the idea of a moving picture. The crazy things I think about.

While Mikey and Leslie fussed about, I thought about how this would transfer to a sheet of parchment. Would the image capture the essence of the day—the faces and the bodies to be sure, but what about this feeling, this emotion? Perhaps not, but it was the closest thing I had to capturing my memories forever.

He told us not to smile, but neither of us could help ourselves. Mikey too looked incapable of a serious face. Realizing it was no use, the photographer finally squeezed his bulb and there was a blinding flash.

"Is that it?" I said.

"That's it," said the photographer.

"Are you sure? Maybe you should take another just in case."

"No. I got it."

"When can we have our photograph?"

"I can have it to you in three days."

"Three days? Why so long?"

"Well, what do you expect? I'm going to make an exposure and the photograph is going to spit out of the camera right then and there. Boy, I'm an artist, not a magician."

"Well, that would be a trick," I said laughing.

"Wait a minute," he said taking on a serious tone." We'll call it...we'll call it instant photography," he said as he panned his hands across the sky.

We both chuckled at the absurdity.

"Oh, Mikey," Leslie said. "I'm so glad to have met you. Maybe you can come to my house someday and help me clean."

This made Mikey very happy. He clapped his hands and gave Leslie a goodbye kiss before climbing down her dress and back onto the camera obscura. I never thought I'd utter these words, but I have to say I envied that monkey.

"You can deliver it?" I asked the photographer.

"Oh, yes," he said producing a pencil and a piece of parchment. "Just write down your address here."

"No need. I'm staying on the other end of Main street. A little boarding house called Clem's. You familiar with it?"

"I'm new in town, so I can't say I am. You say it's down this street a spell?"

"Yes. It's called Clem's; you can ask anyone. Just leave it with the old lady behind the desk. Her name is Lucy. She'll see I get it."

"Will do. You folks have a nice day."

"Now, you said, three days?"

"At the most. I'll try to put a rush on it for you. You and your wife seem like nice folks."

I glanced over at Leslie. She looked at me and blushed.

"Well, be careful," I told the photographer. "I want it to turn out right."

"I'll do a good job for you," he said smiling.

Leslie and I said our goodbyes, then we continued our stroll down the boardwalk. After a few steps, I turned my head and saw the little monkey waving at us. Though I knew it was impossible, he looked like he was crying.

Miss Leslie's eyes suddenly lit up as she pointed to a sign outside a dilapidated structure. The sign was worn, and its lettering cracked and faded.

MADAME SANDY CANDY – FORTUNE TELLER - PSYCHIC

"Look," Miss Leslie said, grabbing my arm. "It's Sandy Candy. Let's go inside and get our fortunes read."

"Sandy Candy?" I said. "You must be kidding."

"C'mon, Dex. I heard she's good. It'll be fun."

"Well, you know fortune tellers, and soothsayers are the work of the Devil. I've exorcised many souls who have ventured into the dark arts."

"Oh, pish posh."

"Pish posh? Don't pish posh me. I'll have you know—"

"Are you still talking? C'mon. Let's go."

Normally, I'd hesitate to engage in such tomfoolery. Talking to the spirit world, garnering information not meant for the living is playing with fire in a very literal sense. Doors open that should remain closed, and through these doors, spirits—bad spirits with nasty temperaments—can pass freely between our world and theirs. Once opened, these doors are difficult to close. I wasn't kidding Leslie when I told her I had exorcised people delving into the occult. These people— fools actually—thought it was harmless fun, and those same people sought me out to rid them of the consequences. I'd be worried if I thought this Sandy Candy was for real, but judging by her name, she was nothing more than a carnival side show. I've seen her kind before. She'll give you a so-called reading, speak in generalities that could apply to almost anyone, fish for information and then make you think it was a message from the other side. Yes, it was all an act, a bit of entertainment on a Saturday afternoon. There would be no real conversation with the other side and thus, no real harm. So I followed Leslie inside. What do they say? A fool and his money are soon parted? I was that fool.

Moving from the brightness of day to the dark interior made me temporarily blind. Miss Leslie grabbed my hand out of necessity as she led the way into this dark cave, slowly inching along as we felt the wall for support and reassurance. I couldn't see worth a damn, but I could sure smell, and a distinct odor made my nostrils flare. I recognized the scent straight away. It's one I used in my own practice. Miss Sandy Candy—or whoever—was burning frankincense.

"Yoo-Hoo," Miss Leslie called out. "Hello? Madame Candy? Is anyone here?"

A voice responded off in the distance. It sounded like it came from another room. "Who's there?" it said.

"It's me. Leslie Reed. I brought a friend. We came to get our fortunes read."

"Oh, well, come on in."

"Where are you?"

"I'm over here."

"Yeah, well, that doesn't help," I yelled. Then, beneath my breath I whispered, "You old hag."

I didn't see the blow coming, but I sure felt it land flush against my temple. "Hey!" I shouted. "What the Hell?"

"Would you mind your manners?" Leslie scolded.

"Just follow the corridor to the end," the voice said. "Take the room on your right."

My eyes had adjusted by this time, and I could just barely make out Leslie's face. "Come on," she urged. "I heard lots of stories about her."

"Yeah, I bet you have. Can we get something to eat? I'm starving."

"Hush now. Follow me."

We inched forward, feeling the wall as we walked. We finally reached the room; it was sectioned off by colored, glass beads. Miss Leslie was first to break through, and I followed close behind.

The room was poorly lit, but I was grateful for any amount of light at this point. I looked around and immediately sensed a woman's touch, a rather bizarre woman's touch, but a woman's touch, nonetheless. There were lots of pink pillows strewn about, and lacy female privates hanging from a stretched rope across the center of the room. Paintings of people— I presumed dead people—hung from the walls in fancy gilded frames.

They were a ghastly site that made the hair on the back of my neck stand on end. Remember, I'm a demonologist. It takes a lot to scare me.

There were books everywhere, laying sideways on shelves, scattered on tables. They were dusty and musty smelling books that looked like they hadn't been opened in centuries. Their spines read: *The Art of Witchcraft, Learn the Tarot in 28 Days and Beginner's Guide to Divination. Good God*, I thought. What have we gotten into?

However, the books were the least of my worries. The doll-like-creatures with glass eyes that followed me as I walked gave me quite the start. One of the dolls looked like an African warrior. It had big teeth, and he held a huge phallic spear between its legs. From my travels, I recognized it as a ritualistic Voodoo doll, one used to cast spells on unsuspecting people; it only got worse from there. The other dolls were baby dolls like the kind a little girl might play with, only these baby dolls would scare the shit out of any normal child. They were a ghastly sight with faces fabricated from tanned hide; some of them were missing eyes, and a few were absent of a face all together.

I've encountered some strange things in my line of work, but this place rivaled anything I've seen previously. I reconsidered the notion that this was harmless fun, and I would have run out of there, Leslie in tow, if it weren't for the transfixed, fascinated expression on her face.

"Well, this is nice," Leslie said.

I didn't say a word. I just squeezed Leslie's hand tighter.

"Hello?" Leslie called out. "Is anyone here?"

A women's voice came from an adjoining room. "Yes, yes," it said. "I'll be right there."

Leslie gave me a questioning look. "Well, you wanted to come here," I said.

"No, no," This will be good she said patting my hand. "This will be good. This is all good."

The door from the adjoining room opened, and out walked an old woman. Her face was wrinkled, she wore too much makeup, and her black hair was piled higher than Leslie's (which, before now, I hadn't thought possible). The woman smiled like she was extremely happy to see us, but I suspected she was happy to see anyone.

"Hello, hello," the woman said. "Welcome to my home. I am Madame Sandy Candy and to whom do I have the pleasure of addressing?"

"Well, I'm Dexter James, and this here is Miss Leslie Reed. You can call me Dex."

Madame Candy's face lit up. "Oh, Mr. Dexter James. I've heard of you."

"You have? See there, Leslie? Miss Candy has heard of me. My reputation precedes me."

"Hmm," Leslie grunted.

"Yes," Miss Candy said. "You're that fella that stands on that ridiculous soapbox, shouting about devils and demons."

Leslie laughed. I decided then and there, I did not like Madame Sandy Candy.

"Yes," I said. "I'm also the fella that cast a demon out of the Radley girl. Perhaps you've heard of this?"

"Yes, of course you did," Madame Candy said with more than a hint of disbelief in her tone.

"Oh, Madame Candy," Leslie said. "We saw your sign and—"

"And you've come to get you your fortunes read."

"Yes, that's right."

"Of course it is," Madame Candy said, her eyes narrowing on Leslie. "I am a fortune teller extraordinaire. I knew you were coming even before YOU knew you were coming."

"Oh yes, of course," Leslie said gushing.

"Oh, brother," I mumbled.

"I'm a certified psychic at the First Spiritualist Society of Laona," Madame Candy said.

Leslie looked duly impressed. I, on the other hand, bit my tongue. I wanted so badly to tell the Madame she indeed looked certifiable.

"Which one of you would like to go first?" Madame Candy said.

"You go first, Dex and then tell me how it is," Leslie said.

Before I had a chance to answer, Miss Candy whisked me away. "You have a seat out here in the waiting room," Miss Candy told Leslie. 'I'll come get you shortly."

I followed Madame Candy into a back room; she closed the door behind us and we both took a seat at a round table. I looked nervously around, but the lighting was poor, and I couldn't see much beyond the Madame's face. I suspected this was probably a good thing.

I had never had a reading before, and this was all very strange to me. I was leery to be sure. One could not always discern between good and evil spirits for an evil entity will masquerade as something else, taking the form of loved ones to gain trust and then gain entry into the soul. I've seen this too many times in my line of work. For this reason, I never sought to make contact with the other side, and I counseled others to do the same. Allow the dead to rest I always say.

I would have taken Miss Leslie by the hand and dragged her out of here, if I thought the Madame was a real psychic, one that can actually talk to the dead. However, there was no real danger here. Madame Sandy Candy had every bit of the charlatan in her, a woman of show rather than substance. She was no more psychic than I was. I guessed she'd prattle on about some nonsense, speak in vague generalities, and I'd be out a few bucks; no great loss. An entertaining way to spend an afternoon I suppose, and if it made Miss Leslie happy, so be it.

"Okay, let's get on with it," I said.

Madame Sandy Candy cleared her throat loudly. "There is the matter of my sitting fee," she said.

"Oh yes, of course," I said laughing. "How much? I'm paying for my friend too."

"Ten dollars."

I nearly fell out of my chair. "Pardon me? I might be a little hung over, but I thought you said ten dollars."

I started chuckling and Miss Sandy Candy and I enjoyed a hearty laugh that lasted for several seconds. Then, Miss Candy stopped suddenly and stared blankly at me.

"Oh for God's sake," I said. "Ten dollars? You're kidding?"

"Well, times are hard."

"Apparently, times are not so hard for you."

Madame Candy shrugged and against my better judgment, I handed her a ten-dollar bill. It was my only option at that point. If I backed out now, I'd look like a cheap scoundrel in front of Leslie.

"Thank you," Miss Candy said taking the bill and stuffing it down her dress. "You know, I caught your act once. I liked it. You're good."

"Act?" I said. "And what act is that?"

"Oh, come on slick. We're in the same business. No need to be coy with me."

"I'm not being coy. I really don't know what you're talking about."

"You know. Up on that soapbox of yours, calling all sinners, casting out demons at five bucks a head," she laughed. "That's a good business."

It took me a while to catch on, but when I did, I felt the back of my ears turn red. Apparently, this woman, this fraud, had mistaken me for her own kind, and I felt compelled to set her straight.

"Wait a minute," I said. "What are you saying? I'm putting on a show as you call it?"

"Oh, don't get so upset. It's nothing bad. You have a good act, very entertaining, and you're charging people for it as you should. There's nothing wrong with that."

I shot straight up from my chair. "Listen here," I said. "Don't confuse me with a scoundrel such as yourself. I'm an exorcist, I cast out demons—"

"Oh sure you do," she said in a condescending tone. "Of course. Of course you do."

I wanted to argue with her, but I didn't know what to say. I could tell her about my training and my former standing in the Roman Catholic Church, but I felt it would be lost on her. I just stood there feeling hurt and stupid and shaking like a leaf; I couldn't stand her insolence, so I turned and stormed out of the room.

Miss Leslie looked surprised when she saw me. "What's wrong?" she said.

"It was a mistake coming here. C'mon let's go."

Sandy had followed me out to the waiting room. "Come back," she said. "I didn't mean to upset you."

"Give me my money back," I demanded.

Miss Candy pulled the ten out and gave it back to me.

"Wait a minute," Leslie said. "I want a reading."

"You'll not get a reading from her," I said. "Not a real one at any rate. You'll get generalities and vague suggestions that apply to most anyone. You'll get a—what did you call it, Madame Candy—a show?"

Madame Candy's eyes teared up. "Please," she said. "I didn't mean to upset you. Let me offer my services to your lovely wife."

"My wife?"

"No charge."

Leslie looked at me with her puppy-dog eyes, and I threw up my hands. "If you want to waste your time, go ahead," I said. "I'll wait here for you."

Miss Leslie smiled and followed Miss Candy into the back room. I waited patiently, and fearfully in the creepy doll room. At that moment, I wished I had my demon-fighting bag with me. Roughly, thirty minutes had passed before Leslie and Madame Candy came back out, but instead of smiling, talking away as usual, Miss Leslie looked downcast as she brushed past me without a word.

"So, how was the reading?" I asked cautiously.

"C'mon, Dex," Leslie said. "We should go."

Miss Leslie walked out, but I lingered behind, waiting for a reaction from Madame Candy. She gave me a sympathetic smile and with her eyes, said, "Ask Leslie."

CHAPTER 16

The walk to Miss Leslie's home was long, but it was made longer by Leslie's silence. Her usual buoyant character was gone, and replaced with a sober soul, and unsmiling countenance.

"What's wrong?" I said.

"Nothing. Tired."

"No. You're not tired. It was that sad excuse for a psychic. She told you something. What did she tell you? It doesn't matter. She's not real, you know. She can no more predict the future than I can."

I laughed and expected Leslie to join me, but she didn't. She just walked along in cold silence, distant almost aloof. I fed off of her energy. Unfortunately.

I hoped to lighten the mood and so I changed topics. I talked, or more accurately, I chattered like that stupid monkey. I pointed to the ground and up at the trees as I effervesced over the most obvious and ridiculous things.

"Look," I said. "There's a rock, and up there are birds. I think they're finches. They look like finches."

My overt attempts to cheer her up went unnoticed, so I took a different approach. I just shut up and listened to the sound of nature as we walked the path through the woods. However, I was never one to be silent for too long. I need to think constantly, create, or invent, and if I don't, I feel like I might explode. It's who I am; it's what I do. But it's not just the inner world that haunts me. I'm hyper-sensitive to what goes on around me. It started in my youth and has only intensified with age. Something would catch my eye: the slightest movement, the slightest change in the wind, a raised eyebrow, or downturned lip, and I'd know something was amiss. It comes in handy during a game of poker, but it can be overwhelming at other times. It's like I can sense someone else's pain.

It sounds crazy, I know, but there was something about Leslie I had noticed even before visiting the daft psychic—something I could not describe, but I knew was off.

"Are you Ill?" I said.

Leslie looked startled. "Why do you ask?" she said.

"I don't know. You look gaunt. Your cheeks are not as full. Your eyes droop. There's a tone in your voice that was never there before."

As if by magic, that wonderful smile of hers appeared, but I did not trust it for a moment. It was a trick, and she was merely putting on a show for me.

"Oh, I'm just fine. I'm tired. Just tired."

"What did Madame Candy say to you. She said something. You were different when you came out."

"Nothing I didn't already know." Leslie stopped as if she were hoping that would satisfy my curiosity, but it did not. I continued to press her with my eyes. "I just need to take a break, you know, from working."

My heart skipped and I momentarily felt elated and then confused.

"Wait. Stop working. That's wonderful, but how will you support yourself? Do you need money? We made a killing at Clem's. Half of it is rightfully yours anyway."

"No," she said waving me off. "I have some saved up. I'll be fine."

I felt like for the first time in Titusville (or maybe in my lifetime) things had finally come together. I had money, a measure of respect, the beautiful Miss Leslie next to me, and now, it seemed like God had moved mountains to make sure Leslie and I could be together. I could never imagine such a day would come. I, a mere mortal, could never make such events happen; never in a million years, but God in his infinite power and grace has done just that. It's like after all these years, my faith, and my servitude would pay off. We'd soon arrive at her house, alone. I'd been thinking about it for some time, and though we'd been alone before, this time will be different. Miss Leslie and I had a history, stories, and common experiences. We knew each other. We liked each other. There was no doubt in my mind. We were meant for each other, and I had finally summoned the courage to think as much.

"There are a lot of oil derricks here," I said nodding to a distant hill dotted with the menacing wood, steel contraptions.

They made for an odd site, like a forest of deranged trees with symmetrical limbs stained black from oil. In a big city, they could pass for abstract art. Perched on farmland, they looked out of place, odd and foreboding.

The mention of oil derricks jostled Leslie from her thoughts. "Yes," she said in a soft and mournful voice. "They seemed to sprout up overnight. One day they weren't there and the next day they were. It's like the people too. I woke up one morning and no longer recognized my town."

"This makes you sad?"

Miss Leslie grabbed my elbow and squeezed it. "You know," she said. "I lived here all my life. That little shack I live in, it's my family home. I know it ain't much, but I have so many memories, my momma, my poppa…"

"What was it like?" I asked her. "When you were a little girl?"

"I remember I was playing near the edge of the creek. I was about five or six, and somehow, I stumbled and fell and landed in the water. I yelled for my momma; my little doggy heard me, and he fetched Momma and Momma fetched me out. Funny what you remember."

"Your Momma, she passed?"

Leslie nodded. "I was twenty-seven when Momma passed," she said.

"Did she know about your husband, how he treated you?"

"No. I never told her. I kept it hidden."

"Why?"

Leslie shrugged. "I don't know. Too embarrassed I guess."

"Embarrassed? But you did nothing wrong."

"Yeah, except marry him."

"What was the town like?" I said. "Before all this oil business?"

"It was just a town. Nothing fancy; farms, hills, horses, cows. I don't know. I ain't never been anyplace else."

Up ahead I saw Miss Leslie's little shack—my destiny. I fell silent, and deep into my mind as thoughts began to swirl like a storm. My breaths came shallower and my skin felt clammy as we hiked the final steps to her house and stood at the front door. There was an awkward pause in which I didn't say anything. Miss Leslie, well, she was no help. If I could feel the air, thick and stifling between us, then I'm sure she felt it to. I swallowed hard, but there was hardly any spit left in my mouth. Quickly, I ran through a series of emotional progressions: nervousness turned to fear. Fear turned to excitement. Then, like a bolt, the adrenalin kicked in and overwhelmed my inhibitions. I seized the moment and placed both my hands on her shoulders and started spewing without thought; words spilled from my mouth like rain off a tree branch. I was out of my mind.

"Miss—Miss Leslie," I stammered. "You and I—I've seen it. We work good together..."

Miss Leslie's face dropped, and the blood emptied from her cheeks. "No," she said shaking her head. "Get that notion out of your head."

A dagger straight to my heart could never hurt as much. I stood there in shock, dumbfounded.

Leslie rose up on her toes and planted a soft kiss on my cheek. "I had a wonderful time," she said. "Let's do it again, soon."

Her condescending smile, her attitude, it was like a kick to the testicles. But I was determined. I waited so long, bided my time and behaved myself in a way I've never behaved before. And if she thought I was about to give up so easily, to allow myself to be deposited to the side of the road like old trash, she had another thought coming.

"What do you mean?" I said. "May I come in? I've been in your house before." Miss Leslie hesitated. "I have a long walk back to town and I could use a drink to warm me up."

I mustered all the charm I had left and gave Leslie a big smile. She smiled back and nodded. I had wormed my way in. It was something. The night would not end; not yet.

Leslie prepared a pot of coffee while I sat and watched. I was deep in my head now, thinking about my next move, thinking about a lot of things, actually. Who am I, an old man, a fraud, a keeper of useless knowledge, dead languages and ultimately, a failure at everything I've done? As far as looks go, I'm gangly and a bit scruffy. I was never much to look at, but age had taken its toll. She could have anyone she wants. What did she need me for? I needed her far worse than she needed me, and this was a frightening thought.

Even so, something inside made me persist. Besides, there was nothing waiting for me at the boarding house, just a lonely room, a cold bed, a lifetime of memories and regrets left to ponder during the empty,

THERE ARE NO SAINTS

dark hours. I traveled here to conquer this oil town, and now, finally, I was on the verge of something wonderful. The town lay prostrate at my feet. I was on top, a king, a demigod and yet, it wasn't enough. I wanted one more thing, the most important prize of all and she was just a few feet away. I could see her, close yet far. I drank in her scent; it was light, flowery and intoxicating.

"Coffee is almost ready," she said.

Her tone sounded odd to me. Her already-pale complexion was much paler than I remembered. Her eyes were dark, swollen and lifeless. I almost felt guilty for inviting myself in.

"Leslie," I said. "Is there something wrong? Do you feel all right? That psychic...she said something that troubled you."

Miss Leslie walked over to the table and took a seat next to me. She closed her eyes and rested her cheek against her palm. "I'm fine," she said. "Just tired, I guess."

I felt every bit the selfish, little prick I was. The right thing to do was to leave her be and let her rest. There would be the next day and the day after that. Yet, I planned for this moment, wished for it, prayed for it, thought of nothing else for days on end. It wasn't the perfect time, but I was so close. She was so close, and even in her tired state, she was lighting up parts of my brain that had been dark for some time. I reached forward and in one coordinated move, I cupped her face in my palms, closed my eyes and planted a kiss on her chubby lips and held it there.

At first, I thought we were good. She seemed to respond by pressing her lips against mine. I swear I felt the earth move but it was probably just the heart palpitations. Then, as suddenly as it happened, it unhappened. Leslie pushed me away. She shoved me is more like it. When I opened my eyes, I read the harsh sentiment of regret written on her face.

I spoke first, but I didn't have the words, just some jumbled ramblings came from my mouth. It was meant as an apology. It turned out as gibberish.

"Dexter," she said shaking her head.

She was going to tell me something, perhaps offer me an explanation. I didn't want to hear it. I stood up and donned my hat.

"I really should be going," I said trying to avoid her eyes.

"Dexter, wait—"

"No. I get it, Leslie. If I were you, I'd rather not be with an ugly, old man like me either. Good evening."

"Dex, sit down. Let's talk. What about your coffee?"

"Give my coffee to the cat," I said.

I rushed out the door and down the steps; the last thing I heard was Leslie's trailing voice from inside: "I don't have a cat!"

CHAPTER 17

I didn't mind the broken lock, or the fact Boo didn't even knock before letting himself in. I felt alone, depressed and a little suicidal. Seeing his face warmed my heart. He looked foggy, however, disheveled and unbalanced and it took a moment to realize that it was my sleepy eyes and whiskey-soaked brain that was at fault and not the boy's appearance. He smiled at me and waved, and I managed to return a weak smile from my bed. I don't remember the last time I stood on my feet or had a solid meal and despite the blankets wrapping my body like a cocoon, I felt the chill of a nonexistent breeze.

"Close that goddamned window," I ordered Boo.

Boo looked around. "There are no windows," he said.

"Oh, yes. Quite right."

The whiskey was supposed to make me forget, but the only thing I forgot was to pay my room and board. Miss Lucy's been after me all week. I waved her off and told her I'd get her damned money to her, but I never did. The liquor only masked the pain and it did a poor job of that.

I've spent hours in front of the mirror, looking for a clue, stroking my face, tracing every bump, crevice and imperfection. Am I homely? Yes. I must be. I'm attracted to women beyond my grasp; they are like the moon in the night sky—pretty, but unreachable. Why would God play such a trick, make me desire beauty I could never possess?

At first, I blamed Miss Leslie. I was angry with her, but I knew better. She was blameless, like a beautiful bird, colorful, talkative and wild. I wanted to hold that bird and, well, she wanted her freedom. I can't blame her. I don't know her or what she's been through, not really. I could only imagine what she's had to endure, the mocking, the scorn, people pointing fingers and talking behind her back. It must be awful. She doesn't need another man in her life. She has too many as it is. I regret showing my true feelings. Best to keep them in. When will I learn? It's like the Monsignor used to tell me: for a smart man, you sure are dumb.

Boo sauntered to the table and took a seat like he owned the goddamned place. Then he picked up an empty bottle, peered inside and took a whiff. The smell made him jerk his head back in disgust. He pointed the bottle at me and said, "This why I haven't seen you?"

"You little peckerwood. What business is it of yours?"

I was angry because Boo was right. It didn't matter; he was still a little peckerwood, a smart peckerwood, but a peckerwood all the same.

"It's plenty of my business," Boo shot back. "You haven't been exorcising no demons. People been asking about you. They say, where that demon-fighting man be? I got customers lined up. Customers mean money for you. They mean money for me."

Boo placed the bottle on the table. Our eyes locked momentarily, but I looked away.

"Is that right?" I said.

"That's the truth. There's more too."

"What's that?"

"Miss Leslie. She's been asking for you."

"Miss Leslie's been asking for me? You've seen her?"

"Yeah, I been doing work for her, even though Momma told me not to."

"How is she, Boo?"

"I don't know," he shrugged. "She seems kind of sad. Not like she used to be."

"Sad?"

"She said she won't be needing me anymore, and not to come around again."

Boo hung his head.

"Well, what did she have to say about me?" I said.

"Said you need to stop by and visit."

"Why doesn't she come visit me?"

Boo shrugged. "I don't know," he said. "Maybe she's scared."

"Scared of what?" I snapped. "I mean, there's nothing to be scared of."

"Did you do something mean to her Dex?"

I sat up in bed with some difficulty.

"No," I said. "I would never do anything to hurt her. Never."

I picked up the bottle sitting on my stand and tried to drink from it, but it was empty.

"You need to stop drinking," Boo said. "Else I'll need to exorcise the demon of drink from you."

I don't know what it was, his astute comment or his deadpan delivery or both, but that was the funniest thing I've heard in a long time. The irony wasn't lost on me either. I laughed, hard, like a belly laugh that shook me and the bed. It sent an ache through my body, but it felt good. Boo looked at me like I was mad.

"So, you're going to exorcise me?" I said.

Boo smiled and nodded. "Yes," he said. "I'm going to exorcise the demon of drink from ya. Just like you taught me."

"Well," I said. "I think you can find a better teacher than me. Teach you the right things at any rate, not some broken-down drunk like me."

Boo smiled and shook his head. "Naw," he said. "You're about the best teacher there is. You taught me how to read, Dex."

"I didn't teach you how to read. You taught yourself. I just helped that's all. Did you finish those readers I gave you?"

"Yes, sir. Momma helped me at first, then I read them two, three times on my own. I'm ready for some bigger books."

I picked up the Bible sitting on my stand and held it up for Boo to see. "Here's a big book," I said.

Boo's eyes grew wide. "That's too big," he said.

"You don't have to read the whole thing, just bits and pieces. I can help you."

"Did you read the whole Bible, Dex?"

The weight of the book made my arm tremble and so I placed it back down on the nightstand. "Yes," I said. "I read the entire Bible, more than once."

"Damn," said Boo drawing out the vowel in a long, sustained breath.

"Hey, mind your tongue boy. Who taught you how to speak like that?"

"You did Dex."

"Never mind that. What are you doing here anyway?

"I told you. I came to get you. Demons need exorcising. The whole town has gone crazy. They need you."

"They need me?" Boo nodded his head. "All right, Boo. Let's go exorcise some demons. Fetch my soapbox. Bring it downstairs. I'll be there straight away."

Boo and I set up shop on Main street. It was morning, sunny and warm; the light hurt my eyes, and I felt wobbly. I steadied myself on Boo's shoulder until I found my balance, but when I did, it felt good up there. I felt tall and I could see for what seemed like a mile. The people were walking about, scurrying like little ants. A few looked my way even before I spoke a word. Today would be a good day. I sensed it.

My voice was deep, and steady. I spoke with an authority that commanded people's attention. I saw it on Boo's face and all the faces as they gathered. My reputation had grown despite my recent absence or because of it. In seconds, an eager crowd gathered in front of me practically salivating for my sermon. I did not disappoint. I waved my hand across their heads as if I were conducting an orchestra. I swayed side-to-side to a beat only I could hear as I began to preach.

"Come everyone!" I shouted. "Gather ye sinners. Boy, do I have your salvation at hand."

All those shiny faces stared back at me with their mouths hung open. They reminded me of stringed puppets, and I was the puppet master.

"Ma'am," I said pointing an elderly woman. "Are you a sinner?"

"Well," she replied. "I reckon we're all sinners."

"This is true. But I'll tell you all. Hear me now. Satan has come to your town." I paused and allowed a gasp to punctuate the air. "It is so," I continued. "You all know it. With the black gold came woe, heartache and sorrow. Your town has changed, and not for the better. Who, my dear friends, is responsible?"

A man shouted and punched his fist to the sky. "The Devil!" he yelled.

I pointed to him. "Yes," I said. "The Devil is in charge of Drake's Well as if he drilled the hole himself. The Devil has captured this town's soul. This town is possessed. You who drinks is possessed, you who seduces is possessed, you who lies is possessed."

A man's voice rose from the crowd. "Aw, that's a bunch of hogwash," he said. "Tain't no devil around here. We struck oil. That's all. Town's never been so prosperous."

"Shut-up, Virgil," the woman next to him said. "Listen to the man. He healed the Radley girl. Don't you know anything?"

Everyone buzzed in agreement, then the woman knocked Virgil a good one sending his hat flying. Virgil retrieved his hat and held it reverently over his heart.

"No, no," I said to the crowd. "My good man is right. Business is booming. Money flows like the very gusher that brought it here in the first place. This much is true, but at what cost? Sure there's prosperity, but there's more fallen people, saloons, drunks, women of ill-repute, robbery, fights…"

"Sure," Virgil said. "But what's that got to do with the Devil?"

I started laughing. It was infectious and the rest of the crowd joined in. Even Virgil laughed, though I'm sure he didn't know what was so funny. I held my hand up to silence the crowd.

"My good man," I said. "It has everything to do with the Devil. The Devil looks for footholds and when he finds one, he unleashes a wave of evil and terror, death and destruction in all forms of avarice."

I scanned the crowd of ashen faces and dark mouths that hung open like empty pits. No one said a word and you could hear the wind blow. I had them. I had them where I needed them to be, a place of fear. The Church knows this too. Where do you think I learned? Fear is the driving force of all religions, not just the Catholics. The Jews are just as bad, so are the Muslims. Make them afraid of the Devil, of the afterlife, or the most neurotic fear of all—the fear of almighty God himself. Once they're afraid, they will hand over their money—the money that feeds the religious order. It's like when Jesus kicked the money changers out of the temple. Jesus was crucified, and the money changers came back.

I continued in a soft voice that would have been inaudible if it weren't for the silence. "How many of you?" I said. "How many of you have seen your crops die, your loved ones get sick, or die, or have taken to the bottle, or have left their homes and families for personal sin and glory? Perhaps you are one of those people."

No one said anything; their heads just swayed back and forth like scarecrows on a windy day.

"That, my friends, is the Devil. You are unclean whether you realize it or not. This town has been infected"

"You can clean us?" a women's voice cried out.

"I can and I will. I am the only one who can make this town great again."

There was a hesitation in the crowd. I sensed they needed one last push, a final twist of the knife.

"Line up," I commanded. "Boo, here will take your money."

Like a wave, the crowd came pouring in. They surrounded Boo, who looked like he was about to wet his pants. The wild-eyed look on his face was precious, but I wasn't worried. No harm would come to him. I was sure. People shoved bills in his face and not just dollar bills. I saw five's and twenties too, and I almost thought I saw a one-hundred-dollar bill. Boo snatched them up as fast as he could and then shoved them him into his pockets. A less trustworthy boy, and I would have been worried. Boo's heart was pure as gold and so I had no such fears.

"Now, now," I said. "Everyone calm down. You don't want to hurt the boy. Line up everyone. I'll take you one at a time."

"I'm lonely."

"I have the rheumatism."

"I'm missing a leg."

People pushed and shoved to be first in line. My box was jostled nearly knocking me off balance, and I had to scold a few folks. I whacked people with my hat so they would keep their distance. Jesus, I felt like Moses up there commanding the seas.

"Make sure you give the boy your money," I shouted. "I will perform your exorcism one at a time. Form a line in front. Form a line, I tell you."

It was a feeding frenzy, like piranhas devouring a carcass. I quickly realized I needed to alter the rite of exorcism a bit to satisfy this mob. I pulled out my holy water and splashed it over their heads, and I prayed loudly in Latin. I saw an elderly woman pressed up close to me and so I placed my hand over her forehead.

"I cast ye out, Satan," I yelled as I pushed on her forehead. She fell like a tree, and I heard a gasp from the crowd as she landed hard on her back. "It's okay. This is the power of our Lord."

People shoved their way forward and shouted their demons at me, and one-by-one I exorcised them. The demon of drink, lust, greed all slain under my touch. As one body was hauled off, another would take its place. It's what I've always dreamed of.

After about twenty minutes, the crowd had thinned, and I had a chance to catch my breath. I looked off in the distance and noticed a pale, thin woman walking towards me. I did not recognize her at first, but as she approached, I saw it was Miss Leslie.

"Dex, Dex," Boo said pulling at my pant leg. "What you doing?"

"What do you mean? I'm exorcising demons. How much money do you think we pulled in thus far?"

"That ain't exorcising no demons."

"Sure it is."

"No it ain't. You're standing up there throwing well water on people's head and pushing them down."

"Like you would know."

By this time, Leslie was at my soapbox. I thought maybe I could ignore her, but she had this look on her face telling me she was not going to be ignored.

"Dex," she said. "Come on down. I need to talk to you."

"What is it?" I said stepping down from the box.

"Didn't Boo tell you to come see me?"

"He did."

"Well, why didn't you?"

"Because I'm busy."

"Doing what I wonder?"

"Doing what? I'm exorcising this godforsaken town, ridding these people of their demons. That's kind of what I do."

"Hmm," Leslie scoffed.

"No you ain't," said Boo. "You're just splashing water—"

"Oh, why don't you shut up?" I shouted.

Boo had an eat-shit smirk on his face. "Why don't you make me?" he said.

It was a reflex. I didn't think; I reacted. I pulled my hand back and laid it down across Boo's cheek. There was a loud crack, and he fell backwards on his ass. I watched as dollar bills flew in every direction at once.

For a moment, I heard nothing but the sound of blood rushing through my own ears. I looked at Boo lying on the ground; his face was dirty and stained with blood. His mouth hung wide open and his eyes mirrored both terror and disbelief at once. Then, I looked at Miss Leslie. If I thought I couldn't feel any worse than I already did, I was wrong. She stared at me, and she said nothing. However, her eyes conveyed everything: *what have you done?*

I tried to help Boo up, but Leslie slapped my hand away.

"You keep away from him," Leslie said as she helped Boo to his feet. "What the hell is wrong with you? I thought you were a decent man, not like these hayseeds around here. I guess I was wrong about you. You're nothing but a coward, hitting little boys. You're nothing but a scheming, snake-oil salesman. Even worse because you're not even giving them anything. You're just preying on their fears and heartache."

Leslie knew just where to plunge the knife.

"Oh, c'mon, Leslie," I argued. "The boy was insolent."

"The boy was astute. C'mon, Boo; let's go."

"Hey, wait a minute. He still has my money."

Leslie stopped and turned around. "Oh, oh," she said. "Your money? Boo, empty your pockets."

Leslie grabbed the dollar bills from Boo, wadded them up and threw them, handfuls at a time until they lay crumpled at my feet.

"There you go," she said. "Now, go buy yourself another bottle."

I watched them walk away. Leslie's arm draped Boo's shoulder, consoling him as a mother would. I hoped they would look back one last time and see the regret on my face, but they never did.

CHAPTER 18

I pushed hard against the swinging double doors and sent them flying in opposite directions. It was Friday evening and the place was packed with every cockroach and maggot this town had to offer. There were businessmen and oilmen, and businessmen pretending to be oilmen, and vice versa. There were women there too—lots of them—not the nice, fluffy kind, but the hard women, heavily made-up, looking to score their meal ticket. Oh Hell, let me just call them what they were. They were whores every single one of them, whether they took money directly for relations or not; they were all whores and all the men—not to be outdone—were their clientele. And in this entire maggot pool, I counted myself as the biggest maggot of them all, perhaps no worse; certainly no better.

I strode up to the bar and cut the line ahead of me while I made contact with the scruffy, bearded barkeep. I barked one word at him. "Bourbon," I said.

He looked at me suspiciously while he poured my drink.

"How much for the bottle?"

"That be two-bits," he said.

I shoved a dollar bill against his chest and said, "Open a tab."

I turned my head and scanned the smoke-filled room. Even if I wanted to be alone, there were no empty tables that I could see, so I did the next best thing. I spotted two women sitting at a table with two empty chairs. They weren't the ugliest women I'd ever seen, but pretty damn close. I picked up my glass and bottle, and feeling more confident than I ought to, I waltzed up to their table.

"Howdy, Ma'am," I said to the prettier of the two. She was blonde and if I squinted hard, I could almost see Miss Leslie's face in hers. "This seat taken?"

She looked me up and down and with a wry smile, said, "As a matter of fact it is."

This was a clue for me to get lost, but I didn't care what she had to say. I went ahead and took the seat next to her.

"What are you two fine ladies doing here alone?" I said. "Shouldn't you have some men folk protecting you?"

"Like I was saying, these seats are taken."

"Oh yeah?" I said looking around. "Who's taken them? I don't see anyone."

"We're with two gentlemen friends," the other woman said. "They're filling our glasses for us."

I smiled at the Miss Leslie lookalike. Her legs were crossed at the knee and she bobbed her toe up-and-down quickly and rhythmically. To my surprise, she wasn't wearing any shoes, and I could see her red nail polish peering through her black, sheer stockings. I looked up at her, caught her eye and let out a big grin.

"How much?" I said to her without really thinking nor caring about what I was saying.

I saw her eyes grow wide and her forehead wrinkle. "What do you mean?" she said.

"C'mon, missy. You know what I mean."

The expression on her face told me she may not have known what I meant.

I looked at her less pretty friend for some help. "You know what I mean?" I said to her.

"I think I do know what you mean," she said. "And I don't like what you're implying."

"Oh c'mon. I got plenty of money," I said pulling a cash-wad from my pocket.

I waved the bills in front of the two women and that was akin to waving a red sheet in front of an angry bull, but much worse because there were two of them and they were women, not bulls.

"Mister," the blonde one said. "You better march yourself right on out of here before our friends get back."

I smiled and took a sip of bourbon straight from the bottle. I always got stupider and braver when I drank, and this time was no exception. "Listen, here," I said peeling off dollar bills and laying them, one-by-one on the table in front of their noses. "How many of these is it going to take?"

I watched their eyes as they intently watched the bills float lightly down.

"Aw, why don't we make this simple," I said while slapping four, five-dollar bills on the table. The two women looked at each other and exchanged knowing glances. "See, there. I found your price. That ought to buy me the two of you for the evening. Hell, by the looks of you, twenty dollars should get me a whole week."

I started laughing and then took another swig from the bottle. That's when I noticed there was trouble standing next to me, and he wasn't alone. He had an even bigger friend standing next to him.

"Well hello, Betty," I started to say.

And that was the last thing I remembered.

CHAPTER 19

Through swollen eyes, I could barely make out the faint outline of big hair, but it was the sweet smell of lilac that gave her away. It was Miss Leslie, thinner than I remembered, but just as lovely, just as pretty. I thought I might have died and was now in heaven, but a quick glance over Miss Leslie's shoulder told me otherwise. Lucy's scowling face glared at me like a snake about to devour a jackrabbit. *Oh shit*, I thought. Lucy hates me. Understandable, I suppose. I don't remember the last time I paid rent. Come to think of it, I don't recall ever paying rent even when I had the money to do so. I suppose I haven't been the best tenant. I've been drunk most of the time, nearly thrown in jail after a brawl and hosted a known prostitute in my room despite Lucy's repeated objections; I suppose I'd hate me too if I were her. I did my best to focus on Miss Leslie.

"Miss Leslie," I said. "What are you doing here?"

"That's what I keep saying," crowed Lucy. "I told her; her kind wasn't welcomed here."

Miss Leslie turned on Lucy and spat back, "Oh, why don't you shut up, you old hag? My kind is your kind It's just the price and terms are different."

Lucy appeared momentarily stunned. "What darn fool told you that?" she finally said.

Miss Leslie thought a moment. "Dex told me that," she said smiling at me. "Ain't that right, Dex?"

Lucy glared at me, her eyes were cold and murderous. I smiled and wiggled three fingers at her, which only served to further provoke her more.

"You're a mess," Lucy said to me. "Look at ya."

"I can't look at me. I don't have a mirror."

"Oh, you don't want a mirror," Miss Leslie said while grimacing and shaking her head.

"No?"

"What was the fight about this time?" Lucy asked. "Someone insult your Ma?"

Lucy slapped her thigh and began cackling like a hen. I had no idea what she was laughing at; her joke wasn't funny, and I had no recollection of a fight let alone a reason for said fight. After some quick deliberation, I did what I'm good at; I made something up.

"Oh—oh, the fight? Yes, well the fight. Some people were bad mouthing Miss Leslie, and I gave them what for and that's what happened, yes."

I winked at Leslie and she smiled back even though she knew I was bullshitting her.

"Did you get any good licks in, Dex?" Leslie said.

I thought for a moment. "I don't know," I said. "Did I?"

"Oh, saints alive," Lucy said. "From the looks of things, you didn't get any licks in, good or bad."

Now, I remembered what happened, the moments leading up to the fight, not the fight itself. I then made the mistake of sharing this memory with my audience.

"Oh, yes," I said. "I was trying to buy the services of two prostitutes and their clients didn't like it so much, and they got real pissed."

It was a small miracle neither woman said anything. They just stared blankly at me with blinking eyes. I supposed it was just as well.

"Ooh, ooh, my head," I said trying to illicit some sympathy.

Miss Leslie swabbed my open wound with a cold cloth. It stung like the devil and made me wince in pain. I tried to repel her hands away, but she was steadfast in her onslaught.

"Sit still," she said. "Let me wash your cuts."

"Maybe you can use something to eat," Lucy said. "I'll go fetch you some soup."

I wasn't hungry, but I was eager to be alone with Miss Leslie. "That sounds great," I said. "Take your time."

"I'll bring some soup for you too, Leslie."

"Oh, that's okay," Leslie said. "I'm not hungry."

"You're looking scrawny and pale. I'm bringing soup and bread and you're going to eat it. You mind me, young lady."

Leslie smiled and nodded her head. "Yes, Ma'am," she said.

"You know, Leslie. Your mother and me were friends. We used to attend church functions. She wouldn't be happy if I didn't watch after her little girl."

I was a little shocked by Lucy's admission, and by the look on Leslie's face, she was too. That's Lucy for you. One minute, she's at your throat, ripping you to pieces. The next she's coddling you as if you were her only child.

"Yes, Ma'am," Leslie said.

"And no funny business while I'm gone; ya hear?"

"Oh, good God woman," I said. "Look at me. What funny business can I be involved with in this delirious state?"

"Just you mind yourself."

After Lucy left, I grabbed Leslie's wrist. It was hot to the touch. I felt her cheek with the back of my hand.

"You're warm," I said.

"It's the room," she said. "It's stuffy in here."

"You know something; Lucy is right. You're looking thin and pale, not your usual self. Are you feeling well?"

Miss Leslie shook her head and closed her eyes. "Yeah, I'm fine," she said. "I'm just tired."

Leslie wasn't lying exactly. She indeed looked tired, but there was something else too. She looked like an imitation of Miss Leslie. Her once cherub face had lost its curves; it was flat and defined by sharp edges. Her hair looked dry and scraggly. The Leslie I knew would never be caught dead in its present unkept state and yet here she was. However, it was her eyes which caused me the greatest concern. Those once sparkling jewels that conveyed life and beauty were now dark and flat.

"Tired my ass," I said. "There's something wrong. Tell me."

"No. You're wrong, Dex."

"You're sure? You'd tell me if there was something."

"Uh, huh."

I didn't know whether to believe her or not, but something else tugged at my heart, and I needed to set things right before it was too late. I reached out and held Miss Leslie's hand in mine as I spoke.

"Miss Leslie," I said. "I want to say I—I'm so glad you came. I thought I'd never see you again after yesterday. I apologize for how I acted. Really, I am so sorry, so sorry. I assure you I'm not like this normally. It's just that—it's just—"

"Hush, now," Leslie said wiping my tears away.

"It's just that I came to this town, and I never expected to meet anyone like you, and I thought...oh, never mind what I thought. I know I'm nothing to look at even before my face was bashed in. I'm a fool—"

"Hush, now."

"Can you forgive me? I—"

I broke down and bawled like a baby. My shoulders heaved and my body shook the bed. My face felt wet with tears; snot poured into my open flesh, and it stung like the fires of Hell, but the pain, well, somehow it felt good. There was darkness inside of me. I've tried to hold it back for as long as I could remember and now it gushed forth like waters through a busted dam.

Leslie's eyes welled up, then she buried her face in my chest, and I felt her tears stream down my skin. I didn't mind. I placed my hand on the back of her head and held her tight as lilac filled my senses; we laid there, holding each other while our breathing synchronized. It comforted me like a warm, spring day.

After our tears had dried, Leslie lifted her head and smiled at me. "There's nothing to forgive," she said. "There are no saints. Only us sinners."

There are no saints, I thought. Indeed.

"What about Boo?" I said. "I want to talk to him. Have you seen him?"

"I have."

"Where is he? Is he mad at me?"

"Everything is fine. He's the one that came and got me after hearing about your fight."

"Are you sure? I've been a real ass. Not only to Boo, but to you as well. I'm not this. I don't like myself. I don't like the man I've become. I—I know you're not attracted to me. Why would you be? I'm old and ugly. You're young and beautiful."

Miss Leslie produced a handkerchief and carefully wiped away my tears. Then, she placed her hands on my cheeks and said, "Dex, for a smart man, you are so dumb."

"What?"

"You think you're old and ugly. I think you're beautiful."

I was speechless. I know *dumb* wasn't a compliment, but somehow, I think she meant it as one, and no one ever called me beautiful. Even if they thought it, they'd never tell me. Men are handsome. Women are beautiful. That's Leslie. She could take the earth and place it on top of the sky and then convince you it was meant to be that way.

"Then why?" I said. "Why not you and me? I make you laugh, and you make me happy. I know you're afraid Leslie. I know you don't want a man in your life, controlling you, telling you what to do and how to live. You're a free spirit, Miss Leslie and that's what I love about you."

Shit. I heard myself utter a word I had only said to one other woman: my mother. It didn't seem to faze Miss Leslie, but I could see by her shaking head that she was already protesting.

"That can't happen," she said. "Not like that. We can be friends and that's all."

"But why? Tell me this much. Is it because of what you do?"

"It's not that. I'm quitting. I'm never going back to that. I can never be with a man again. You or anyone else."

Leslie had a remarkable ability to speak without words. It was in her countenance, but her eyes spoke most eloquently. As I stared into them, they told me to back away, to leave it alone. I wouldn't listen.

"Look," I said. "I can help. You don't have to marry me or even like me. I still want to help and now I'm in a position to help."

"Look, Dex. You need to forget about me. I'm no good for you or any man. There's no future for us."

I reached down through the bed covers in search of my pocket only to discover I wasn't wearing any trousers.

"Did you take my trousers?" I said.

"What? Of course not."

"Well, who took my—" A terrifying thought crossed my mind. "Wait, you don't suppose Lucy took them, do you?"

"She might have. She probably didn't want you sleeping in them all night and took them off. Don't worry. I'm guessing you don't have anything she hasn't seen a thousand times before. You got your skivvies on, right?"

"Yes, but what do you suppose she's done with my trousers?"

Leslie looked around the room. "They're hanging over the back of the chair," she said.

"Ah. Be a dear and fetch my billfold. It should be in my back pocket."

Leslie sat up from the bed and walked over to the chair. I watched as she fished for my billfold, checking one pocket and then the other until they were turned inside-out. Leslie gave me a perplexed look and shrugged.

"What's wrong?" I said.

"There's no billfold here. Are you sure it's not in your coat pocket?"

I tried to remember. "No," I said. "I didn't wear my coat. Do you remember seeing me in my coat?"

"I don't remember."

"Go ahead and check it please. I may have worn it."

Leslie picked up my coat from the floor next to the dresser, and after, a thorough search, she turned to me with a blank stare; the hairs on the back of my neck stood on end.

"It has to be somewhere," I said. "Look again. Look on the chair; on the floor."

Leslie dutifully looked but to no avail. I was on my feet now, in my drawers, but too frantic to care. I looked everywhere. I checked my pants again and my coat. I opened up drawers and pulled out clothing. Every garment I owned was now strewn on the floor. I even dropped on all fours and like a dog, panted about the room, in hopes of stumbling upon my billfold. I found nothing.

"Where is it?" I demanded. "My billfold? I must have had two-hundred dollars or more, from the past few days."

Leslie looked stricken. "Dex, I don't know."

"Do you suppose Lucy took it?"

"Why would she take it? She's not that kinda person."

"I don't know," I said rubbing my hands through my hair. "I owe her money for room and board. Perhaps she took it as payment."

"Dex, I don't think she'd do something like that. She's a cuss all right, but she ain't one to take people's money."

"I wouldn't be so sure. You'd be surprised what money does to people. It twists them up inside and turns them into people they ain't. Besides, she'd be right to take some of it. Some of it is rightfully hers I suppose. I'm not mad. I just want to find out what happened."

Leslie was right; Lucy wasn't a thief. I had that much going for me. She probably took her share for the rent I owed and was keeping the rest for safekeeping, so no one else would get their greedy paws on it. That's what happened. It must be.

I limped out of the room, ignoring Miss Leslie's plea to return. "For God's sake," I heard her shout after me. "You're in your drawers."

When I reached the banister at the stop of the stairs, I leaned over and shouted for Lucy to come up right away, and then I returned to my room.

"That's it," I said. "Lucy has my billfold. She took it for safekeeping. She has it. Everything will be all right."

I sat on the edge of my bed in a cold sweat, ringing my hands while I waited for Lucy. After a minute, the door swung open and she walked in. "What's all the commotion about," she said.

I hobbled over to her and grabbed her by both shoulders. "Lucy," I said. "Did you take my billfold? It had money in it. A lot of money." Lucy frowned. "It's okay," I said. "I'm not mad. You took it for safekeeping, right? Besides, some of it belongs to you. I was going to pay my rent. Honest. I have money, now. Please tell me you have it. Please tell me. Please."

Lucy stared back at me like I had lost my mind. She shook her head and said, "Dex, I don't got your money."

I stood dumfounded for a moment as a cold chill swept my body. Then, I collected my thoughts and spoke in a calm, deliberate voice. "You undressed me last night?" I said. "The billfold was in my pants pocket."

"Dex, I didn't undress you. The Sherriff and the Doc dragged you in and put you into your bed. Don't you remember? You were drunk and had the piss beaten out of you. Maybe one of them knows where your money is at."

I found my way back to bed and plopped my ass down on the mattress. "Yeah, maybe," I said.

I knew better. The money was gone. I was robbed—a fool and his money. I would have cried again, but I had nothing left inside. Leslie and Lucy had nothing to offer but their sympathetic smiles. A lot of good that does me.

CHAPTER 20

I sat on my soapbox. My clothes were dirty. My eyes tired, lids hung heavy and low over my pupils. I sat with a hunched back. My elbows supported on bony knees and my chin rested in my palms. It must have been about three in the afternoon, but you'd never know it by the sun or more like the absence of it. It looked like night was about to fall. I could barely make out the forms that sat at the road's east end; they were like shadowy ghosts trudging around, looking for something to do or somewhere to belong. It was as though the darkness had turned the entire town into a gray mass and the people into dust, what few people I could see.

I half-suspected one of the oil-derricks had sprung a leak spewing ink-black rain into the air and blotting out the sun. A quick scan of the sky told me it was only thunder clouds. I was tired all right. I don't know why. I had one customer, and he only had two-bits. I told him to keep it, and I performed the rite of exorcism on him anyhow. I made sure it was a good and proper exorcism; no short cuts. It was a minor demon—wasn't much trouble.

Maybe the weather kept the customers away. That's what I told myself, but I think my reputation had turned to shit again. People saw how I behaved with Boo and what had happened at the saloon. They saw and they talked. It's a small town. Word gets around.

I felt lonely and sorry for myself. I wanted to make amends. I wanted to pay my debt to Lucy even though she told me not to worry about it and that she knew I was good for the money, but I couldn't agree. Just three short weeks ago I was flying, miracles seemed to shoot from my eyes and ears, money rained from the sky. Now, the well ran dry. It's like a fishing hole. You catch fish, and soon, they get wise to you: no bites. The fishermen have to move to another hole. Towns are like that. Oil wells, too, I suppose. One day, they'll have sucked all the oil from the ground and when that happens, there won't be any people left either. Funny to think about, but it's true. People have it good, and they want it to last forever—jobs, money, relationships. Problem is nothing ever lasts—the good, the bad. I suppose I can take some solace in this: *and this too shall pass, Dexter James.*

There was no point in waiting any longer. Besides, my heart wasn't in it. I started to pack up my things when I saw a lone, black-clad figure approach. It was an old woman and her dog and as she neared, I saw it was Lois and Runt. Lois had the sweetest smile on her face as she waddled up to me.

"Ma'am," I said taking my hat off and waving it to my waistline in an act of exaggerated reverence.

"You were a priest?" she said abruptly.

For a moment, I couldn't say anything. I had thought about denying it, but she obviously had been speaking with someone and seemed certain in her convictions.

"You've been talking to the local clergy?"

Lois shrugged. "No need," she said.

I looked into her eyes and they spoke to me with kindness and compassion. She smiled and I was enveloped by a warm glow that seemed to emanate from her spirit. There was something about Lois, something I couldn't explain. I had felt it in our earlier meeting, but it was stronger now by a thousand-fold.

"What brings you here?" I said.

"I'm here for a friend of mine."

"A friend?"

"She's actually a friend of yours too."

I was puzzled and intrigued. "And who might that be?" I said.

"Her name is Leslie. Leslie Reed."

Hearing the name caught me off guard. I had not seen, nor heard from Miss Leslie in several days.

"You know Miss Leslie?"

"Yes. I sure do."

"You've seen her? What does she need? How is she?"

Lois' face grew long, and her bright smile dimmed. "Not well I'm afraid."

"What do you mean?"

"She needs you. Go to her, Dex."

She called me Dex, which strangers never do, and though this struck me as peculiar, there were more urgent matters to attend to.

"What do you mean?" I said. "She needs me? What's wrong? How do you know this?"

Lois grabbed my sleeve, but her touch was light and airy, and I could not feel it. "Go to her," she repeated. Her smile returned but this time it was weak and sad.

There was something in her tone, in her countenance and inner being that commanded my attention. She held me in a vice grip—not a physical hold mind you, but one that existed in my mind, or more accurately, my soul. I could not escape even if I tried. She didn't ask me to go as much as she demanded in a quiet, yet powerful way. It was as though this diminutive woman was speaking with the force of God almighty himself. I have heard this voice once before when I was a young man— it was my mother's. "You should enter the seminary," it told me. I listened to that voice and nodded my head. Four years later I was ordained as a Roman Catholic priest. Three years after that, I was appointed to the rank of exorcist, one of the youngest at that time. It was the proudest moment in my mother's life.

I thanked Lois, then I picked up my bag and hurried down the road leading to Miss Leslie's. I thought about bringing my soapbox with me, but it was heavy, and I was in a hurry, so I left it behind. I had a feeling I wouldn't need it anymore anyway.

I was no more than twenty steps down Main Street when I looked back one last time. I was shocked to see the old woman and Runt standing on my soapbox. They were both smiling.

CHAPTER 21

As a boy, I ran fast for long stretches. I was lanky, too skinny for other activities, but my weightless frame served me well for running. My gangling legs ate up the ground allowing me to float above the ground. It would take only a few minutes before my body found its rhythm. When this occurred, I'd experience a state of bliss similar to the ones I would only come to know in prayer and meditation. I never got tired; it felt like I wasn't running at all but rather carried along for a ride as passenger in a buggy. With my body removed from the endeavor, my mind was free to drift like a leaf on a pond. In those moments, I would think of things, fantastic things, wonderful things. These were flights of fancy and imagination. I dreamt of faraway places I wanted to visit, money, beautiful women, adoration, and love. I dreamt about the natural world, science and mathematics, engineering and religion and philosophy and of life and death, of this world and beyond. I was curious like Boo. I wanted to know things, how machines worked, what made people happy, how to mend a broken foot, or a broken heart or ease a troubled mind. My thirst for knowledge was unquenchable and running freed my mind and comforted my soul when nothing else did. Running was my outlet, my peace and sanctuary.

When I entered the monastery, I stopped running. It was a huge mistake, but I was young, and what did I know? Afterwards, when I was ordained as a priest, I rekindled my passion for running. Since, I was no longer supposed to have relations, it helped release the tension—at least for a while. I caught hell for it too. People running for no apparent reason (without being chased for example) are looked upon as odd nuts, but a running priest, drew the scorn of townsfolk and the ire of my superiors.

They told me to stop running. I told them to fuck off; only I was a little nicer about it. I kept running. They turned a blind eye. Unfortunately, they couldn't turn a blind eye to the relation I had. Her name was Veronica, and Lilly, and Sarah and...

I wished I could run that way now. It would have made the distance to Miss Leslie's seem less daunting. I'm old and tired. My legs ached, and they protested at the slightest provocation. Nonetheless, I hurried along as best I could. Miss Leslie needed me.

When I arrived at her house, I recognized the gravity of the situation. There was a black carriage fronted, by a chestnut brown horse with a white patch on its nose and white stocking feet on three limbs but not the other. I recognized it as belonging to Doc Brown. If the Doctor was here, it was more than a tea and honey cure.

I barged my way in, plowing through the front door like a runaway bull. As I entered the kitchen, I was immediately taken aback by its distressing, cluttered state. Dirty dishes and rotten food were strewn everywhere as if the owner could care less about tidiness. The odor was so bad, I had to cover my nose with the crook of my arm. *This wasn't Leslie*, I thought. She would never allow this. She always took pride in her home and cared for it as she did everything else: with love. My body reacted by turning cold. I began to shake, then I hurried straight back to the bedroom.

The door was open and when I walked in, Doctor Brown wheeled around to face me. He was sweaty, his face was tired and when our eyes met, he closed them and shook his head. I looked past the doctor. In the bed I saw something that would haunt me for the rest of my days.

"Oh, God," I said. That's all I could say.

I turned to the doctor looking for an answer. With his eyes, he motioned me to the door, but I shook him off, dropped my bag and ran to the bedside where I kneeled. I gently clasped her hand in mine, and I began praying. It's all I knew, and I prayed like I never prayed before, like my life depended on it. I prayed to sacrifice my life for hers. Then I shot my fist into the air and challenged Him. I told Him to come down, to face me like a man. I called Him a coward who picked on the defenseless and the frail.

As I screamed a succession of curse words towards heaven, she opened her eyes and smiled at me. Can you imagine? Through all of this— her obvious pain and suffering—she managed a smile. It was a lovely smile, but everything else was in discord. Her skin stretched drum-tight against her skull and was the most sickening grey I had ever seen on a body that was not yet a corpse. Her cheekbones were pronounced and gave her face a grotesque, chiseled look. The blood vessels popped from her forehead and turned her once smooth skin into a lizard-like membrane. Her eyes were dark; her hair was a tangled bird's nest. Still, that wonderful smile gave her away. I had hoped against hope when I first saw her. Now, to my deepest regret, I knew it was Miss Leslie.

I pulled her hand to my lips and I kissed it repeatedly and chanted repetitively, between sobs. "Oh, Dear, Oh dear, oh dear. Dear God. My sweet, Miss Leslie, my sweet, Leslie."

Miss Leslie's voice was low like a whisper, yet surprisingly strong and reassuring. "Dex, you're here."

"Of course I'm here. I came as fast as I could."

"I didn't want you to see me like this. I wanted you to remember me like I was—beautiful."

I smiled through my tears. "My dear, Leslie, you are beautiful."

Leslie's sweet smile brought just a bit of comfort. I turned my head to look for the doctor, but he was gone. Instead, I saw my bag sitting on the floor where I had dropped it, and I remembered something. I had healed the sick before—the Radley girl. I could do it again. That's why I'm here. The old lady was an angel from Heaven. She brought me here to save my dear Leslie. It all made sense now.

I hurried to retrieve my bag and brought it to Leslie's bedside. I opened it up and pulled out my demon-fighting arsenal. I grabbed my purple stole, kissed the embroidered cross and wrapped it around my neck. I pulled out my iron cross and kissed that too and placed it on the bed next to Leslie. I took out the holy water. I had forgotten it was worthless well water but hoped there was still some magic left in the bottle. I didn't know. I wasn't thinking. I was desperate. Finally, I produced my book of exorcism and I rifled through the pages looking for the right prayer.

"What are you doing?" Leslie said.

"I'm going to perform an exorcism. You have a demon inside of you and I'll cast it out. Wait and see. You'll be better, Leslie. You just wait and see."

Leslie's smile faded and she shook her head. "No," she said.

Her solemn tone alarmed me more than what I already was. "No? What do you mean no? Don't you remember? I healed the Radley girl, of polio no less. If I can do that, I can do anything. You'll see."

I removed my hat, my jacket and rolled up my sleeves. I was ready for the greatest battle of my life, prepared to give my own life in exchange for Leslie's, if necessary. If that's what God demanded of me, well, that's what I'd do.

Miss Leslie was unmoved. "No," she repeated. "I—I'm going to be with Momma."

She didn't know what she was saying. She was delirious. I proceeded without her blessing, convinced it was for her own good. I placed some water on her forehead and when I did, she reached out and grabbed my wrist with a strength that belied her condition.

"You see over there?" she said looking toward a corner of the room. "In the chair?"

I looked back to where her eyes directed me and saw an empty chair.

"I see it," I said

"Do you see the beautiful woman sitting there?"

I looked back knowing full well the chair was empty. "I do not," I said.

"You don't see her? She's dressed in black and she's smiling. Her eyes are smiling. Her entire body is smiling. She has a little dog too. Can't you see them, Dex?"

A woman dressed in black? A little dog? I wanted so bad for this to be a trick played by Leslie's fevered brain, but I knew better. I've spent years as a priest; I've given countless last rites. I've been privy to a world few others knew existed. It was common for the terminally ill to see specters, family members from the other side greeting them as they crossed over. I looked back at the empty chair once more and remembered my encounter with the old woman and her dog.

"Leslie," I said. "Your Momma's name. Was it Lois?" Leslie never took her eyes from the chair. She just nodded her head and smiled. "And you had a dog named Runt."

"That's right," Leslie said.

"Yes. I almost think I can see her."

"Dex. It's time."

"No. I can save you Leslie. Don't give up."

Leslie shook her head. "I'm going to close my eyes and when I do, I'll be with Momma. All the pain will be gone. I'll be happy. I'd appreciate it if you'd say the last rites."

"I can't. You need an ordained priest. I'll call for Father O'Brien, or Father Paco."

Leslie shook her head. "They won't come," she said. "Momma sent for you."

By this time, tears stung my eyes and flowed down my cheeks. I tasted the salt in my mouth. Miss Leslie was right. I was all she had. I gathered myself the best I could. I wiped my tears and read the last rites to my friend Miss Leslie. It had been a long time, and I'm sure I left parts out, but I don't think she cared. Her eyes were closed, and she had an angelic, peaceful look about her.

When I had finished, I leaned in close, held her hand in mine and asked her if she had any last words. Leslie's free hand fell gently over mine. I looked down and, in my palm, I saw a worn, stained cross hanging from a string of Rosary beads.

Leslie opened her eyes and whispered, "Take this. It was Momma's. She gave it to me. It will protect you fighting against demons."

Miss Leslie closed her eyes one last time and wanted so bad to join her. Instead, I stepped out of her house, numb and nearly sick to my stomach. Dr. Brown greeted me and offered his condolences.

"I'm sorry," he said. "There was nothing anybody could do."

"What are you going to list as the official cause?" I said.

The doctor thought for a moment. "I'll say it was natural causes," he finally said.

I nodded my head. "Thank you."

CHAPTER 22

The boy was smaller than me and I was way meaner and a lot angrier. He was wise to step away as I brushed past him and charged through the closed door. The two priests were eating, and I was about to ruin their appetite.

"What are you doing here?" O'Brien protested.

"I'm sorry, Father," the boy said. "I tried to keep him out."

"It's okay," Father Paco said. "Perhaps you can get Mr. James a cup of tea."

"No need," I said. "I won't be long."

Father Paco nodded, and the boy closed the door behind him.

"I'm here to discuss a little matter," I said. "Funeral arrangements for Miss Leslie Reed."

O'Brien rolled his eyes. He took another bite of his chicken leg and chewed his food along with his words. "Leslie's body will be buried in the cemetery outside of town," he said. "It's good enough for her."

My ears burned, but I did my best to control my temper for Leslie's sake as much as my own. I was her voice now.

"Yes," I said. "I was informed as much by the doctor. He said you pompous assess wouldn't allow her in the church yard, nor would she be granted a proper Christian burial."

"Dr. Brown said that?" said Father Paco.

"Well, I added the pompous asses part, but the rest is accurate."

"I see."

"Look," said O'Brien, his words garbled by the half-eaten chicken in his mouth. "You can't expect her to rest in the church cemetery."

"And why not?"

"You know why."

"So you'll allow her to lie with the drunks, the thieves and the murderers?"

"She made her bed; now let her lie in it."

I'm sure Miss Leslie would not approve of what I did next. I certainly didn't approve, but I acted on emotion and was powerless to stop myself. I marched over to the fat priest, grabbed him by his white, stiff shirt and despite his prodigious weight, lifted him clean off the chair. I pulled him in close and was about an inch away from his greasy mouth and chicken splattered face when I spoke to him slowly and deliberately.

"Look at you," I said. "How do you stand in judgment?"

Father O'Brien's lower lip quivered. "I—I'm a priest," he managed to blurt out.

Father Paco was on his feet and managed to wedge his way between O'Brien and me. He gently pushed me back, and I slowly released my grip.

"Please," Father Paco pleaded. "This is our rectory, our home. There is no need for this."

I looked into Paco's imploring eyes. They were soft and green, and I felt ashamed. I felt tears forming, so I turned without a word and walked towards the door. I placed my hand on the handle and paused. I had to try once more. Too much was at stake: Miss Leslie's final resting place.

I removed my hat and made my appeal directly to O'Brien. "Leslie was a good woman," I said. "She and her mom used to attend St. Titus. They were regulars. I know Leslie wasn't much for church in recent times, but that's because she wasn't welcomed. She prayed. She prayed the rosary every day. She even gave me her beads." I paused trying to think of what else I could say to plead her case. "Jesus was friends with Mary Magdalene," I added.

"He who is free of sin, shall cast the first stone," Father Paco said. His soft, compassionate voice resonated with reason.

The room went silent, and I could hear the birds singing sweetly outside the window. They made me think of my walks through the woods with Miss Leslie. O'Brien and Paco looked at each other, each waiting for the other to speak. Then I saw Father Paco lift his chin ever so slightly. It was a small gesture, but it conveyed a powerful message I am sure.

O'Brien turned to me. His shirt was disheveled and his face still red from the altercation. He looked at his shoes as he spoke.

"Leslie will be buried in the church yard," he said in a shaky voice. "She will have a proper Christian burial. I'll perform the ceremony myself."

"You'll perform it?" I asked.

O'Brien and I locked eyes. "You have my word as a priest, as a man," he said. "It will be the finest eulogy ever heard in this town."

There was something in his demeanor, in his tone, and for the first time, I trusted him to do the right thing.

I couldn't speak, and that was probably for the best. For one of the few times in my life, I had nothing else to say.

The day of Leslie's funeral was fittingly dark and wet. The sky was crying as Mom used to say. Not many people attended. There was me, Boo, Jenny and Lucy, and a few people I didn't recognize. I was surprised to see Hank there as well. I hadn't seen him since our fight. He wasn't there to cause trouble. He just wanted to pay his respects. He came up to me afterwards and told me how sorry he was for my loss and what a good woman she was. He even gave me a hug, which was shocking but pleasant. Everyone was so nice to me, and that was the one blessing to come from all of this.

The ceremony was lovely. Father Paco was there and Father O'Brien, true to his word, performed the services. It was a fine ceremony and he was in fine voice. Afterwards, I went up to the fathers and thanked them. Father O'Brien offered his condolences. "I know you're sad," he told me. "If it's any consolation, she's in a better place than we are now."

I was taken aback. "Really?" I said. "You believe she's in heaven?"

Father O'Brien nodded his head rhythmically and said, "She is." His tone was firm and emphatic and made me feel just a little better.

"I know how much you must miss her," Father Paco said.

"You do?" I said.

"I could tell you loved her very much and a love like that never dies. That's why it hurts so much, my son. It's the love you are remembering. If there were no love, there would be no pain."

I felt myself blush. "You could tell I was fond of her?" I said.

"Well," Father Paco said. "I think anyone could see. The way you talked about her, the way your face lit up, and the way you barged into our office and fought for her."

I looked down at my feet and kicked at an imaginary blade of grass. "Yes, about that. I am sorry."

"It's okay. Sometimes, you have to kick down doors, fight for what you believe. You know, you can be really obstinate, but if I was ever in a fight, I'd want you there by my side."

I took Father Paco's hand and kissed his ring, then I did the same to Father O'Brien.

"Bless you," Father O'Brien said.

"Thank you," I said. "It was a nice funeral. Miss Leslie would have been proud."

A lot of tears were shed on this day. I shed a few, but Boo seemed to take it harder than anyone. I tried to comfort him as best I could.

"She's not gone," I told him.

Boo looked up at me with innocent, watery eyes. "She's not?"

"No, not really. None of us really go when we die. We just take on a different form."

"How do you know this?"

"Because we're eternal spirits. We are from God and like God we cannot die. Not really."

"Yes, but how do you know?"

I thought carefully about my answer. I thought about my experiences, my training, and all the books I've read on the topic and not just the Bible, but other sacred texts as well. A beloved seminary teacher once told me, *if you don't know all the religions, you don't know any of the religions including our own.* His comment shocked me, especially coming from an ordained priest—most of whom are as rigid and narrow minded as they come—but as I pondered his words in prayer and meditation, I realized he was right. All religions differ in some ways but are very similar in others. Their message of forgiveness, and redemption ring clear as a church bell across lands, cultures and races. The message of enduring love that survives past death rings even louder.

In the end, I decided this wasn't the time for a theology lesson. What the boy needed was a simple affirmation of love. I lifted Boo's chin and wiped his tears with my handkerchief. "You just have to trust me on this one," I said. Boo nodded his head.

As I pulled Leslie's beads from my coat pocket, I saw the life return to Boo's eyes. "What's that?" he said.

"Here," I said handing him the rosary beads. "These belonged to Miss Leslie."

Boo took the beads and rubbed the cross between his fingertips. "She gave them to you?" he said.

"It's okay. She'd want you to have them. She loved you very much."

For the first time that day, I saw Boo smile.

When most of the crowd had dispersed, Lucy came up to me and asked if I wanted a ride in her buggy back to the boarding house.

"Naw," I told her. "I'd rather walk. I want to be alone."

"You sure? Nearly three miles back."

"I'm okay. Maybe you can swing by Boo's house and drop him off. His Momma may be worried."

"You going to be okay, Dex? I know you're sad. It will take time."

I closed my eyes and nodded my head. Lucy gave me a hug before taking Boo and leaving me alone.

I didn't head back straight away. Instead, I made a detour to Leslie's house. I don't know why, maybe I shouldn't have, but I wanted to see it one last time, touch the door, peer through the window, and maybe beyond all reason, catch one last whiff of lilac. Her empty home was the only physical connection I had left.

Along the way, I thought of her; I could think of nothing else, and when I reached her home, well, all those memories boiled to the surface. They were good memories, happy ones, filled with laughter and vibrant banter. I could hear her voice, prodding me, poking fun while trying to get a rise from me.

When I reached her door, the day came crashing down on me like a torrential downpour. I could no longer maintain my facade. I placed my forehead against her cold, wet door; it helped settle the turmoil raging in my belly, but it was a temporary fix, however. My knees soon grew weak before buckling. I felt weightless as my mind left my body, and I saw myself from a bird's-eye view. I watched myself slide down the door and crumple into a fetal position on the ground. I rocked back and forth as I mumbled something. I couldn't hear what was said.

After a few moments, I returned to my body and looked up at the sky; it was cold and dark.

CHAPTER 23

I stared out over the balcony watching the people move around on the street below. They floated like tiny dancers on a big stage. They looked odd, not like people at all, but animated stone statues. My vision was skewed as if I were wearing thick spectacles made for someone else. I squinted hard and searched for Miss Leslie. I had to remind myself to stop, that I was only making things worse, but I couldn't seem to pull myself away. From this very spot just a few months ago, is where I first laid eyes on her. Now, my mind, my heart, my body, my soul ached. I walked beneath a permanent black cloud, and my once powerful thirst for life was replaced with an overwhelming desire for it to end. I was tired of Titusville, tired of fighting. Mostly, I was tired of me.

A knock on the door pulled me from my trance, and I stepped back inside the room.

"It's open," I said.

Lucy walked in. "Good morning," she said.

"Why did you bother to knock? The lock is broken," I reminded her.

"Oh, I don't know. I thought it was the decent thing to do."

"Really?" I said smiling.

Lucy held out a rolled parchment, which she extended towards me.

"Here," she said. "A gentleman dropped these off. He had the craziest critter I'd ever seen, blabbering away like it owned the place."

"That was Mikey."

With a bewildered look, Lucy handed me the parchment. I unrolled it and immediately lost my breath. As if by some miracle, I saw Miss Leslie smiling back at me. I was there too, and so was that stupid monkey. I could almost hear Mikey chattering in my ear and it made me laugh. Then, all the memories from that day came rushing back. I closed my eyes and felt the sun, the cool breeze; I heard Miss Leslie's voice and the sound of the camera. It was bittersweet, but more bitter than sweet. It took a moment before I could speak.

"I forgot all about this," I finally said. "I was expecting it weeks ago."

I held the photo so Lucy could see. She looked over the image carefully and thoughtfully.

"The man said he ran out of something he needed to make it," Lucy said. "He said he was sorry."

"I'll have to get a frame for it."

Lucy nervously looked around the room. She kept wiping her hands over her apron and pulling imaginary strands of hair from her face.

"Hey, Dex. There's something I got to tell ya. You know I like ya and all. You know it's more Clem than me. I'd let you stay."

"It's okay," I said.

"It is?"

"Yes. I understand. I hadn't paid you in over a month. I'm surprised you didn't kick me out sooner."

"I don't want to do this, Dex. I like you. I like you a lot. Perhaps if you went out and rustled up some of the possessed....well, I thought maybe you could make enough money to pay me, maybe make enough to get a place of your own and settle down, but you just been sitting up in your room drinking, feeling sorry for yourself. I was willing to overlook the rent, but the missing bottles of liquor is too much."

"Yes, you can add thief to my growing list of accomplishments."

"Well, Dex. Me and Clem talked it over and decided it was time for you to leave."

Normally, I'd feel bad about being evicted, but I was actually relieved. Ecclesiastes said it best: to every thing there is a season and a time to every purpose under heaven. This season has passed. There are too many memories here, too much sorrow. Coming to Titusville was a mistake. I see that now.

I smiled and nodded. "It's okay," I said. I'm truly sorry for everything, the rent, the booze. I'd promise to pay you back, but I can't keep that promise. Thank Clem for me and tell him I'm sorry too."

"Where ya going, Dex?"

"I don't know."

Lucy reached down her dress and pulled out a five-dollar bill. I waved her off and told her no, but she was a persistent little bull and she made me take it.

"How ya going to get anywhere without no money?" she said.

"I could hop trains, work odd jobs, play poker. I've done it before."

"Well, now you can buy a train ticket and get yourself something to eat. I'll pack you something for the trip home."

"Home?" I laughed. "I ain't got no home, but thank you, Lucy. You've been more than kind."

Lucy smiled even though she looked like she was about to cry. "Can I give you a hug?" she said.

"Of course."

We embraced, and I held her tight against my beating chest. When we parted, she looked up at me and said, "Dex, give me the gun."

For an instant, I had no idea what she was talking about, but then I remembered.

"How did you know?" I said retrieving the revolver from my pocket and handing it over.

"Clem's gun is missing, and I felt it poking my ribs."

Clever girl, I thought.

Lucy shook her head and emptied the revolver as she spoke. "What were you going to do with this?" she said.

I turned my head in shame and didn't say anything. As it turned out, I didn't have to. She already knew.

"You know, Dex, things are never as bad as they seem. You need to clean yourself up. Get back on the box and do what you do best."

"And what would that be?"

"Why, kicking the snot out of those demons, of course."

"You must be joking, woman. You think I had anything to do with exorcising demons?"

Lucy cocked her head to the side. "Of course. That's what you do, ain't it? You exorcise demons. You're the, what did you call it, Demonologist?"

"I didn't exorcise any demons," I said softly.

"What you mean? You chased a bushel-full away since you been here."

"Those weren't demons," I argued. "Not the real kind at any rate. They're just the inner demons that all of us carry around inside, demons of lust, and avarice and drink. I didn't exorcise any real spirits. I just told people what they needed to hear, and their minds did the rest."

"That's not true. What about my cousin, Ethel? She was possessed by a chicken and you exorcised that demon for her good."

"Your cousin Ethel wasn't possessed by a chicken," I smirked. "She was suffering from a form of psychosis probably brought on by old age. I just performed a ceremony and planted a suggestion in her mind that she was cured. She believed she was unpossessed and, well, her subconscious mind made it so. You see? It's nothing more than a trick, a magic trick if you will."

"What difference does it make?"

"What do you mean what difference does it make? I'm nothing more than a con artist, and a snake oil salesman. That's what difference it makes."

"So? She's cured ain't she? She no longer believes she's possessed by a chicken. She's happier now and gets out and visits her friends. She was a recluse until you fixed her."

"I never looked at it that way."

"Well, maybe you should. And how about the Radley girl? She can walk now, and she owes it all to you."

"Yes," I said stroking my beard. "I don't know how that happened. I performed another bullshit ritual on her and apparently, it healed her of polio, an uncurable disease. Damned if I had anything to do with it."

"Well you must have had something to do with it cause—"

The sound of my fist slamming into the table cut Lucy's sentence short. "Then why?" I said. "Why couldn't I save Leslie? Can you tell me why? Tell me why I couldn't save Leslie?"

Lucy returned my harsh gaze with her compassionate eyes. "I guess the good Lord just wanted to take her home," she said softly. "It was her time."

I stood in silence for a time, mulling over her words. I thought about the Radley girl, and how, for a brief while, believed my own lies, that I was someone special, anointed by God to do his work, to heal the sick and the broken. I was higher than a kite with my self-importance. Then, a few weeks later, I couldn't perform one tiny miracle to save the woman I loved. No. I was nothing special. I'm still the same, tired conman I was when I got to this town. I'll leave that way, too.

"You know what I think?" I finally said. "There was one person I exorcised in this town. I mean really exorcised."

"Who's that?"

"It was Miss Leslie's friend, Jenny. She had been playing with the spirit board. I believed she was really demon possessed. Everyone else, well, they had normal problems like we all do. They were no more possessed than I am."

"And the Radley girl?"

"I had nothing to do with healing the Radley girl, nothing whatsoever. There was someone or something else in the room that healed her. Wasn't me."

"You're selling yourself short, Dex. You were there. You performed the ceremony and now she's better. The whole town was talking about you. Even the Church thinks it was a miracle."

"The Church?" I said in disbelief. "They think I'm the biggest pain in the ass to come through Titusville, and that includes all the drunks, thieves and scoundrels living here."

"Well," Lucy said nodding her head in agreement. "You are a big pain in the ass, but I asked Father Paco about you and do you know what he told me?" I shook my head. "He told me, some people have a gift, and that you're one of those people."

I chuckled. "Father Paco, he's all right."

"Sure he's all right and you're all right too. You done a lot of good for this town, and don't you forget it."

Lucy's words eased some of my guilt, but still, it wasn't enough. She was kind, and she was a friend and that's what friends do. They stick by you even when you don't deserve it.

I smiled at Lucy and she smiled back. "Thank you kindly," I told her. "I'll pack my things and be out of here by noon."

I noticed Boo standing in the doorway. I don't know how long he was standing there or how much he heard, but he looked about as sad as I felt, so I motioned for him to step in. When he was close enough, I wrapped my arm around him and asked him how he was doing. He cast his eyes downward and shrugged.

"I gotta go," I told him.

"Don't leave, Dex. Who's going to excise all the demons."

"How many times do I have to tell you? The word is exorcise."

Boo look up at me and smiled. "Yeah, I know."

His obstinance, normally annoying, made me happy. "You know, Boo," I said. "I need to excise my own demons for once." Boo nodded his head.

"I'll pack you a nice lunch," Lucy said. "I have a feeling you'll have a long journey ahead."

"Thank you, Lucy."

Boo kept me company while I packed my things. I didn't have much, just the clothes I came with, my demon-fighting bag and the photograph. I worked slowly because talking to him made things just a little better, and I suspected it helped him too.

I was tempted to leave Boo my demon-fighting bag as a remembrance—I had no further need of it—but I decided against it. I didn't want him getting a fool notion he could become an exorcist on his own. The boy looked up to me, and I remember him saying he wanted to be just like me when he grew up. I told him I was the last person he wanted to be like. I told him he had a father and he should be like him.

"Pa can't fight no demons like you can," he said.

"Your Pa is a good, hardworking man," I said. "You grow up to be like him. Forget this demon fighting nonsense. You hear me?"

Boo hung his head and didn't say anything. He's young and has many lessons to learn. In a few years, maybe not even that long, he'd forget all about me, and I told him as much.

"Dex," he said shaking his head. "As long as I live, I'll never forget you, and I'll never forget Miss Leslie."

I was choked up but didn't want to get emotional in front of the boy. "Carry my demon-fighting bag," I said. "It's time to go."

When we got downstairs, Lucy greeted me with a pail. "I chipped off some ice from the ice box and placed the Titusville Herald over it," she said. "Should keep it cool for maybe an hour or two."

I placed my nose in the pail and inhaled. "Ah," I said. "Roast beef and lobster tail. My favorites."

"Oh, Dex. Come here."

Lucy and I embraced, and I felt her body shake. "Stop it," I said. "You're going to make me cry."

"You take care of yourself, Dex. Write sometime."

"I will."

I turned to Boo and said, "Okay, my lad. Where's your trusty steed? I need a ride to the station."

"I walked," he said.

"Oh, that's okay. I hated that beast anyways."

"I could hitch up the wagon for ya," Lucy said.

"That's okay," I said. "The air is cool. It's a nice day for a—"

Before I could finish my sentence, the front door flew open and startled me. A boy, whom I recognized from the parish home, rushed in and was panting hard.

"Mr. James," he said between breaths. "Father Paco sent me. You need to come quick."

"What is all this commotion?" yelled Lucy. "Ain't no one teach you no manners?"

"Sorry, Ma'am, but the Father asked me to fetch Mr. James."

"Why?" I said. "What business does he have with me?" The boy looked nervous and was hesitant to speak. "C'mon, lad. What is it?"

"Well, there's a problem."

"What sort of a problem?"

"There's a girl. Her name is, Anna. She was playing with the spirit board and now she's acting strange."

"Ah, I see," I said nodding my head. "C'mon Boo. Carry my bag. I've got a train to catch."

"What?" Boo said. "You heard him. Father Paco needs you."

"He doesn't need me. O'Brien's with him. I'm sure they have the situation under control."

"No," the boy said clutching my arm. "They don't."

"What do you mean they don't? What does this Anna girl have? Indigestion?"

I started to laugh, but the boy didn't crack a smile. He just looked at me with frightened eyes.

"Father O'Brien's dead," he said.

The boy's words were punctuated by a gasp from Lucy. I looked at her, and saw her hands covering her mouth. It took a moment before I could speak.

"How did he die?" I finally said.

The boy didn't say anything; he just kept shaking his head back and forth.

I placed my hands on his shoulders and said, "What's going on?"

"She's talking funny. No one can understand her."

I felt a prickly sensation run down my spine.

"What language?" I said.

"I think Father Paco said it was Ara…Amarica?"

"Aramaic?"

"Yeah, that's it. He wasn't sure, but he thought it was that and Latin."

"What else?"

The boy closed his eyes and shook his head. "Oh, man," he said. "I was in the room for a minute. Father Paco told me to leave and fetch you. Please come."

"Why does he need me? He's a priest."

"He needs you. He asked for you."

"But I'm not even a priest."

"But you're the best demon fighter there is," said Boo.

"But I'm not."

"Sure you are."

"Are you coming?" said the boy.

"Sure he is," said Boo.

"I have a train to catch," I protested.

"What do you mean?" Boo said in an agitated voice. "The girl's demon possessed. She needs you, Dex."

"I told you, my demon-fighting days are over."

Boo let my demon-fight bag drop to the floor where it landed with a thud. "Coward," he said in soft voice.

"What did you call me?"

This time his voice was strong and sure, and he looked me in the eye when he spoke. "I called you a coward," he said. "You got a chance to help, and you won't even try."

I wasn't angry. Boo didn't understand, and I told him as much.

"I understand they need you. I understand that much."

I wanted to leave, to be rid of Titusville and the memories for good. I had got used to the idea of a new place and new faces, but as I looked around, I saw everyone staring at me, judging me like a man on trial. I was condemned. There was no escape.

I turned and looked at Boo, and those damned eyes sealed my fate. "Carry my bag," I told him. "There's one last exorcism to perform."

CHAPTER 24

It looked like an ordinary bedroom, in an ordinary house. A little girl lived there. I could tell by the toy dollies that littered the place. They were creepy, little things with bulging eyes that appeared to follow my every step.

Yet, the dolls weren't responsible for my goosebumps. There was something else in the air, something you felt in your soul. Imagine an argument had just taken place and though the angry voices have quieted, a residual trace remains like smoke after an extinguished campfire. That's what it was like only a thousand times stronger. The air was alive, I felt it; I sensed it, tasted it on my lips, and felt it in my skin. It made the hairs on the back of my head stand on end like a static charge after a lightning strike, and though I did not know what it was—couldn't see it, couldn't hear it—I sensed it was waiting for me.

I stepped lightly toward Father Paco. Boo was close behind, and the boy from the rectory simply refused to follow us in. I looked at Paco for an explanation, and he just looked back at me with pleading eyes. His normally pristine hair was wet and matted, and he looked like he had slept in his habit for the past several days. I was alarmed by his ghostly complexion. His green eyes were now coal black. I looked more closely and saw his cheeks were wet from sweat or tears; I could not tell which.

I looked around and saw a couple; a husband and wife I presumed. I did not recognize either one. They stood beside the bed, and they too looked at me with a sense of desperation. I could tell the woman had been crying. The man looked to be on the verge of tears.

Then, I saw her for the first time. It was a child who looked no more than nine or ten years old, but her countenance conveyed something different. Her eyes shined with a soul born a thousand years ago. Those eyes. At once, paralyzed my heart and soul. I dropped my bag and it fell to the ground with a loud thud that shattered the unearthly silence.

"Oh, dear, God," I said reaching back for Boo in a protective reflex. "Boo, leave."

"But, why?" he said.

"Boo, you mind me, now." I shoved him hard toward the door. "You, get out of here, boy!"

Boo gingerly stepped backward and out of the room. I turned to father Paco, and though I already knew the answer, I had to ask as a matter of course.

"What is it?" I said.

Paco's breath was heavy and labored, "The girl," he panted. "That's why I sent for you."

I looked at the girl. She seemed transfixed. Her eyes reminded me of the dolls': non-blinking, absent, an imitation of life.

"What do you mean?" I said in an angry tone. "Where's Father O'Brien?"

Paco lifted his chin toward an adjoining room; Through the partially open door, I saw a large, black-clad figure crumpled up next to the washstand.

"What happened?"

"We were performing the rite of exorcism and his heart gave out. He stumbled to the lavatory and never came out."

Oh, God, I thought. What have I gotten myself into? I looked around the room, and it seemed like every eye was on me now, the girl's, Father Paco's, the man and woman and even the dolls stared at me as if I held the answers. Sadly, I did not.

"Look," I told Father Paco in a hushed tone. "I don't know why you sent for me, but I am not your man. I'm leaving town."

Paco's eyes bulged. He rose to his feet, grabbed me by my coat lapels and said, "No, no, no. You can't leave me. I can't do this alone. You were a priest. You were an exorcist. This little girl needs our help."

I looked at the girl. She sat straight up in bed rigid as a metal rod and she wore a slight smirk, which conveyed a hint of superiority.

"Help with what?" I said. "You don't know she's possessed. That's for the Church to decide. Make an official inquiry. Let the Vatican send their people."

Father Paco turned red. "You—you," he stammered. "You of all people are telling me to go to the Vatican? You, who stood on a soapbox and claimed to drive out demons at five bucks a head. Well, here's your chance, right here, right now. An official inquiry would take months or even years, and even then, this poor soul may never get relief."

"But how can you tell she's possessed? She may have a touch of the influenza?"

"She's exhibiting all the classic signs."

A part of me didn't want to know and another part had to know. "Tell me."

"She fears all religious artifacts and blessed sacraments," Father Paco said in a hushed voice. "She speaks a language that is not her native tongue and that she's never studied. She has knowledge of this world and its history that she could not possibly know at her tender age."

As Father Paco spoke, I shut my eyes tight and shook my head in hopes this was some kind of mistake. However, what I heard, what I saw and felt, all pointed to one thing.

"You've seen possession before?" Father Paco said. "I mean a real possession?"

"Of course."

"Well?"

I nodded my head. "Yes," I said. "But what do you expect from me? I'm no longer ordained."

"So? You're the closest thing."

"I'm a fraud. You and Father O'Brien told me as much yourself."

"But you healed the Radley girl." I shook my head. "Are you going to let this poor girl suffer?"

I turned around quickly, took a step toward the door and ran smack into Boo who had been standing right behind me. "I told you to get out of here," I snapped.

"What ya doing, Dex?" he said. "You can't leave. The girl is demon possessed and you're the best demon fighter around. You can't leave her, Dex. You're not going to leave her. Are you, Dex?"

I looked into Boo's eyes and unlike the little girl's, his showed life. I was afraid, but I felt a benevolent presence was with me. It was a steady hand on my shoulder, loving, comforting and it whispered to me like a gentle, distant musical strain: *I am with you.*

I turned to Father Paco and told him to get me ready. Then, I turned to Boo. "Leave the room," I said.

"Aw, but Dex—"

"Now."

"I've seen exorcisms before, Dex."

"Yes, well, this one's different. I looked once more at the girl. "In fact, all of you need to clear out," I said raising my voice.

"I ain't going nowhere," the man shouted back at me. "That's my daughter."

"C'mon, David," the woman said placing her hand aside his chest in a soothing gesture. "Let the priests do their work."

"Well, he ain't even a priest," he said pointing to me as if everyone in the room didn't know who he was talking about.

"C'mon, David," she said, leading him toward the door by his hand.

Before they left, I stopped the woman and asked her how this had happened.

"It was the spirit board," she announced. "She found it near the oil derricks and brought it home and started playing with it. I didn't think it any harm. Next thing you know, strange things started happening. It started with frightening dreams and it got worse every day; she got moody and ill-tempered, melancholy and wasn't eating normal food. I saw her digging up the ground like a dog looking for its bone. She took to talking to people that weren't there."

"You need to burn that wretched board," I told her.

"We already did," the man answered. "Didn't do no good. You've seen her." I nodded my head. "Can you bring my little girl back? We ain't the most Christian folk, but...We struck oil on my farm mister, a big gusher, pumping a hundred barrels a day. I'll pay you whatever you want." The man bit his lower lip and hung his head. "Funny," he continued. "All this money, but I feel broke about now."

I placed my hand on his shoulder and told him I'd do my best. I was honest. It's all I had.

After Boo and the parents left; I turned to Father Paco and said, "Let's pray?"

Normally, the rite of exorcism—a true exorcism—takes days of preparation. The exorcist should attend confession; he should elicit an act of contrition, offer the holy sacrifice of the Mass and implore God's help. Most importantly, he should pray for several days before the confrontation. There was no time for any of that. I knew it and Father Paco knew this as well. This was a race against time. By morning, the girl might be dead. We all might be dead by the looks of things.

I knelt in front of Father Paco and bowed my head. He placed his hand over me and prayed the Litany of Saints, an ancient prayer meant to protect me from evil.

"Lord, have mercy," Father Paco said.

"Lord, have mercy," I echoed.

"Christ, have mercy."

"Christ, have mercy."

"Lord, have mercy."

"Lord, have mercy."

"Christ, hear us."

"Christ, graciously hear us."

Father Paco's voice was strong, soothing and filled me with peace, a peace I had not known for a long time. As he spoke, memories came flooding back. I was lost in my own world, and for a moment, I forgot where I was and the gravity of the situation. That is, until a growling voice yanked me back to reality. Its bass note was so deep, I felt the vibration in my gut.

"Does Dexter want to play?" the voice said.

I turned toward the direction of the voice and saw the little girl. She was smiling at me, not a pleasant smile, but a forced one that looked more like a pained grimace.

"Don't pay attention," Father Paco reminded me. "The Devil distracts us. Focus on me."

I heard Paco well enough, but I couldn't turn away from the little girl. I was drawn to her like a magnet; such a cute girl I imagined and now, her face was a twisted, maniacal stare.

"Father," I heard a voice say. And then again. "Father, Father."

I turned to face Father Paco, but he wasn't there. Instead, my former superior, the Most Reverend Monsignor was speaking to me.

"Father," he repeated. "Get a hold of yourself. I can overlook the drinking but those women, all those women you fucked. It's not becoming of a priest."

I blinked my eyes a few times, trying to clear this vision, but it was no use. I looked around and saw I was no longer in a little girl's room. I was in St. Paul's Cathedral in Hell's Kitchen. It was dark; the only light came from the stained-glass window and the flickering votive candles on the altar to the Virgin. Monsignor's face was old and wrinkled, just as I remembered.

"You know all the drinking, passed out drunk on the altar," the Monsignor said. "I could overlook that, splash some water on your face, clean you up. You cost us a fortune in wine but those whores you fucked—all those whores." The Monsignor shook his head and made a clicking sound with his mouth. "But all those whores you fucked…"

"But lots of priests fucked whores," I said. "You probably fucked a few yourself in your day, when you were young enough to make love to a woman."

"Sure, sure, but you got caught, more than once. Too many people talked. Too many parishioners complained. Can't have that. People stop believing in the church; they stop coming to church. Stop giving to the coffers."

I felt the back of my neck grow hot and flush. My hands trembled. "It's all about the money," I said. "Isn't it? That's all it was ever about. God, Jesus, love, kindness, compassion, forgiveness...none of that...just how much money we bring in."

The Monsignor shrugged and smiled. "Eh, no money, no church. You'll be reassigned."

"Where?"

"A little place called Westerville, Ohio. It will be a dry town soon."

"Mr. James," I heard another voice say. It was Father Paco; he grabbed hold of my shoulders and was shaking me. "Get a hold of yourself. Focus on me."

I turned and looked at the little girl. She was laughing at me—an absurd laugh that reminded me of the hyena's high-pitched cackles I once heard at the zoo.

"What's her name?" I said.

"The girl's name is Anna. The demon inside her has yet to be identified."

"Anna," I called out raising the pitch of my voice. "Anna, can you hear me? My name is—my name is Father James, Father Dexter James. I'm coming for you Anna. Just hold on."

My declaration stirred the demon; Anna's head snapped back violently exposing a neck covered in blue, root-thick vessels. She let out an unearthly howl that I supposed was meant to be a laugh but sounded more like a desperate cry for help. The shocking noise made my ears ring and caused the hairs on my arms to stand on end.

Then, the demon looked at me and in a matter-of-fact voice that exactly matched my pitch and timbre as it recited my words back to me: "Anna. Anna, can you hear me? My name is—my name is Father James, Father Dexter James. I'm coming for you Anna. Just hold on."

Anna closed her eyes and lowered her head as she appeared to fall into deep sleep, punctuated by a loud, rasping snore normally heard in old men.

I looked over at Father Paco and with my eyes alone conveyed a single thought: what is it?

Father Paco shook his head. "It's very powerful, very intelligent," he said.

"Why is she not bound? She needs to be restrained to keep her from hurting herself and others."

"She was," Father Paco said nodding in the direction of the girl.

I looked closely and for the first time noticed the knotted linen digging deep into her bruised, blue wrists. I followed the cloth to their frayed ends which at one time, clearly bound her hands to the bedposts.

"Finish praying," I said. "We have work to do."

"God, the Son, Redeemer of the world."

"Have mercy on us."

"God, the Holy Spirit."

"Have mercy on us."

"Holy Trinity, one God."

"Have mercy on us.

"Holy Mary, pray for us."

"Pray for us."

"Holy Mother of God."

"Pray for us."

"Holy Virgin of virgins."

"Pray for us."

"St. Michael."

"Pray for us."

"St. Gabriel."

"Pray for us."

"St. Raphael."

"Pray for us."

With each call and response, our voices rose, my courage grew and so did my resolve. I was about to battle a nemesis, a force I could not see, nor fully explain and one that does not belong to this realm. Fighting a man is a relatively easy undertaking by comparison.

Despite the odds, I was ready—perhaps it was Father Paco's calming influence or the familiar words I once held so dear, or perhaps it was the same foolish bravado I carried into all of my fights. Whatever it was, the fear had dissipated. I may get the shit kicked out of me or I may die, but I didn't care. Today, I am doing God's work. My place in heaven secured.

When we finished, I stood up and placed both hands on Father Paco's shoulders. "Are you ready," I said.

He smiled and nodded his head. "I'm right behind you."

I grabbed the stole from my bag and handed it to Father Paco. He held the embroidered cross up and I kissed it. I did the same, then he carefully draped the garment around my neck and smoothed out the wrinkles.

"How do I look?" I said.

Father Paco smiled and shook his head in disbelief. "You look great."

I picked up my bag, and we carefully made our way toward the bed. Father Paco, true to his word, was right behind me and using me as a shield between me and the demon. The diminutive priest didn't inspire a lot of confidence, but he was all I had, and I was grateful he was there.

We reached the side of the bed, and I took advantage of the girls sleeping state to retie the restraints. I knew she was only a little girl, but I tied them tight, as tight as I could until the cloth dug deep into her skin. It pained me to do so, but it was for all of our safety, including hers.

Next, I pulled the holy water from my bag. However, when I uncapped it, I was met with the strong smell of alcohol, the drinking kind, not the rubbing kind. I sprinkled some in my hand and held it up to my nose to confirm my suspicions.

"What's wrong?" Father Paco said.

"It's the holy water. It smells like gin."

A deep, haunting voice interrupted us. "More like Bourbon," it said. "Don't you think?"

I looked up and faced the speaker. Now, with an up-close view, I saw details I could not see before. Her eyes were completely black, and unblinking like two lumps of coal. I could not distinguish at all between the iris and the pupil. Her skin stretched tight as a drum across her skull causing the blood vessels to pop. Her smiled reminded me of a wild animal's bared teeth; there was no real humor or joy behind it.

I raised the bottle to the demon's eyes and said, "Did you do this?"

"Well," the demon said, its voice sounding like a bass drum. "A man, his name shall go unmentioned, turned water into wine. I thought I would make something stronger for you, Father. You are fond of the strong drink, are you not?"

The demon laughed as if it were pleased with itself.

"Bastard," I said. "This was holy water blessed by the Cardinal."

"No, no, no, no," the demon answered in a sing-song voice. "Allow me to refresh your memory. You ran out some time ago. It was replenished from a well. It is nothing but ordinary swill. That's how I was able to turn it into something more palatable. Go ahead, Father, James. Take a drink. It's good and strong, the way you like it. You'll be passed out on the floor shortly, just the way you like it."

Arguing was no use. Instead, I threw the alcohol in its face, bottle and all, and this made the demon laugh hysterically.

"It's okay," Father Paco reassured me. "I have real holy water from the church."

The demon watched closely as Father Paco handed me a new bottle.

"Oh, what's wrong?" I said to the demon. "You're not laughing anymore."

I uncapped the bottle and raised it above my head. The demon's eyes were as big as silver dollars.

"Wait. I have someone here with me," it said in the little girl's voice. "A friend of yours. Leslie Reed."

I froze. "Miss Leslie is with you?"

"Yes, would you like to speak with her?"

"Don't be stupid," Father Paco," said. "It's a trick."

I looked at Father Paco; his eyes were pleading with me, but I had to hear for myself. "Let me speak to her," I said.

The girls face softened ever so slightly; she opened her mouth and the familiar twang I once held dearly floated past her lips like a song. "Hi, Dex."

It was Leslie's soft voice all right and hearing it again, as plain as day, sent a tear streaming past my cheek and onto my lips.

"Leslie?" I said.

Father Paco had a hold of my coat sleeve and was shaking me hard. "It's not, Leslie. It's a trick. The demon is—."

"Shut up, you fool."

I turned to the girl. "Leslie? Is that you? Are you okay?"

The demon smiled at me and I swear it was Leslie's smile, the beautiful one that I remembered. I smelled lilac too and had no doubt I was talking to my beloved.

"Yes, Dex it's me. Come here sugar and give us a kiss."

Leslie invited me in with widespread arms and I wanted so much to accept the embrace for it was Miss Leslie, my beautiful Leslie. I was certain of this. Then, I heard Father Paco chattering like a squirrel, calling me back, scolding me, but his voice trailed off and the walls collapsed and I was no longer inside, but outdoors, sitting on the bank by the edge of a stream; in front of me was Leslie, in her pink dress, wearing red lipstick that glistened in the morning sun like honey.

"Leslie?" I said.

"Sure, it's me, Sugar. Come in and give Miss Leslie a kiss. You want to kiss me, right?"

"Oh, of course, I do, but—"

"Lots of men have kissed me."

"What?"

"Yes, they kissed and fucked me, and I bet you wanted to do the same, but you never got the chance, Sugar. Well, here's your chance, Sugar. We have this nice quiet spot near the brook and though it may be unbecoming of a lady—well, I reckon I'm no lady."

I felt every bit the fool I was. I allowed myself to be tricked.

"No," I said shaking my head. "You're not Leslie. You're a cheap reflection."

The demon's face went gray and slack again, and I was suddenly back in the bedroom. Father Paco had grabbed the holy water from me and doused the demon's face and head, causing the girl's body to convulse and writhe in pain. Her menacing grimace had returned.

"Stop it," I said, tugging Father Paco's arm away. "You're hurting her."

Father Paco turned on me, grabbed my lapels and pulled my face an inch from his. "Listen," he said. "I sent for you to help this little girl. Are you up to it or not? If not, there's the door. Go. Leave now. Get drunk and rot in the street for all I care, but if you're going to stay, you'll need to be strong."

I turned and looked toward the door. It would be so easy. Leave. Steal a bottle and get drunk. I'm not even a priest anymore. This is not my problem. Then, I looked at the demon—past him, actually—and I imagined the sweet, blue-eyed, blond haired girl playing with her dolls. She was in there, held captive as a slave. I pictured her mom's arms around her daughter's shoulders, rocking her to sleep while singing a lullaby. I imagined Miss Leslie and her mom and how it must have been between them, the love between a mother and a daughter. It reminded me of something the Monsignor told me: *love conquers all*.

What's it going to be, I thought? *How are you going out, Dex? Walk away and get piss-stinking drunk or stay here and fight this evil piece of shit?* Either way, I'll probably be dead by morning. Well, I've always wanted to be a hero.

I threw my shoulders back and looked into Father Paco's eyes. "I'll stay," I told him.

"Are you okay?"

"I am."

"Are you drunk?"

"I—I'm a little hung over."

Father Paco turned me loose. "Let's pray over her," he said.

The father opened his Bible and leafed through the pages until he found what he was looking for. Our eyes met; he gave me a nod and we prayed.

Things went smoothly at first. The demon was well-behaved as demons go. He watched us through that ever-present, stupid grin plastered on the girl's face. He appeared to listen, quite unaffected and even a bit amused by our efforts to eradicate him. The only time we got a rise is when Father Paco doused the beast with holy water. The demon hissed and its head twisted left and right when the droplets touched its skin.

I knew this would not be easy. We may be here all night and into the next morning; we could be here for weeks and even this didn't assure our victory. Yet, we continued to pray over the girl. Sometimes, I'd look up and think she was normal, but then a shrill voice reminded me that this was anything but normal.

"Camptown races sing that song, doo da, doo da. Camptown races five miles long, all the doo dah day!"

The song was a joyful one, but under these circumstances, it sounded ghastly to my ear. I stopped praying, but Father Paco continued.

"You have a horrible singing voice," I told the demon.

"Speak for yourself," it snarled back at me. Then, the demon changed its tune: "I'd like to teach the world to sing, in perfect harmony. And I'd like to buy the world a Coke and keep it company. It's the real thing. Coke is. What the world wants to be. It's the real thing…"

"What is that?" I said cocking my head to the side.

"Oh, this? It's a ditty I picked up somewhere," the beast answered.

"Oh? Funny. I have a good ear for a song; I don't recall ever hearing that one."

"That's because it's more than a hundred years into the future."

"The future, you say?"

"Yes, from a Coca-Cola commercial. I believe it was the seventies."

The demon spoke in puzzles as plenty of demons do, but I decide to play along. "The eighteen seventies, you say?"

"No. The nineteen seventies."

While I engaged the demon in nonsensical conversation, Father Paco dutifully prayed: "Fight this day the battle of the Lord, together with the holy angels, as already thou hast fought the leader of the proud angels, Lucifer, and his apostate…"

The demon's dark eye's shifted from left-to-right. I sensed unease and so I pressed forward.

"You don't like hearing the Lord's name?" I said.

"Have another drink," it spat back. "Or fuck another whore. That's what you're good for, Father James. That's why you were demoted to that shithole parish in a dry town, but you couldn't even make it there."

The demon's breath wafted deep inside my nostrils and conjured up images of Hell. The stench was so putrid, I gagged and buried my nose in the crook of my elbow to keep from puking. I nodded to Father Paco. He took the cue and doused the demon. It threw a fit, throwing its head from side-to-side like a rabid dog. Its legs rustled violently beneath the yellow-stained sheets. I wanted to leave, to run actually, but then I remembered there was a girl named Anna in there. I would not leave her.

Father Paco and I continued to pray, speaking nearly in unison.

"St. Michael the Archangel, defend us in the day of battle; be our safeguard against the wickedness and snares of the devil. May GOD rebuke him, we humbly pray and do thou, O' Prince of the Heavenly Host, by the power of GOD, cast into hell Satan and all the other evil spirits, who prowl throughout the world, seeking the ruin of souls, Amen. In the name of the Father and of the Son and of the Holy Ghost, Amen."

I looked into Anna's eyes, hoping to recognize a faint glimmer of life. There were times, I thought I saw her staring back at me. It would last a moment, then the demon returned with its hollow gaze.

A wave of darkness fell over me. I was tired and weak and Father Paco, who had been fighting much longer than me, looked to be on the verge of collapse. Sweat dripped from his forehead, despite the preternatural cold. I tried to engage him with my eyes, to convey a silent message of fortitude.

Father Paco, however, was in his own private hell. He never acknowledged me. Instead, he grabbed a washcloth from a basin resting on the nightstand. As he applied the cloth to Anna's forehead, I saw the Demon's hand slowly rise like a cobra's head. Then, as if watching a dream, I saw its fingers curl around Paco's neck. It happened with such nonchalance, such grace, that the act was done before we had a chance to react. The demon's grip was like a vice. Its nails buried deep into Paco's skin causing a bright stream to trickle down his white collar and staining it red.

"Camptown ladies sing dis song, Doo-dah! doo-dah! Camptown racetrack five miles long, Oh, doo-dah day!"

As the demon sang joyfully, he stared directly into my eyes.

"I come down dah wid my hat caved in, Doo-dah! doo-dah! I go back home wid a pocketful of tin, Oh, doo-dah day!"

Father Paco pulled, then scratched at the Demon's wrists, but it had no effect. The Demon's arm was locked rigid as a metal pole and he appeared to exert little effort. The nails sunk deeper, and I watched as Paco gasped and his face turned blue.

I am not proud to say this, but I did not react right away. I was afraid and in shock and thinking too much. How did the demon get free? I had tied the restraints myself. *Never mind that*, Dex. *Move*! I instinctively grabbed the demon's wrists and was about to rip its hands away from Father Paco's throat, but to my surprise, I didn't have to. The demon had already let go, and I heard a relieved gasp escape from Paco's mouth.

Suddenly, I struggled for my own breath. There was a searing pain followed by the sensation of warm fluid running down my neck. Time was distorted; a second seemed to last a day. It was strange, because despite my precarious position, I was not afraid. In fact, I wasn't the least bit frightened. I was calm, maybe the calmest I had ever been and for the moment, I was able to think clearly as I listened to that wretched voice.

"Gwine to run all night! Gwine to run all day! I'll bet my money on de bob-tail nag, somebody bet on de bay."

I dug my thumbnails into the demon's wrist, but no matter how hard I pressed, the demon bore down harder. My eyes watered, and I struggled for air. That bit of calm was fleeting. I was now desperate. I grabbed its wrists with both hands and pushed with all my strength to break the hold. I might as well have been pushing against a fortified wall. With one hand alone, the demon held me firm and with seemingly little effort.

My breathing grew shallow, and I knew blackness would soon follow (which meant certain death). I flailed widely, first with my fists and then with the bony part of my elbow. They were short, powerful blows that landed with a resounding thud against the demon's cheek and jaw. It would have shattered a man's bone into a hundred pieces, but it seemed to have no effect on the demon. As I rained down elbows, my arms became bruised and tired; the demon's smile only intensified and it's singing became louder.

"It's the real thing! Coke is. What the world wants to be. It's the real thing…"

I was tired and barely able to lift my arms anymore. It was easier to drift off to the hypnotic strains: "Coca-Cola. It's the real thing."

Father Paco bless him. I saw him through wet, blurry eyes. He did his best. He shouted something intelligible at the demon, then he pounded its head with his fist, narrowly missing my skull. When that didn't work, he smashed the holy water bottle against the Demon's temple where it shattered like ice and left a bright, cherry stain behind. The bottle was empty, and it just made the demon laugh as he sung that ridiculous song. "I'd like to buy the world a Coke…"

Everything went dark for a moment and I closed my eyes. I was happy, almost relieved that my struggle was over. I opened my eyes just to have one final glimpse, but all I saw was the grotesque demon staring back at me, and Boo.

I must've been hallucinating; oxygen had been cut off to my brain I reasoned, but as much as tried to convince myself, Boo was there, standing on the other side of the bed, holding Leslie's rosary out for me. Boo reached forward and I felt the rosary in my palm. I closed my fingers around the strands, and felt they were hot to the touch.

I walked my fingers over the beads, one-by-one as if I were praying the Rosary. I was going as fast as I could, but everything seemed to move slowly like time itself had been magically slowed down by the hand of God. It gave me time to think and of all things, I thought about Leslie and how I came to hold her rosary in my fingers at that very moment. I imagined her by my side, fighting next to me like she had in the saloon. I may have been delusional, but I swear I smelled lilac.

Finally, my fingers found what they were looking for. I grabbed hold of the cross and suddenly, time sped up. I balled my hand into a fist and shoved the crucifix against the demon's forehead where it sizzled like cold water on a hot greased pan. The demon's eyes closed, and he spoke to me in a surprisingly calm voice. "Faciam te in inferno, Patri, James," he said.

The demon relaxed its grip and I could breathe again.

"Ne ego ante te, porcus," I replied.

Using all my weight, I forced the crucifix deeper into its skin, pressing it as hard as my thumbs would allow. The demon arched its back before going limp and letting out a long breath of air. The fight was gone from him, but I wasn't going to let up. I held continuous pressure until Father Paco tapped me on the shoulder.

"It is done," I heard him say.

I rolled onto my back and panted desperately for a full breath.

"Dex?" I heard Boo say.

"What is it?" I rasped back.

"What's Coca-Cola?"

"I have no fucking idea."

CHAPTER 25

The picture hung cockeyed, so I adjusted it and took a step back. I closed my eyes and I allowed the memories to wash over my brain like a morphine bath: that day, our walk, the silly monkey, Sandy Candy and most importantly, Miss Leslie. I'll never forget her. She lives in my heart and will do so till the day I die. I may be crazy, but I sense her presence; she watches over me and Boo. Occasionally, I'll catch a whiff of lilacs and sometimes I think I hear her laugh when I do something silly. Other times, I hear her scolding tone when I'm about to do something stupid. I haven't done anything stupid for some time.

I felt a tear in the corner of my eye. *None of that*, I thought as I wiped it away.

"She was pretty," Boo said admiring the photo.

"Yes, she was," I said. "But who's that brute sitting next to her?"

"You mean the monkey?"

"I meant me."

Boo laughed. "Are you sad?" he asked.

"A little. I think about what a gift she was."

"A gift?"

"Yes. She was a gift. I'm a gift, you're a gift. In fact, we're all gifts to God, from God. It's just that some gifts shine more than others." Boo nodded his head. "You know she's still around," I said placing my arm around the boy.

"I know."

"You do?"

Boo grew quiet. "I got cold one night," he finally said. "And Momma pulled the covers over me. Only when I opened my eyes, Momma's not there. Nobody is."

A chill raced up my spine. It sounded so much like Miss Leslie. She loved Boo as her own.

"Dexter James?" a voice from behind me said. I turned around and saw Carpenter John standing in the doorway. "I finished hanging your sign. Want to have a look?"

"Let's go look at our new sign," I said to Boo.

We stepped outside into the bright sunshine. With a week of rain and dark clouds, I had almost forgotten what the sun felt like. Its warming rays brought hope, and I took it as a good omen, a turning point, not only in my life, but in the town's too. I've traveled this country and have seen other nations. I've been blessed to learn about different religions, cultures, food and people. Now, it's time to settle down.

Boo and I looked up and studied the newly minted sign. Its fresh coat of black, green and gold paint glistened in the sunlight:

Dexter James
Apothecary & Counseling
Walk-ins Welcomed

"So, what do you think?" Carpenter John said.

"Oh, it's marvelous," I said. "Simply splendid. Shall we settle up, then?"

Carpenter John nodded his head, and I handed him a packet containing a vial of blue pills. He took the packet from me and winked. I smiled at him and winked back, then he got into his wagon, whipped his horse and he hauled out of there as if he was shot from a cannon.

"Hey, you be careful with those," I yelled after Carpenter John. I don't think he heard me.

After the dust settled, I turned to Boo and said, "What do you think?"

Boo's forehead wrinkled in concentration as he read the sign. He worked carefully and had difficulty with only one word.

"I know what it says," he replied. "But what does it mean?"

"Well, it means I'll be helping people," I said. "That's what it means."

"But what about demon chasing? That's what you do."

"Well this is sort of demon chasing, but in a different way, different kinds of demons. You see?"

"Not really," Boo answered.

"We'll be helping people, curing them. That's all you need to know."

"We?"

"Sure. You don't think I can do this without you?"

Boo smiled. "But I liked how it was, Dex; you on the soapbox, casting out demons. That was the best time I ever had in my entire life."

"Oh, don't worry, Boo. We'll be casting out more demons than ever. Father Paco and I reached an agreement. I'd help him out from time-to-time when he needs assistance with a particularly bad demon, and he's helping me exorcise my own demons. You know, keeping me accountable and such."

"Oh, that reminds me." Boo reached into his pocket and pulled out a piece of folded parchment. "Here," he said handing it to me. "It's from Pa."

I unfolded it and read the crude, yet very legible inscription: *thank you*. Next to the writing were two dots and an arching line made to look like a smiling face. It made me smile.

"How is your pa?" I said.

"He hasn't had anything to drink since you exorcised him."

"So the twelve-phase program has been working?"

"Yup, and he said to send this back with me if you ever want to take another drink. He'll come any day, any time."

I nodded my head, folded the parchment and tucked it carefully into my coat pocket. "Thank you," I said. "I'll do just that."

"It's looking mighty fine," a voice said.

I turned around and saw Anna sitting in the arms of her father. There was a radiance about them; they smiled, and Anna looked as cute as I remembered. There wasn't a single mark on her.

"Ah, Mr. Ames," I said shaking his hand. "I'm so glad you came down to see the place."

"It's my pleasure," he said. "I'm so glad you decided to stay in Titusville. This town needs a good man like you."

"I couldn't have done this without you. I used the money to order more supplies for my apothecary business and I paid my long overdue debts."

"Well, the Lord saw fit to put a lake of oil beneath my farm, so it was the least I could do for what you did for Anna."

I accepted his compliment, but I knew better. The demon had me body, mind and soul. I should be dead, but I had help, an angel, a very special one. She was there and her love was fierce and more powerful than anything Hell could ever dream of. Love conquers all. It conquers evil. It transcends death and that's just the way it is; always was; always will be.

"And how is Anna, today?" I said.

The girl flashed her toothless smile. "I'm fine, mister," she said, and we all laughed.

"Anna," I said. "Do you remember anything from when you were sick? Do you remember talking to me, or Father Paco, or anything from when you were ill?"

"I remember seeing you there, and another man, and…" She stopped and smiled at Boo; Boo smiled back. "I remember seeing him there and Momma and Poppa too."

"Is that all? Do you remember anything else?" Anna shook her head and sent her blond locks flying across her face. "That's okay," I said laughing. "I want to show you something, Anna, your real benefactor and you too, Mr. Ames. Follow me."

We all went back inside, and I led them to the photo hanging on the wall. I pointed to the picture, but before I could speak, Anna immediately piped up. "Oh, I know her," she said. "That's Leslie."

I was stunned as I imagined everyone else was.

"You know Miss Leslie?" I said.

"You never met her," said her dad.

"Yes I did; when I was sick. I forgot she was there, but I remember her now. I saw her in like a dream, but it wasn't. She told me to sit tight, that her friend would save me. She said she would help him."

I looked over at her father and our eyes met. "Children say some crazy things," he said.

"Yes," I replied. "They say some truthful things as well."

"Hey, Dex, it's missing one thing," Boo said nodding toward the photo.

"What's that, Boo?"

Boo held up Leslie's rosary. "This," he said.

I took the rosary from Boo and draped it over the frame making sure the crucifix was centered over Leslie's heart.

"There," I said. "Now, it's complete."

CHAPTER 26

Leslie and Lois stood arm-in-arm beneath the portrait.

"You think they'll be okay?" Lois said.

Leslie smiled and her face radiated like the morning sun. "Oh, I'm sure," she said.

"I reckon you'll see to it."

"I will. I'll watch after Boo, and we'll both watch after Dex."

The two women thought this was the funniest thing and even Runt appeared to laugh. If you were walking by the little building on Main Street, you might have heard their giggles through the closed door and darkened windows.

"Well," Lois said. "We better hope Dex stays away from the demon drink."

"I don't think we'll have to worry about that. He threw out a near-full bottle he had stashed under his bed. You know, he really is a good man, Momma."

"Oh, I know. He'll be fine and so will Boo. I'm more worried about the town. What do you think is going to become of Titusville?"

Leslie cocked her head to one side and said, "You know, Momma; this will all go away someday. The oil will dry up, along with the money and eventually most of the people. There will be nothing left but old derricks, millionaire mansions and maybe someone will build a museum to remember when they struck oil here."

"You think so, Leslie?"

"Yes I do. No one will remember us Momma, not me nor you, Dex, Boo, or the time we drove the Devil out of Titusville. It's like it never happened."

Momma held her daughter's hand. "We'll remember it, Leslie," she said smiling. "We'll remember it."

"Yes, Ma'am. We will."

Lois looked around and sighed. "It's a lovely evening for a stroll by the creek," she said.

The two ladies locked arms and exited through the closed door; Runt followed close behind. If you happened to walk past the little building on Main Street, you would have heard tender voices in the night and smelled the scent of lilacs wafting in the cool, fall air.

THE END

ABOUT THE AUTHOR

Stephen Kanicki enjoys thought-provoking, reality-based science fiction. His novel, *The Seven Experiments*, explores religious, spiritual and metaphysical themes woven into an imaginative and frightening narrative. Kanicki is a father, a teacher, and an award-winning photographer. When he's not writing, he likes to run and if his aging body can stand it, he would love to complete his third marathon.

Note from the Author

Word-of-mouth is crucial for any author to succeed. If you enjoyed *There are No Saints*, please leave a review online—anywhere you are able. Even if it's just a sentence or two. It would make all the difference and would be very much appreciated.

Thanks!
Stephen Kanicki

Thank you so much for reading one of **Stephen Kanicki** novels. If you enjoyed the experience, please check out our recommended title for your next great read!

The Seven Experiments

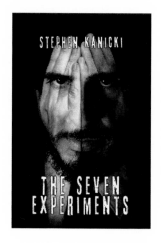

"An engrossing and tension-filled imagining of what would happen if Jesus had stopped adhering to The Ten Commandments and started reading *The Secret*."
–Rick Treon, author of *Deep Background*

Made in United States
North Haven, CT
13 February 2022

16077883R00131